::a minute before friday

THE LIGHTFOOT TRILOGY

A Mile from Sunday

A Quarter After Tuesday

::a minute before friday

book 3

jo kadlecek

NAVPRESS®

For a free catalog
of NavPress books & Bible studies call
1-800-366-7788 (USA) or 1-800-839-4769 (Canada).

www.NavPress.com

ISBN-13: 978-1-60006-051-9
ISBN-10: 1-60006-051-X

Cover design by studiogearbox
Cover illustration
        Woman: Steve Gardner/Pixelworks Studio
        Subway: Chris Gilbert
Creative Team: Cara Iverson, Darla Hightower, Arvid Wallen, Kathy Guist

Unless otherwise identified, all Scripture quotations in this publication are taken from the HOLY BIBLE: NEW INTERNATIONAL VERSION® (niv®). Copyright © 1973, 1978, 1984 by International Bible Society. Used by permission of Zondervan Publishing House. All rights reserved.

This novel is a work of fiction. Names, characters, places, and incidents are either the product of the author's imagination or are used fictitiously. Any resemblance to actual events, locales, organizations, or persons, living or dead, is entirely coincidental and beyond the intent of either the author or publisher.

Published in association with the literary agency of Alive Communications, Inc., 7680 Goddard St., Suite 200, Colorado Springs, CO 80920.

Library of Congress Cataloging-in-Publication Data

Kadlecek, Jo.
  A minute before Friday / Jo Kadlecek.
    p. cm. -- (The Lightfoot trilogy ; bk. 3)
  ISBN-13: 978-1-60006-051-9
  ISBN-10: 1-60006-051-X
  1. MacLaughlin, Jonna Lightfoot (Fictitious character)--Fiction. 2. Reporters and reporting--Fiction. 3. New York (N.Y.)--Fiction. 4. Missing persons--Fiction. I. Title.
  PS3611.A33M56 2008
  813'.6--dc22
                              2007051980

Printed in the United States of America

1 2 3 4 5 6 7 8 9 10 / 11 10 09 08

For my writing students at Gordon College,
who inspire me.

He said to them, "Do you bring in a lamp to put it under a bowl or a bed? Instead, don't you put it on its stand? For whatever is hidden is meant to be disclosed, and whatever is concealed is meant to be brought out into the open. If anyone has ears to hear, let him hear."
—Mark 4:21-23

::Chapter One

They didn't look like witches. Not a pointy hat or broomstick in sight. And yet the more I stared, the more I noticed something else was missing: light.

I didn't know how they'd managed it, but the fifty or so people gathered at the intersection of the sidewalk and the university entrance looked as if the darkness of a movie theater had somehow spilled onto them, even while sunlight flickered on the leaves and buildings behind them. They stood motionless by a tall oak tree, an odd contrast to the busy pace around them.

Granted, it was only 7:56 in the morning and I wasn't exactly awake. It didn't help that, despite the sunny blue sky, the February temperatures had dropped to eighteen degrees. My cheeks stung. The early-morning sidewalk traffic of students and professors hurried past with heads down and hands stuffed in pockets to keep warm.

I swallowed the bitter air and stepped toward the dark corner, yanking the earflaps of my cap as far down as they'd go — which made my hair stick out sideways — and pulling up the collar of my coat, which made my neck disappear so that I must have looked like a clown. A few of the night people suddenly smirked as I walked toward them. Or maybe the crunch of the snow beneath my boots signaled to them, "Danger, outsider approaching."

They shifted. I stopped where I was and smiled toward them, one of those hopeful little smiles you developed the first day of class when you were the new kid and wanted someone, anyone, to like you. Of course, it rarely seemed to work then. And it sure wasn't working now.

Sometimes religion reporting was a lonely job.

An hour before, I'd barely rolled out of bed, and so was hardly in the mood for an encounter with the dark side—beyond my own mirror, that is. Our apartment had been freezing, so I'd tossed my red parka over my flannels, stumbled into the kitchen, and dumped yogurt in a bowl, when my phone rang. I poured some coffee and answered.

"You busy?" It was my editor, Skip Gravely. I looked at my mug and the clock.

"Uh, well . . ." This was not a good sign. Instinctively, I reached for pen and notebook.

"Just got an interesting call about the Wiccans who are—"

"Did you say Wiccans?" I asked, gulping the rest of my coffee. "You mean like witches . . . with cauldrons and wands and—"

"Yes, those Wiccans. Seems they're tired of being discriminated against and want to be treated like every other law-abiding religion so they're going to—" Skip paused as if he were looking for something. "They're holding a rally right now and are going to—"

"A rally? In this weather? Now?"

"Apparently, the U.S. Department of Veterans Affairs won't allow Wiccan symbols on headstones," he said. "So they're rallying at the steps of Regal University, where I guess they thought they'd get both support and press."

I blinked. "Couldn't they wait until spring?"

Skip laughed. "Devotion requires sacrifice, doesn't it? Anyway, got a pen?" He gave me names and an address of where they were on the campus. I knew the university wasn't far from my apartment building, though I hadn't actually visited it since moving here. It was one of those places nearby that you always intend to see but never quite get to.

A bell rang in my head, reminding me that I knew someone who either worked there or took classes there, though I was too groggy this morning to remember whom.

"Why Regal, Skip? Why not city hall or the park?"

"Are you kidding? The university loves this sort of thing. They've got a long history of civil disobedience and protests and cheering the underdog. See what you can find out, okay?" I stared at my breakfast. "Oh, and dress warm."

Who invented cell phones anyway? Or mornings?

I jumped in and out of the shower, traded my flannel pajamas for a wool sweater and jeans, and threw on my parka and cap. The frigid air slapped my face when I hurried down the steps and across the street. My brain was sleepy. I was fairly sure my parents hadn't dabbled in Wicca during their early spiritual pilgrimage—at least not that I could recall. I did remember a classmate in college named Wanda who'd given a speech once in a communication class on being a member of a Wicca congregation. A guy in the class teased her from that point on, calling her Wanda the Witch. I had felt badly for Wanda, but at the same time I hadn't tried too hard to find out any more about her religion.

Now, standing near this strange dark corner of the campus, I wished I had.

I lit a cigarette, the organic kind, for backup. Tobacco always seemed to reverse my central nervous system from full throttle, and for some reason it tasted better in the elements of a winter day—just like cigarettes were always the best on chairlifts above a ski slope back home in Colorado. Granted, the Surgeon General's warnings had helped me quit twice already since taking this job. But on this cold sunny morning, as I approached an organized number of prospective spell-casters who stood in the shadows of one of the country's most prominent Ivy League universities, it seemed as good a time as any to light up again.

"Lord, have mercy," I said out loud. I saw my breath; that was how cold it was.

The group stood ghostlike at the entrance of the college. They'd turned a tall cardboard box into a podium and stenciled a large five-point star in a circle across it. People stared blankly at the snow-crested branches above them, threatening to sprinkle snow on their heads anytime a breeze passed. Each of them wore black, though I wasn't sure if that was because of their beliefs or because it seemed the most fashionable color to wear in this city. I inhaled my cigarette, feeling suddenly self-conscious of my red parka and green hunter's cap, and took in the crowd.

A middle-aged woman in a long black skirt, jacket, and scarf was at the podium. Her short-cropped hair was dyed blue-black, a stark contrast to her chalky face. She held a bullhorn to her lips but rested her other hand in her jacket pocket. The crowd—comprised primarily of women her age—offered an occasional nod or chant, but mostly they seemed as unresponsive as the mannequins in the Fifth Avenue windows.

" . . . because it's time this country accepts us for who we are. Wiccans. Humans. Divine. And citizens with as much right to wear our beliefs on our sleeves—and our tombstones—as Catholics or Protestants," she said. Her voice hummed. I dropped my cigarette to the ground, stepped on it, then picked up the butt and tossed it in a trash can. Then I shoved open my notebook and jotted down the speaker's words. The cold air pricked my fingers.

"Why do our children have to hide the fact that their mommies are witches? It's the twenty-first century! Why do some of us here today have to keep our Wicca a secret for fear of losing our job? Or our friends?" I scribbled while her volume increased. "And what's so wrong with our religion that in the land of the free we must believe and practice our rituals in private?" A delicate applause rose from the crowd—though I suspected some were simply warming their hands or waking up—and I jotted more notes. A few college students shook their heads as they passed us. Others stopped to listen. But everyone came to an abrupt halt when a shrieking noise cracked the morning air behind us.

"What's so wrong?!" Behind us, a skinny pale man in a hunting jacket threw his fist in the air as he screamed at the woman—making the boy in my college class look like an Eagle Scout for how he treated Wanda. "What's wrong?! You sacrifice children for their blood! You have orgies with the Devil!" Then he shoved a sign high above his head that read, "Hell Is for Sinners Like You!" And in a voice that reminded me of a thousand fingernails against a chalkboard, he screeched, "God hates witches and Satan worshippers and homosexuals! You are an abomination to the Lord of the Universe!"

I sighed. Men like him did not make my job any easier.

Two campus security officers quickly emerged from the crowd, gripping the man's elbows and ushering him toward the street. The people around the podium merely tossed him a glance before looking back at the woman with the bullhorn.

She continued as if she'd not heard a thing the man had

bellowed: "We bring no harm to others. We only want to be heard. Don't we deserve the freedom to worship as we want and to be remembered for what matters most to us? Just as our soldiers deserve to be buried with dignity." She bowed her blue-black head and stepped backward, passing the bullhorn to an older man, whose crew-cut hair and shaved face had a military style to them. He cleared his throat and brought the contraption to his chin.

"My name is Griffin Lewis," he said, his voice low and tunnel-like. "I'm here this morning to tell you that we will appeal every decision the government inflicts on us until brave soldiers, like my son, can have the Star of our Center go with them to the other world." He dropped the bullhorn to his side for a moment and glared at us as if he were trying to recognize a face in a darkened room. His eyes squinted, then widened and narrowed again. He pulled back the megaphone to his lips and continued with his speech, attracting a few more passersby. He was met with slight affirmations from the crowd, and I tried simply to write down my observations, though I wasn't doing a very good job. My hands were shaking and there was a strange sensation in my stomach. But the winter cold wasn't the only thing making me shiver. I rocked back and forth to stay warm. And I glanced at the sun to remember it was there.

When the military man stopped talking, he and the woman with blue-black hair began to pass out petitions for the crowd to sign. Only a few took out a pen. Some handed the papers to the next person and hurried off, while others tucked the papers into their pockets. Shadows fell across their faces. A few made small talk to those standing beside them. The rally was ending, and I remembered Skip's charge to see what I could find out.

I adjusted my green earflaps and approached a tall woman

who was wearing a baggy black leather jacket that made me think of a motorcycle rider. When she saw my notebook, she shook her head and turned away. I tried talking with a younger woman carrying a backpack, but she did the same. Each time I asked someone about the rally or their religion or why they were standing out in the freezing cold on a February morning, I got a vacant stare. Most simply looked toward the star on the podium or smiled flatly or pretended not to hear.

Finally, Griffin Lewis, the man who'd spoken, approached me.

"Is there something wrong?" he asked, though his tone didn't sound like a question.

"Not sure. I was just wanting to find out a few things for the—" I began, holding out my hand to shake his. But he interrupted and slipped a petition into mine.

"We're glad to talk with anyone who'll treat us as they want to be treated." It was the clearest sentence I'd heard yet, but I couldn't ignore the caution inside it.

"I can appreciate that." I nodded. "My editor sent me out here this morning, Mr. Lewis—which is no small thing, believe me. Anyway, he'd heard the recent DVA ruling and wondered why it was so important to have the Wiccan pentacle—"

"Why is it any different from the cross or the Star of David?" Anger now laced his voice before it dropped in pitch but not volume. "Why can't I put it on my son's grave?" His eyes darted somewhere else, as if he were remembering something he did not want to. The woman speaker, who'd come up beside him, intervened.

"Griffin's son was killed in combat," she said calmly, stepping toward me as if to protect her friend. "And since the government doesn't think much of us, it hasn't seen fit to add us to its 'approved' list; our religious symbols aren't allowed on our tombstones." She licked her lips. "We think that's wrong. In fact, it's evil."

I tried to wake up a little more, in case I hadn't just heard a witch calling the government evil.

"I'm sorry for your loss," I said to Griffin Lewis. He offered a quick nod. I shifted toward the woman at the same time the crowd began breaking up. "Somehow I missed your name. You won't mind if I quote you in an article I—"

"I have nothing to hide, although I can't expect you'll be any different from the others," she said. A vertical line formed between her eyebrows, and she lifted her shoulders, tying her scarf on her neck. "I'm Lady Crystal Lenowitz, High Priestess of the Eastern Order of the Pagan Sanctuary."

I wrote her name in my notebook, expecting she'd continue to tell me what else her group hoped to achieve. I'd covered enough protest rallies to know that was usually how it worked: say a few words, hand out flyers, and find the reporters to convey exactly what you wanted to communicate. But Lady Crystal stopped after she introduced herself. I looked up and her lips went tight. I tried again: "So you—and the Eastern Order of the Pagan Sanctuary—are hoping today's rally accomplishes . . . ?"

She glared. I waited. Finally, she sighed as if I'd asked the silliest question in the world.

"I want to send Griffin's boy—and all others—off with pure enlightenment. Nothing more or less. That's all. Perhaps you can print that . . . correctly." She crossed her arms, signaling the end of our discussion.

"Excuse me?"

"You know, without all the other . . . lies."

"Lies?"

"The stereotypes. The judgments. We get it all the time, you know."

"You do?"

Lady Crystal smiled faintly. "Course we do. We're *witches.* . . . You yourself were probably afraid to come this morning, weren't you?"

A bristly quiet formed around us like that in a cemetery at dusk. I felt a cold breeze across my face at the same time a branch above me thumped snow onto my head. I took it as a sign.

"Okay, well, I'll do my best. And since it isn't exactly chatting weather, here's my business card. Feel free to call me later if you . . . if there's anything else that might enlighten me, okay?" She took my card as I smiled the new-kid smile again but with no effect. I turned toward the street without looking back to see what the Wiccans were doing or if that corner of the campus was still thick with night. I was too cold.

I ducked first into a corner deli for a coffee warm-up, then headed down into the subway station, where I fumbled through my bag for my MetroCard. Finally, I found it and swiped the turnstile. Not many commuters were standing around the subway platform, which meant I'd either just missed a train and that was why the underground shelter was so empty, or it was a slow time of day, or both.

I sniffled from the cold and guzzled my coffee. They'd served it in one of those little blue paper cups with a Greek goddess sketched on the side that seemed to be everywhere in this city. Then again, there were a lot of things that were everywhere here all the time: Yellow cabs. Chinese take-out menus. Tourists with shopping bags. It was New York City after all, home of the fastest minute on earth. The capital of the whole world. As my colleagues at the newspaper called it, the City of all Cities. The Big Apple.

And Coffee Mecca of the Universe, as far as I was concerned. If I was desperate for a mocha or hazelnut, an espresso or cappuccino, I didn't have to look more than a block to find it. Even the traditional blue cup French roast I held in my hand made me feel lucky. So did the constant flow of pizza shops, pretzel stands, and bagel joints on every block. Some days it was hard choosing, so I'd pick up one of each and enter carb heaven. Between the bakeries and hot-dog stands, coffee bars, Godiva specialty shops, and secondhand bookstores, this city was a nonstop smorgasbord every day I walked out of my apartment—not to mention a minor heart attack waiting to happen for folks whose membership card to the local fitness center was three months expired but who carried it in their wallets anyway, just in case.

Like me.

"Jonna Lightfoot MacLaughlin."

I whipped my head from side to side. No one.

"Okay, God," I whispered. "I promise I'll start exercising again. Soon." I shifted uneasily, guzzling some more, hoping the caffeine would soon take effect. This was turning into a weirder morning than usual. I peered down the tunnel to see if a train was coming. Nothing. I decided that as soon as I got in to the office, I'd call Mrs. Green's Fitness Planet on Eighty-ninth to see if she still had that monthly special.

"Jon-na . . . Light-foot . . . Mac-Laugh-lin!"

I was in trouble now. Had Lady Crystal followed me from the rally? My eyes darted around the benches and platform. Though a few more people had trickled into the subway, I didn't see anyone I knew, let alone anyone who resembled a witch. Then again, Lady Crystal looked like an ordinary New Yorker, so that didn't help. I gulped the last of the coffee and tossed the blue cup into the trash can. I had to wake up. I was hearing things.

I clapped to get the blood flowing, when a loud clicking sound came over the speakers. I expected an announcement from the transit agent that a southbound Number 2 train would soon be approaching 110th Street. Instead, I heard a worried voice bellow, "If there's a Jonna Lightfoot MacLaughlin waiting on the platform, please come to the window immediately. Jonna Lightfoot MacLaughlin to the ticket booth."

I looked back through the turnstile where I'd come in and saw the soft silhouette of the clerk behind the window. She was moving the microphone to the side and resuming her place behind the counter. I backtracked my way through the gate.

"I'm Jonna MacLaughlin," I hollered into the tiny window speaker, my breath fogging the glass.

The woman with a round wrinkleless face and gray streaks in her hair smiled. She brought the microphone back to her chin and leaned toward me. "Did you lose this?" She held up a laminated New York state driver's license with my frizzy-headed mug shot taken last summer when I first got here. I fumbled through my bag.

"I guess I did," I said. "How'd you find it?"

"It must have fallen out when you were looking for your subway pass and someone turned it in," she said, still smiling. "Sugar, you might want to be a little more careful."

"I might want to be a lot of things." I sighed, feeling the red of my Irish cheeks give me away. She slipped the license into the tray and laughed.

"You just be yourself, Jonna Lightfoot," she said into the microphone, a silver lining in her voice, a steady wisdom in her eyes. "Just as the good Lord made you." The light grabbed the golden name tag on her jacket and I made out the letters: "E-m-m-a J-e-a-n T-i-p-t-o-n." She caught me reading.

"Call me Emma. Nice to meet you, Jonna."

"A pleasure." I nodded. "And thanks for . . . this." I waved my license in the air at the same time I heard a train screeching into the station. She tilted her head toward me as if she were, well, Glinda, the Good Witch of the North about to send me on my trip home. Then she pulled the pencil from behind her ear and pointed it like a wand toward the gate for me to hurry toward the train.

I had witches on the brain.

Just as the doors of the subway slid apart, I glanced back at Emma. She waved. And for the first time that morning, I felt awake. And warm. I waved back, thankful for a friendly face in a city that sometimes felt tougher to navigate than the moguls on a Colorado ski slope back home.

I found a seat next to a man in a Sikh turban who was reading today's *New York Clarion*. I couldn't help myself: I peeked over his shoulder at the Metro section page and saw my boss's handwriting all over it. From the profile about the local cabdriver-turned-activist for safer streets to the story on a small-businesswoman's innovative recycling effort, as well as the dozen other headlines, I could spot his "kinder and gentler" approach to news 5,280 feet away. In fact, if it hadn't been for Skip Gravely, I thought as I pulled off my cap, I wouldn't be sitting here reading the *Clarion* on my neighbor's lap on the Number 2 southbound train — after I'd already covered a chilly rally for witches on an Ivy League campus.

My first editor at the *Denver Dispatch* and longtime mentor in all things newsworthy, Skip hired me right out of college. I might have stayed a Mile High granola girl forever if he hadn't been the first to suggest this beat. I'd spent a lifetime training for it, he said, after listening to all my stories of how my mom and pop fiddled or faddled with just about every belief system when I was growing up in Summit County. How they taught my brothers and me about Buddhism, pantheism, Judaism, and all other *isms* they explored before settling on Presbyterianism. Skip thought these early spiritual encounters had uniquely prepared me, so he promoted me to be the number one—and only—religion reporter at the *Dispatch*. After a couple years of page-one stories, his old friend Hattie Lipsock recruited me to the *New Orleans Banner*. But when the *New York Clarion* called him and offered him this job as managing editor, Skip was determined to bring with him as many of his own reporters as he could.

By then, the Southern charm of the Crescent City had worn off for me. I'd watched a few too many "fine Christian men" flatten the only good stories I could find. God, I'd come to learn, might have once established the Bible Belt of the South, as folks liked to claim, but the belt no longer held up many people's breeches. All who lived near the Mississippi River were automatically good Christians, just like they were members at the local country club, city council, or Ladies Auxiliary—regardless of who got hurt along the way. When Skip made me the offer, I was more than ready for a new adventure.

I was still covering religion, only now it was New York style. Which meant—as I discovered again this morning—everything qualified for my beat. Even my subway neighbor with the turban might have been an interesting story, until we stopped at

Ninety-sixth Street and he hurried off with his *Clarion*. An enthusiastic subway preacher stepped in at the next stop and called me to repentance. And by the time we pulled into Thirty-fourth Street/Penn Station, I'd also heard a Hare Krishna chant for inner tranquility, and a Catholic priest appeal for dollars.

At least, he looked like a Catholic priest. Until I told him I'd given at church last Sunday and he cursed me. He shook his collection jar next to his ear like it was a tambourine, mumbled about his daily quota, and shoved an unlit cigarette between his teeth. That, I had to confess, seemed like a pretty good idea.

Outside, on Thirty-third Street, across from Madison Square Garden, I yanked down my flaps and pulled out a cigarette. A light snow had begun to fall, reminding me of a Rocky Mountain winter morning. Tomorrow I would toss the pack—even if it was organic—and I would join Mrs. Green's Fitness Planet—even if there wasn't still a special. I would. Tomorrow.

As I turned onto Seventh Avenue, I caught a whiff of hickory coals from a hot-pretzel stand. I breathed in gently and bought another breakfast. After a few bites and a couple more steps, I was in the lobby of the *New York Clarion*, an old eight-story factory building in the fashion district that had been converted fifty years ago. As the number three daily newspaper in a city with over half a dozen, plus scores of weeklies, everyone believed the *Clarion* was on its way up the ladder of influence and eventually uptown in location as well. For now, though, our neighbors were tiny clothing and fabric boutiques, theater rehearsal studios, a small kosher deli named Goldwasser's, and various modeling agencies. Not another newspaper, magazine, or publishing company for at least ten blocks.

Skip Gravely was standing peacefully in the newsroom

talking to a features reporter. The tall lanky editor wore a dark green suit and tie that hung neatly on his frame, as wrinklefree as his attitude. His chin was a trimmed blend of brown and white whiskers, and his glasses reminded me more of a professor or a banker than of an editor for a daily newspaper. While most editors and reporters in the newsroom were a frenetic combination of high-octane caffeine under looming deadlines, Skip had always been a calming presence. Chamomile tea with a beard.

He grinned when he saw me, finished his conversation, and came over to my cubicle.

"So? A magical morning?"

"Spellbinding," I said, not able to resist. I plopped my bag on my desk and logged on to my computer, then took off my coat and cap, wondering if my hair looked as funny as it felt.

"I expected such. Anything interesting?" he asked, adjusting his glasses.

"Too early to tell."

"What, they're holding more protests?"

"I meant it was too early in the morning for me to tell what in the Wiccan world was happening." And as if another drop of snow fell on my head and woke me up all over again, I looked at my boss and wondered aloud, "How in the world did you know about the rally?"

The corners of Skip's mouth curved. "An old friend tipped me off early this morning. I sent a photographer just after you to —"

"You have a friend who's a witch?"

"Hardly. Just a professor at Regal. We're old classmates. He stayed to study ancient religions; I joined the newspaper business."

"What? You're a Regal grad, Skip?"

"Shhh! I have a reputation to maintain," Skip whispered. He glanced at his yellow pad, took the pen from behind his ear, and wrote something I assumed was related to this assignment. Again, Regal sounded familiar. I knew someone linked to it but couldn't for the life of me remember who. It would pester me until I figured it out. Skip looked up from his paper.

"Reputation aside, Lightfoot, let's try to run something on the rally for tomorrow, okay? I'll call you when I get the photos." It was the kind of tone that didn't wait for a response, a gracious but firm authority that simply expected—and received—compliance.

I watched Skip walk through the newsroom maze of desks and cubicles toward his office, stopping to talk with reporters and editors along the way, his gait deliberate but slow. How was it that even after knowing him my whole career, I just now discovered he'd been educated at one of the oldest universities in New York? It had never occurred to me that Skip had gone to college in the first place, let alone an institution like Regal.

I shrugged, my own mysterious connection to the campus nagging in my head.

I flipped through my drawer of business cards I'd collected over the years. The buzz around the newsroom grew. Reporters were coming in from the cold, and editors were handing out assignments. I flicked the next business card and the next, but no one's card jumped out. None had the university's logo—a king's crown—or seemed remotely connected. Was I hearing things again? Who had talked with me recently about Regal?

I shut my eyes, trying to imagine the answer, and a series of faces popped up randomly in my mind: Matt, my eldest brother; Griffin Lewis, the Wiccan man I'd just met; Mrs. Widener, my ninth-grade English teacher; the subway faux-priest; a sports reporter named Chip; my mother with my pop; Emma, my new subway friend; David Rockley . . .

My eyes shot open. David Rockley worked at Regal, in the library with rare books and old files. That was why I recognized the name. But this was a fluke, I reasoned, a strange coincidence, and all the incentive I needed to pick up my *Cromwell's Encyclopedia of World Religions* and focus on the W's.

Wiccans, I read, worshipped the divine in nature. That sounded close to my parents' experimentation with pantheism, which said God was in all of nature and nature was all of God. During that season on their spiritual road trip, every day in the mountains became a worship service. My mom loved to hold up her hands to the clouds, and my pop always claimed nothing could beat the scent of evergreens. But that was where the similarity seemed to end. Wiccans, I read, carried their practice further into the magic arts and witchcraft so they could exert what they believed would be a distinct influence over their destinies.

Most Wiccans viewed themselves as pagans who worshipped pre-Christian deities found in the universe around them, but they didn't seem too interested in demons. The more I read, the more I realized Wiccans were as different from each other as Protestant denominations. The image I'd had of pointy hats and broomsticks was clearly out of date. It seemed instead that witches professed balance and harmony as life goals, eliciting the help of many gods or goddesses, and were offended if anyone called them Satanists. The confusion, I guessed, was in part because the Wiccan pentacle, the five-pointed star inside a circle, was sometimes associated with symbols of Satanism. Each point on their star represented the elements of nature—air, fire, earth, water, and the spirit

—within the eternal circle of life, not like the symbols of the biblical enemy. One paragraph in my *Cromwell's* even said that Wiccans were not allowed to "dominate, manipulate, control, or harm others, unlike Satanists."

That was a relief. At least I didn't have to worry too much if I wrote a story Lady Crystal didn't like. But the line was still a little blurry for me, in part because what I was reading about their ancient customs sounded more like New Age spirituality than a bona fide religious tradition. Which made me wonder why a witch's star should be considered a sacred symbol any more than a pitchfork or a scythe? Christians had a cross to remind them of Christ's death, Jews saw the Star of David as a link to their Hebrew heritage, and Muslims had a crescent moon and star. But what was the point of a symbol that was pagan, not religious, as Lady Crystal had said?

Then again, when I clicked on the Web site for the Department of Veterans Affairs, I saw that even atheists were included on the list of approved religions. Their atomic-looking symbol with an "A" planted in its center was featured alongside the thirty-five other sacred signs, half of which I recognized from growing up, and the other half from religions I'd barely heard of. So, according to the government, a belief in no god—or many gods, for that matter—qualified as a religion.

I didn't know if this made my job easier or harder. How would I ever know which stories to cover if everyone's beliefs were considered official religions?

My head hurt. I clicked off the Web site, shut the encyclope-dia, and realized I'd been so busy studying Wiccans that I hadn't yet checked my e-mails since I'd come into the office. There were the usual spam messages, denominational announcements, and invitations to church potlucks. I scrolled through most of them, deleting the potlucks, and listened to the only voice message waiting for me. And that was when the morning escalated to an all-time high in terms of weirdness: David Rockley was hoping I would join him for dinner.

He had something to tell me that could no longer wait.

::Chapter Two

There was no other word for it really. Unlike words such as *special* or *bad* or *cute*, I decided as I watched the snow fall outside the newsroom window that *nice* still meant what it was supposed to. Nothing flashy or sensational, just nice. Pleasant. Polite. Good. It fit David.

His face flashed again in my mind. It, too, was a nice-enough face to think about on a cold morning, though I didn't want to admit it. Not like the faces you'd see on the hunky models in the style section of the newspaper or the underwear billboards in Times Square, if you noticed their faces at all.

But David's was a face square with kindness, and whether or not he was smiling, he had one of those perpetual expressions of niceness, as if he'd been born that way. From the neat goatee on his chin to the thick glasses that slipped occasionally down his nose, David Rockley's face mirrored his character: simple and cheery and mostly, nice.

He was the type of guy who'd wear nice clean jeans, shirts with button-down collars, and a haircut so close to his scalp it couldn't look out of place. He had a nice job as an archivist in Regal's library, where from what I imagined, David probably treated old documents and rare books with a nice touch — carefully and curiously — each like a person who deserved proper attention. No matter what.

You couldn't find much nicer than that.

At least that's how Matt, my eldest brother, explained it when he'd first met the man. Matt taught history at Denver College, and David was a visiting researcher there one year. They met in the library, started a conversation about some western author who had New York connections, and within days Matt had a friend for life.

"You've got to meet this guy, Jon," he'd say each time he called me at the *Denver Dispatch*. Until finally one night at The Pub of Saint Agnes, my favorite eatery on the planet, I joined my brother and his wife, Mary, for burgers, and David Rockley sat down beside me. But I was too busy with other projects — romantic and otherwise — to take much notice.

The next time I saw David, he was visiting New Orleans. He'd called my brother Mark — who lived only "spittin'" distance away in Mobile — hoping we could show him a local's perspective of the Crescent City. David had come south for a university archivists' conference — which seemed about as exciting as the obituary beat I'd had when I first started in journalism — and reasoned that all MacLaughlins were like family because of Matt. So Mark and I took him around to the Garden District, but I was preoccupied then, too. One too many Southern gentlemen had caught my eye — which, it turned out, really was one too many for me.

David, apparently, had promised both Matt and Mark that he'd connect with Luke back in New York. The youngest of my older brothers, Luke taught music at a private high school across the river in Hoboken, New Jersey. Of course, David followed through on his promise by inviting Luke, his wife, Sarah, and their boys to a basketball game at Regal. He'd been "Uncle David" ever since.

So Mr. Nice had more than earned high ratings on my brothers' approval chart as both good friend and "long-term" potential for little sister. They'd begun scheming long before I'd noticed the guy's existence, or his face for that matter. Not that there was anything wrong with either their scheming or his face. It was just that I wasn't seeing what they saw. And I wasn't wanting to.

My last few adventures in the dating world had given me plenty of reasons to avoid it altogether. Southern gentlemen had morphed into demon-like gargoyles before my eyes, Catholic hunks turned into monks, and all-round good guys became, well, the stuff of fantasy. With a track record of broken hearts, I concluded, why not consider a lifelong calling to singleness?

It wasn't hard to imagine, especially after an early assignment I'd had when I first arrived in New York. Skip had sent me to cover the one-hundredth anniversary of the Convent of Saint Helena on Manhattan's Upper West Side, a quiet brownstone building where seventeen Episcopalian nuns — who'd taken vows of chastity, poverty, and obedience — lived and worked together. They looked happy. They didn't seem to mind being single. And they never had to worry about what to wear.

I could do that, I thought when I wandered up the street from the convent. After all, I already lived out the first two vows, whether I wanted to or not. They came with the territory for a newspaper reporter. Long hours and low salaries made for limited relationships on many levels. Chastity and poverty were already familiar features in everyday life for me. It was that obedience thing that was tricky.

So I began to convince myself that I could be single for a

lifetime. After all, I'd survived the first thirty years of my life; why not the next thirty? Who needed a man? Or a date? Give me convents or witches, Buddhists or Methodists, any day. Those I could understand, or at least find some answers for if I had questions. Religious beliefs and subsequent lifestyles had become my beat, my area of expertise, even if the definitions kept shifting. But there was no *Cromwell's* for dating or romance, and relationships with men—beyond my brothers, my pop, and my boss—took on another language I wasn't entirely competent speaking.

Yes, David's message could wait this morning. I had other more pressing issues. And thankfully, when I walked into the employee lounge on the second floor, there was just enough coffee left in the bottom of the pot to keep me motivated. I poured the black gold into a mug, emptied the filter, and dumped a new one into the coffee maker. I was a good Girl Scout when it came to coffee. I always left the pot better than I found it.

"Nice of you to make it today, Lightfoot," a voice echoed behind me.

"I always make the coffee," I said, stirring sugar into my mug.

I glanced up to see my roommate and friend, Hannah X. Hensley, standing with hands on her hips.

"I meant to the office. It's almost noon, give or take an hour or two." Hannah stood a few feet from me, dressed in a short black jacket and matching slacks, and smelling like the perfume counter of Macy's. Her nails were perfectly red, matching her Valentine's Day lipstick. For Hannah's sake, I'd always thought it poetic that the *Clarion* sat in the middle of the fashion district. I'd mostly shopped at the Salvation Army thrift store with an occasional trip to the Saks Fifth Avenues of the world. But Hannah

X. Hensley was the most professional-looking, stylized reporter I'd ever known, able to mix and match silks and cottons from the boutiques all around the *Clarion*. Her outfits, shoes, and hair were as classy as her journalism, and each had long ago earned my deep admiration. She'd been my first friend in the newsroom back in Denver, and though she covered local politics and city government, she wasn't afraid to take on any story that needed extra coverage. Like religion.

"Dang, girl, I thought you left the apartment right behind me," she said, replacing the glass pot with a mug so the coffee could drip directly into it. "What took you so long?"

"A couple of witches," I said, sipping. "And a hot pretzel."

"I should have known." She smiled for a second as if the thought of a hot pretzel were as equally pleasing to her as it was to me.

When Skip had told me he'd recruited Hannah as well from the *Dispatch*, I was relieved. I'd never quite found the secret to fitting in at the *New Orleans Banner*, so coming to New York with Hannah would be ten times easier. Given our salaries and the shocking rents we discovered we'd have to pay for a Manhattan apartment, we'd even decided to share a place. Because Hannah wanted to live in the neighborhood she'd always read about in African-American literature, she found us a two-bedroom walk-up in a Harlem brownstone. She said it was just around the corner from where the journalist and author Zora Neale Hurston lived in the 1920s and about six blocks from the mosque where Malcolm X preached in the 1960s. She felt connected to Harlem, and I felt glad for a familiar and fashionable friend.

She returned the pot to the burner and started down the hall. "Want you to meet somebody, Lightfoot. You'll like him."

I stiffened. "What? Not you, too." I thought of my brother's matchmaking schemes as I struggled to keep up with her pace.

"Not that kind of 'like.'" Hannah dabbed her lips with a tissue while she talked over her shoulder to me. "I mean, you're the one who's always whining about how you never find any good news to report, how religion is supposed to have at least some positive, upbeat, inspirational something or other in it, though for some reason you can't seem to find any, so—"

"So? What are you getting me into now, Han—"

We stopped suddenly at the newspaper's mail room, a small room off of the newsroom that looked even smaller because of the boxes, envelopes, and catalogs scattered around it. Reams of paper, gray mailbags, and various machines sat on counters and chairs. A portable radio played hip-hop music. Loudly.

"Lee Cheung, meet Jonna Lightfoot MacLaughlin, our number one religion reporter. Jonna meet Lee, the *Clarion*'s new mail clerk." Though Hannah had to shout over the music, she looked enormously pleased as she pointed back and forth as if she'd just pulled off the first miracle of the day. A young Asian man in sneakers, blue jeans, and a baggy T-shirt turned down the radio, then nodded toward me, his shoulders still moving to the rhythm of the music. I bobbed my frizzy hair forward at the same time I put out my hand to him. He grinned and shook mine with cupped fingers and a tap with his knuckles.

"Whoa. It's dope to meet you, Jonna."

"It is?"

Hannah glared at me. "Of course it is. You're a big-time journalist in New York City, remember?"

"Oh yeah." I pulled up my shoulders and tried to look professional, like Hannah. "Well, it's an honor to meet you too,

Lee Cheung." He nodded. I nodded back. He nodded again, his straight black hair bouncing forward. I shrugged. Then the old heater system started to hum.

Hannah rolled her eyes. "So, Lee's a recent convert to . . ." She waved at him to finish the sentence.

"Yeah. Lots of us dudes in Chinatown are down with Jesus Christ. He's . . . radical." He said it with such sincerity that I suddenly wanted to be a young man from Chinatown too. Lee waved his hands around the mail room as if his friends were there with him, amongst the piles and the papers and the radio.

"When I picked up my mail this morning, Lee and I had a nice visit," Hannah said. Her eyes, dark brown and lined with soft tan eye shadow, moved smoothly from mine to Lee's. "He told me quite a few of his friends are becoming what he called 'on-fire believers,' even though their parents aren't, well, you'd better explain it, Lee."

"Yeah, they're, you know, into Confucius. Always have been," he said, his enthusiasm waning. I took him to be about nineteen or twenty years old, though the reverent expression he made as he spoke of his parents seemed much older.

"What do they think of your conversion?" Hannah prodded gently as if she already knew the answer. His emotion changed slightly as he raised his shoulders.

"Ah, it's alright. They believe Jesus and Confucius are both cool. For us," he said. "See, Jesus got us off the streets, so they're, like, really glad we get to church now more than . . . uh, other places." He rearranged a pile of catalogs at that point, his face a tension of emotions, I guessed, over those "other places" he'd mentioned. I slurped my coffee, impressed by his ability to sort and talk and organize at the same time.

"Don't get me wrong, dude," he said, jumping from package to package, sorting and scribbling and stamping. "I wouldn't have it any other way. I got saved, see. I got this job. Everybody's cool—and Chinatown's hip now. No lie. You should see it."

His face was so earnest that I couldn't help but wonder what Chinatown looked like . . . hip. I'd been a few times already, and it had been crowded with tourists, vendors, and fish markets. The food was great, but I hadn't noticed much that resembled the kind of attitudes Lee was describing. Still, this did have the scent of a good-news story.

I asked Lee to tell me a little more about his life in Chinatown, pulled my notebook from my bag, and started an official interview. Hannah tapped my elbow as if dotting the bottom of an exclamation mark. "I told you you'd like him. You can thank me later," she said, strolling back through the newsroom as if she owned it.

In between stacking packages and classifying letters, Lee talked. He'd spent his first three years of life in China before his parents brought him to New York, where they lived with his uncle on Mott Street. Soon after they arrived in the U.S., his brother was born. But by the time they'd entered their teens, both brothers had grown tired of the strict traditions of their parents' beliefs. The White Tigers—"a very un-cool gang" according to Lee—made them feel important. They started staying out each night on the streets, guarding their territory against other gangs, even cops. He learned to fight. He saw a few friends killed.

Lee's eyes clouded, and he paused from his story while I wrote. If he started to cry, I knew I'd be blubbering as well within seconds. Thankfully, though, when I looked up, he collected himself before poking his head into the hallway, looking right, then left. Then he retreated to a spot by a filing cabinet and lifted his elbow above his head to show me the tattoo of a tiger's head on the inside of his arm, no bigger than a quarter, with two Chinese characters next to it.

"This was all about loyalty, man," he said quietly. "But no more. Not after —" The phone rang in the mail room. He held up his index finger toward me and answered. After an English greeting, he broke into Mandarin, laughed, paused, and then abruptly hung up.

"Sorry, but the boss is coming," he said, nodding toward another pile of packages I hadn't noticed. "Tons of work to do so, uh —"

"No problem," I said. "I'm on deadline too. Maybe I could come with you to Chinatown sometime soon?"

Lee put his fist on his heart to affirm my presence with him and nodded enthusiastically. I nodded back and we agreed to meet Friday after work when his church held special services for youth, where he said things "rocked with Jesus." I could join him if I wanted — which, of course, I did.

Because good news in the world of religion reporting was not easy to come by, I followed any hint of a lead I could. No problem finding witches protesting a government ruling I'd never heard of, or discovering pious ministers stealing from honest parishioners, or racist graffiti scrawled across synagogues or churches. All these I'd covered over the past five years because bad news in the world of religion was normal. But *good news* stories? They'd been as hard to come by as, well, a good date.

They probably existed, I reminded myself as I left the mail room and walked back to my desk. I knew in my bones that religion should be good for us. Like aerobics and broccoli. It should be sunshine, not dark clouds.

That was what I'd always been taught, after all; the picture back at my desk reminded me of a thousand conversations about spiritual goodness. Rested against a dictionary by my computer, between a coffee mug and back issues of the *Clarion*, my family's photograph was a steady friend who'd come with me first to Denver, then New Orleans, and now New York. I settled into my chair and stared at my three brothers, their wives, and me standing on a mountain in Colorado. Next to it I had set a snapshot of my parents with coffee farmers in Costa Rica. The more I looked, the more I could almost hear my mom's and pop's voices: "*You live what you believe, kids.*" Religion and faith in their world were the same as good character or positive vibes or at least organic lifestyles. I supposed they were the reason I kept looking for the good.

They were proof positive, after all. With each new faith they'd embraced when we were growing up, my parents found something helpful to hang on to. So had my brothers. Granted, they'd be the first to admit that none of those other religions fully captivated their souls, but that didn't stop them from grabbing some transcendent insight along the way. And when they'd discovered that Jesus was what they'd been after all along, they laughed at how well prepared they'd been, as if these other spiritual encounters had been a sort of boot camp for believing.

God, they'd now come to believe, was not contained in a religion that required they live right or else suffer the consequences. Rather, they said he was a person with a name and a story—and a love they could never have imagined.

I admired their faith.

I dusted off the picture with a tissue and swallowed back the nostalgia as a stack of press releases that had been accumulating for a week pulled my attention away. The first was for a meditation workshop, the next three announced pastoral changes in pulpits around the city's boroughs, and half a dozen after those advertised astrology, numerology, and Scientology conferences happening in New York during the coming months. Each was a lead to a potential story I'd need to cover, though today they'd all have to wait.

Witches were calling. I flipped through my notes and felt again the dark frigid air around the podium where Lady Crystal had delivered her message. The stony faces of the crowd dropped into my mind; so did Griffin Lewis's anger about his son. I made a quick phone call to the Department of Veterans Affairs office and reached a weary-sounding clerk named Rob Beckwith.

"Yes, I can confirm the ruling that Wicca is not included as an approved religion," he said dryly.

"How exactly does the Department of Veterans Affairs define religion?"

He cleared his throat so that he sounded slightly annoyed and responded, "Mmm . . . that information is . . . honestly, all I can tell you, Miss, is that the DVA is firm in its position toward witches. Anything else?"

"But I'm not exactly sure why Wiccans don't qualify, while others — like atheists — do."

"I'm not at liberty to say. Sorry. Only that they don't."

I couldn't think of another way to ask the man, and he wasn't budging. I thanked him for his time and hung up. This was an odd one. I knew I needed more than *Cromwell's* to understand, so I headed toward Skip's office.

"Hey, Skip, what's the name of your friend who —?" I stopped myself when I saw someone sitting opposite Skip in his office. I didn't recognize the man as either another editor or one of the advertising executives. His short white hair was gelled neatly back and he wore a bow tie that made his pinstriped suit seem all the more distinguished. If he was a newspaperman, he was setting a new standard. Though he looked to be about ten years older than Skip, something about him made him seem like a peer.

"Oops, sorry, Skip. Didn't know you were busy," I said, turning 180 degrees before my boss called me back.

"The door's always open, Lightfoot. Besides, now I can introduce you to someone who will probably be playing an important role at the *Clarion*."

The bow-tied man stood dignified and gentlemanly, nodding a single time toward me as I reentered Skip's office. I put out my hand.

"Jonna Lightfoot MacLaughlin," I said, using my most professional-sounding voice.

"Walter Wood," he responded, his hand gripping mine. A quick fragrance of cologne confirmed his class. His voice and energy were low, an even match to my editor.

"Walter works in finance," Skip said slowly, adjusting his glasses. "His firm is interested in media investments."

"That sounds important," I said.

Walter grinned but didn't bite. Instead, he put one hand under his chin, the other under his elbow, and looked at me as if he were studying a picture. A few seconds seemed as long as winter. Finally, he responded.

"Oh yes. You're the religion reporter, aren't you?" My cheeks took flame. He continued, "You wrote that series a few months ago on Muslim and Jewish conflicts in Brooklyn, right? Religion in a place like New York City must be fascinating."

"No shortage of interesting stories, that's for sure," I said. "Speaking of stories, Skip, would you mind giving me the name of your professor friend at Regal? I'd like to get my head around this witch thing, but I need a little extra help. I figured your friend would be just the—" I cut myself off when the two men exchanged glances; I felt as if I'd just confirmed the adage that three was indeed a crowd.

Nonetheless, Skip scribbled a name on a notepad, found a phone number in his files, and handed me the information. Then he sat back down in his chair and gestured for Walter Wood to do the same.

"Anything else?" Skip's gentle nature returned.

"That'll do." I read the name—*Dr. Evan Hartman*—and nodded toward the bow tie. "A pleasure to meet you, Walter."

"And you, Joanie," he said. "Keep up the good work."

I glanced at Skip to see if he'd caught the mistake, but he was already reading a document Walter had set on his desk.

"First things first, Walter Wood," I said under my breath as I walked back toward my cubicle. "It's Jonna. Not Joanie, for Pete's sake."

Names were important to MacLaughlins. After all, my brothers and I had been specially christened by our parents, so we took names seriously. Mom and Pop loved to recount how they'd heard some funky folk band in their hippie days on San Francisco's Haight Street, like Peter, Paul and Mary, a band they were sure had been called Matthew, Mark, Luke, and Jon. They'd been uniquely inspired by the group, and we were, therefore, reminders of that inspiration. And in fitting with their activist years, they'd gone to great lengths to show solidarity with Native Americans by imparting Matthew with the middle name of *BigBear*, Mark

RunningWind, and Luke *EagleWing*. I, of course, was Lightfoot for all the right reasons, and though we were as Irish as potatoes and Guinness, we were proud of each aspect of our identity.

Names mattered. And I was immediately suspicious of anyone who got mine wrong. Especially men in bow ties.

I sat down at my computer, resolved not to let it get to me, and set to work. Just as I picked up my office phone to call the professor, my cell phone rang, startling me so that I bumped my knee. I slammed down one phone and scrounged in my bag for the other. *Ring.* I was finding everything but the critter: Gideon, my tiny green New Testament, was on top, along with receipts, postcards I'd been meaning to send, an empty Krispy Kreme bag, two reporter's notebooks. Still ringing. Finally, underneath a stash of Hershey's in the bottom of my bag, I nabbed it.

"Hi. This is Lightfoot," I answered.

"How's my favorite sister?" Luke's voice was as familiar as a double latte.

"Oh, you know, the usual. Enchanted," I said, unwrapping the chocolate and letting it melt in my cheek to calm my soul. He laughed in my ear.

"You?" I asked.

"The kids are on a weird vibe this morning."

"My nephews or your students?"

"Yes. Must be the weather," he said. I looked toward the window. Still snowing. "But that's not why I called, Jon. How 'bout dinner?"

"It's kind of early, don't you think? I just had a pretzel, which was after some yogurt, but I'm always open for—"

"I meant tonight. David e-mailed and called first thing this morning. Says he's got some big news that we all—including you—need to hear, so we told him to come over tonight . . . ah, just a second, Jon." He paused before telling one of his students not to play with the cymbals yet. I clicked open my e-mail and read a forwarded message from Luke.

"Okay, I'm back. Where was I?"

"David e-mailed and called," I reminded him.

"Right. Did you get his message?"

"I'm reading it as we speak."

"What? You weren't late to the office again, were you?"

"The call of duty," I said, hearing an increase of musical burps in the background. "Mom and Pop were never Wiccans, were they?"

"Wiccans? You mean witches?" Cymbals crashed. "Don't think so. Hey, you're not changing the subject, are you? You can't keep avoiding David, Jon. He's such a—"

"I know, he's such a nice guy."

"Well, at least give him a chance," he said. "Besides, Sarah's making enchilada casserole. And brownies—from scratch."

"That was mean." I deleted the e-mail along with three other spam-looking e-mails. A tuba blasted in the background. "I don't know, Luke, I, uh, well—"

"Good. Just come after work." Students began hollering. I heard more cymbals clang, horns blast, and a piano pound. "Band practice just started, Jon. See you tonight!"

He hung up, and I went back to my witches. I called Professor Evan Hartman at Regal but only got his voice mail. I left a message and began typing:

> *Visit the grave site of a fallen soldier, and*
> *depending on his faith you'll see on the headstone*

a Protestant cross, a Star of David, or the Virgin Mary. What you won't see is the five-point star in a circle, known as a Wiccan pentacle.

The Department of Veterans Affairs, which determines the military's list of approved religious symbols, ruled yesterday that the Wiccan star could not be included on government-funded headstones. The decision cast a bad spell on a local group who protested this morning at the entrance of Regal University. Leaders of the witches say they're tired of the discrimination and just want to be included with . . .

I stopped typing and stared at the lede, but after a paragraph, curiosity pulled me away from my screen. What could be so important that David would call and e-mail my brother so early in the morning? Why did he want me to know too? The man worked with old records and documents day in and day out, in a world where nothing seemed to move except the dust on the books or the occasional researcher who visited the library. What breaking news could he possibly have?

Outside the window, I watched the snow drop lightly on the city. The sun had disappeared behind gray clouds that reminded me of swirls of whipped cream melting into hot chocolate. It was a different sky from the western ones I'd grown up with, where the color was always ocean blue and the sun would shine even while the snow fell. How were such things possible? And why did I keep getting distracted, by clouds and snow and David wanting to meet with me, with us?

My stomach and shoulders grew tense. I rubbed the back of

my neck, pinching the muscles like pizza dough and thinking of enchilada casserole, nice-enough faces, and convents.

"Everything okay, Lightfoot?"

I zipped around toward Skip, who stood behind my desk, a puzzled look on his face, a water bottle in his hand.

"Sure. Why?"

"When I didn't see the usual flames coming out of your computer, I got a little worried," he said. He twisted the cap and swallowed some water.

"No, I was just . . . thinking."

"Don't let them get to you. There are far scarier characters in this city than witches and warlocks rallying, believe me." He shook his head as if he'd personally met such villains, and I wondered about Walter Wood. "Let's go with this for the Metro section, okay? By four o'clock?"

"Maybe. But I'd like to talk first with your professor friend," I said, "and I haven't been able to reach him."

"Makes sense. Keep me posted," he said. "We can save it for tomorrow if we have to." Skip tipped an imaginary hat toward me and went to his meeting.

The four o'clock deadline came and went, and I still hadn't heard back from the professor. I decided instead to send my editor the backup story I'd been working on during the week, a 415-word piece about the controversies surrounding a Pentecostal yoga class being held at a church in Times Square. That would have to do for now. Hopefully, I'd be able to interview Professor Hartman tomorrow morning and finish the story for the weekend edition. I gathered my parka and cap, told Hannah I'd see her later at the apartment, and took the elevator downstairs. The snow had stopped outside, but the cold still bit my face.

I walked down Avenue of the Americas toward the New Jersey PATH subway station, hoping the motion and the February air would do me good. The sidewalk crowd rolled quickly along each block and kept me moving with it. Though I'd lived here now almost a year, I still marveled at the many different faces I saw and languages I heard each time I entered the streets. Sometimes I listened to conversations in sounds and syllables I couldn't recognize, reminding me just how far this city was from the parks of Denver or the lakes of New Orleans. At the same time, I knew it was only a tiny piece of the world and I was simply riding along on its wave.

It wasn't hard to feel small here.

Maybe it was the combination of the witches rally, the messages from David, and the pastrami sandwich I'd inhaled from Goldwasser's deli for lunch, but the subway ride under the Hudson River seemed longer tonight than usual. I'd never quite gotten used to the idea that I had to go beneath a river to see my brother and his family; tunnels for me had always, and only, been carved inside mountains. That seemed logical to me—that someone could dig a long narrow hole through dirt and rocks so the rest of us wouldn't have to climb 13,000 feet to get to the other side. In New York City, however, someone had actually figured out how to conquer a flowing river with the same objective as the mountains back home—so we wouldn't have to go up and over. Or, in this case, get wet. But it never made sense to me. How could you dig a hole in water? I held my breath every time I rode the train until I emerged in the little urban village called Hoboken.

I climbed the hill from the PATH station to my brother's apartment, a pre–World War II building that sat in the middle of Sinatra Drive. Its steps had a postcard view of the river and

Manhattan's skyline, though Luke and Sarah's apartment faced the opposite direction. Sometimes I'd stand and look before pushing the buzzer in their entrance, if for nothing else but to remind myself where I was. Tonight it was still light enough to see the trees on top of some of the high-rises along the river, but it was too cold to stand looking for long. In about an hour, the lights would come up across the city, and the entire island would look from here like a midnight sky with a million stars.

Sarah was pulling a long blue ceramic pan from the oven when I walked in.

"Hey!" we hollered at the same time. Her thin blonde hair was tied back in a single braid that hung in the middle of her back on her tiny frame. She wore a dark green wraparound skirt and a black sweater. Whenever I saw her, I got the impression that she'd just stepped from her closet. Even with two children, Sarah was perfectly arranged, a trait I admired but could never aspire to. I knew my limits.

She set the pan on the counter, but just as she stepped toward me, two boys — miniature versions of my brother Luke, with moppy brown hair and thick arms — jumped out from behind the couch to scare their aunt. I screamed as if I were afraid before tickling my youngest nephew, Garrett, and high-fiving his brother, Jesse. Sarah joined in, and we'd have kept the giggle fest going except that the buzzer suddenly filled the apartment. Jesse skipped over to punch the button and let in whoever was downstairs, while Sarah, Garrett, and I collected ourselves and moved around the oak table across the living room. I pulled glasses from the hutch and set plates on the table. Sarah folded napkins and talked about her new recipe. Garrett shot across the floor when he heard the front door open.

The six-year-old boy bounced into his dad's arms to welcome him home. As he did, another man entered behind Luke. But he wasn't looking at my brother or my nephew.

Instead, David Rockley was looking straight at me.

:: Chapter Three

He stood a few inches taller than my brother, though Luke's shoulders were broader. When he pulled off his coat, David's red wool sweater almost seemed to swallow him up as if he'd bought it at a time in his life when he was eating more than he had been lately. His eyes seemed tired, but there was no mistaking the squareness of his perpetual expression. It was still a face that oozed nice.

I'd seen it only a few times since taking the *Clarion* job. The first time was the Saturday morning I'd just rolled into Harlem when he joined Luke to help unpack my U-Haul truck; the others were in this apartment for Sunday lunch after we'd all visited Second Presbyterian of Hoboken. It wasn't without his trying; he'd left plenty of voice mails for me at work inviting me for coffee and e-mailed the occasional book-reading announcement, church event invitation, or trendy café he thought would make my transition to the city easier. My schedule, though, had always been conveniently full.

"I'm glad you could make it tonight, Jonna. Really glad." David's voice revealed a genuine lilt of pleasure that did not go unnoticed by anyone in the room. Even my nephew's eyeballs were on me, sending the color in my cheeks up like a thermometer.

"What's the matter, Aunt Jonna?" Garrett's little face peered up into mine as he grabbed my hand. "Your face is all funny."

"You're just now noticing that, Garrett?" I tried to divert. I leaned into him, crossed my eyes, and pursed my lips together into a pretzel twist so that he had to laugh. Then he mimicked my face, which triggered the same reaction from me. My brother greeted his wife with a kiss, Jesse led "Uncle David" to his fish tank, and Garrett and I competed with funnier faces. It was a normal start of a MacLaughlin evening.

Five minutes later, we all congregated in the kitchen, a small but colorful room with a high ceiling and cupboards and shelves that lined each section of the walls. Because Sarah worked from home baking artistic cakes and pies for local cafés—though I never understood how she stayed so petite—she knew how to utilize the space. Between the triple hanging fruit baskets and the pans hooked on a metal rod above the stove, the kitchen always reminded me of the type I'd see in European culinary magazines. But it was as comfortable as a family memory.

Luke poured Brooklyn lagers for us as Sarah tossed a salad. The boys helped by pouring their own glasses of milk and dumping a bag of tortilla chips in a bowl. We rested against the counters, taking in the aromas and warmth from the stove, and raised our glasses.

"To old friends," David said, holding up his mug before clinking ours. He took a sip, and the froth of the beer stayed like a mustache above his lip. Jesse thought that was cool, so he did the same thing with his milk, and of course Garrett followed until all three were gloating over their soggy mouths.

"To old friends," Luke repeated. "And you can never have too many of those in the world, right, hon?" He toasted his wife, who toasted him back, and offered the chips to me. I obliged.

Then my brother, never one to miss an opportunity, went straight to the point of our gathering.

"So, David, what's happening? I've been curious all day."

David wiped the foam—and the silliness—from his face and stared at his shoes as if they had a scuff mark he was suddenly embarrassed by.

"Let the poor man finish his beer first, Luke," Sarah said as she ushered us to the table. "And let's eat some dinner, for goodness' sake. After that, who knows?"

I took the chair next to Jesse, a safe distance from David, and reminded myself that I hadn't come over here just because a nice single man had some secret message he felt compelled to reveal. I had ulterior motives, and they were flavored with chocolate and nuts. At this time of night and after a stranger-than-usual day, the idea of eating brownies made from scratch with my nephews had all but sustained me through the afternoon.

We joined hands, bowed our heads, and listened as Luke said grace: "Dear God, hear our prayer from grateful sinners as we thank you for our dinners. Amen."

"Amen!" the boys shouted. Sarah's enchilada casserole was dripping with cheese and salsa, a pyramid of sour cream plopped on top, a taste as comfortable as her kitchen. Luke asked his sons about their days at school and then recounted cymbal and trombone stories with Shakespearean drama. When Sarah's plate of brownies was finally emptied and the boys had gone to bed, the four of us sat contentedly over coffee in the living room.

David's countenance turned grave. His glasses kept slipping down his nose, and he kept pushing them back with his index finger, an anxious gesture I'd never noticed before. Luke slurped his coffee and put his arm around Sarah, who leaned against him on the couch. My neck muscles felt tight again. It was so quiet that I could hear the sound of the refrigerator humming from the kitchen.

"There's something I've needed to talk about . . . with friends I trust," he said quietly, staring into his cup as if there were secret codes hidden in it. I gulped my coffee, though my fingers—and nerves—were really itching for a cigarette. Luke looked at his friend and waited. Sarah smiled gently.

I resisted the urge to dwell on the happy nuns of Saint Helena's convent. Thinking of their simple life and my possible part in it would have been easier than hearing what I was sure would be a ridiculous pronouncement of David's intentions, which wouldn't exactly be the best ending to a day already filled with awkward encounters. But I pushed away the image and waited for the worst.

"I've discovered something I can't keep secret any longer. I couldn't live with myself if I didn't tell . . . someone." His voice dropped to a whisper and his eyes met mine. I glanced at the books on the shelves.

"What is it, David?" Sarah asked softly.

He nodded, took a big swig of coffee as if that would fortify him for what he was about to say—which I had to admit I could relate to—and swallowed. Loudly. His Adam's apple jiggled.

"It might change everything, but here goes." He paused, then continued. "Something is really wrong . . . at Regal." He let go a breath like he'd been holding it in all day and now felt ten pounds lighter for having released it.

Regal? A wave of relief teased out the tension in my neck and shoulders, and the coffee warmed me.

"Well, you're not kidding about that," I said, then chuckled.

"It's downright creepy. I know I shouldn't say that, but that's how it feels."

David's eyes grew wide, though a hint of liberation fluttered from behind his lenses. "You know about it?"

"They haven't exactly kept it a secret, have they?"

"But I thought I was the only one who knew."

"Not anymore. I was over there this morning and—"

"You were at Regal?"

"Sure was. My boss sent me over to cover the—"

"Your boss knows about this?"

Sarah and Luke turned back and forth as if they were watching a tennis match. I set down my coffee and pulled my hair off my neck before letting it drop again. Sometimes rearranging the frizz helped me think better.

"Of course he knows. He wanted me to see what I could find out, but I have to tell you, it wasn't pretty. In fact, it was like a dark cloud had descended, but only on that spot on the campus, and it had this weird ripple effect."

David almost dropped his cup. "That's exactly what I've thought. But how did you . . . how did your editor . . . ?" David paused and tilted his head. He rubbed his chin. "Wait a minute. Are we talking about the same thing?"

"Witches, right?" I answered as I reached for my coffee.

And in wildly different tones, Luke, Sarah, and David all exclaimed at the same time: "Witches?!"

Sarah nestled in closer to her husband as if the idea frightened her, while Luke sat up straight, looking both brave and mildly unimpressed, both attributes he'd learned most of his life. Each time our parents visited a new temple or hosted a guru, Luke became both courageous and cautious. Sometimes we met characters who were genuinely daunting: long beards, dark eyes, expressionless faces. In hindsight, that exposure had come in handy.

"What are you talking about?" Luke said and pointed his finger at me. "Wait a minute. Is that why you asked me on the phone if Mom and Pop were ever Wiccans?"

"Yup. About fifty witches held a rally bright and early this morning at the university's entrance," I said. "Except it wasn't bright at all."

David began to laugh. Snort really. Like milk had gone down the wrong way. The snort turned into a chuckle and then a laugh that seemed such a relief he could no longer help himself. It became so contagious Sarah joined in, and Luke couldn't help himself either. Soon we were all laughing—though we weren't sure why—until Sarah passed around a box of tissues as we tried to stop.

Finally, Luke staggered off the couch and down the hall. Sarah decided we needed another pot of coffee to sober us up, and David and I were facing each other. Alone. He wiped his eyes and cleaned his glasses. I leaned back into a pillow to catch my breath. And I was completely unprepared for what happened next.

"You're beautiful when you laugh," he said softly. "I hope you don't mind my saying so."

My stomach did a flip and I knocked over my cup. The last few sips left in it splattered across the hardwood floor. I bolted to the kitchen to get a dish towel, and by the time I returned, Luke had happily resumed his place on the couch. I cleaned up my mess while Sarah poured me a refill. I didn't know what David was doing because I couldn't bring myself to look at him.

It was Luke who got us back on track. "So, Jon, what's with your witches?" he asked. "I missed why they were there in the first place."

"Oh, you know. The usual: protesting the government, who won't let them put Wiccan symbols on soldiers' headstones," I said, gathering my defenses. "Seems they're not considered an official religion and — "

"But that didn't stop Regal from allowing them to protest, did it?" David's interruption surprised me; his tone clipped back to serious, not a hint of laughter anywhere. He shook his head fervently, though no hair went out of place, and poked his glasses up his nose again before saying, "Which is what I don't understand."

Luke shot me a questioning look and shrugged. Sarah sat down beside Luke, who rested his hand across her back.

"Here's my big secret," David said. "Regal will allow every type of thinker, protestor, or fringe believer you could imagine to use its campus for anything they perceive as a good cause — or good publicity for the university. But guess who's been pushed aside in the process?"

"Who?" Sarah asked.

"You."

"I have?" Luke's voice was a mix of confusion and wonder. "I haven't been up there since we went to that basketball game — "

"I mean, you, as in Presbyterians. Or Baptists. Or Methodists. And the ultimate irony? Even Episcopalians." He dropped a heaping spoonful of sugar into his coffee and stirred it over and over, more from passion than necessity, in my estimation. But I heard the pattern he was talking about. Protestants. Bible-believing Christians. I bit. I'd heard these conspiracy theories before.

"Come on, David. Are you saying Regal is intentionally pushing Christians aside?"

"We're invisible. A thorn in the side of most of the administrators or faculty. Nuisances because we don't fit their intellectual objectives."

"Which are?"

"Rigorous thinking, lots of evidence. Science and equality, which are all fine. Important even. That's what higher education is all about." He took a breath. "Except they go a step further. Who has proof for God? No one, they say, and therefore biblical faith today is irrelevant in the academy. It's like they've scratched out anything—and anyone—remotely linked to Christianity."

Luke widened his eyes at the same time he perched his foot across his opposite knee. "Whoa, David, what triggered all this?"

"My job," he answered, his tone firm but soft.

For the next hour or so, David Rockley told us exactly what he'd discovered in the archives at Regal University: It began seven months ago when the university president, Dale M. Coen, and his board of trustees decided to implement a restructuring plan across the urban campus to match their vision for growth. New space had to be created for new programs and offices, which meant anything that could be either eliminated or absorbed into another department was instructed to do so. Because of new technology, the college archives where David worked was given the tedious task of transforming many of the old documents, which had been stored in massive freezer-like rooms in the historic library building, into digital archives that took up no space and made the old rooms available for offices. Once they were digitized, the documents were to be either shredded or shipped to storage space in White Plains, depending on the nature and status of their contents.

"At first, my colleagues and I didn't think it was a big deal.

But it's been months now that we've been sorting through thousands of folders, forms, letters, manuscripts, and yearbooks that we've accumulated since the college began in 1754," he said. He paused and pushed his knuckles against the palm of his hands, cracking each.

"That's impressive," I said. "I can barely keep track of the press releases from last week. I can't imagine organizing letters from the past three hundred years."

Luke agreed, but David simply looked at his knuckles. I settled back against my chair, wondering why this was so personal to David, or even why we needed to know.

"The original charter of the university," he continued quietly, "was filed carefully in a folder that anyone could access. When I went to transfer it to the digital archive, a letter fell out. It led me to a bunch of other files, and before I knew it an entire story was coming together, one I knew would spell trouble for the college—if anyone ever found out."

Luke and Sarah sat now on the edge of the couch, like children hearing a mystery for the first time. They ignored their coffee. David grew more animated with each detail. He rose from the couch and began to pace.

"Like most Ivy League schools on the East Coast," David told us, "Regal had been founded as a Protestant seminary—Episcopalian to be exact—to train and equip young ministers in the Scriptures. Its entire purpose was religious, largely because the culture at the time was one that valued at its center Christian doctrine and biblical values. Churches were the heart of communities and their buildings used regularly as schools, town halls, council gatherings, and of course Sunday morning worship venues."

His glance shifted toward me, and I couldn't help but hear the passion in his voice as he continued: Like Princeton, Yale, Harvard, and the others, he told us, Regal's initial purpose had been consistent with the time in which it was established, and like the others, a simple glance around the campus confirmed its mission. Latin inscriptions were carved at the entrances of the buildings, and biblical verses were etched below images, statues, and shields. Even the school mottos reinforced their original purpose.

David stood beside the lamp. "Harvard's was 'Veritas Christo et Ecclesiae,' or 'Truth for Christ and the Church.' Princeton's was 'Dei sub numine viget,' or 'Under God's power she flourishes,' and Dartmouth's 'Vox clamantis in deserto,' or 'A voice crying in the wilderness,'" he said, driving home the point. "You can't miss it, really. It's everywhere on the campus."

I looked at Luke and Sarah, whose attention to David was as fixed as the statues he described. Then David sighed deeply before he pulled out of his shirt pocket a piece of Regal stationery with its traditional coat of arms at the top. He unfolded the paper neatly and held it up as evidence. I recognized the symbol from T-shirts and coffee mugs I'd seen around the office.

"If you look closely," he said, "Regal's motto is spelled out underneath the lion's head. See it? 'In luce Tua videmus lucem.' 'In Thy light we see light.'" Luke and Sarah peered in closely and shook their heads as if what they were seeing was hard to believe. It was.

"That's straight out of the Psalms, isn't it?" Luke whispered, leaning back on the couch and stretching his elbows behind his head as if this were something he'd have to keep thinking about. "Wow. I guess we've come a long way since then."

"I guess we have come a long way," I repeated. But the reporter in me pushed another response. "Sorry, David, but I still don't get it. So Regal was once a seminary, now it isn't. Lots of things have changed over the years. What's the big—"

And that's when David Rockley became an altogether different man. Nice no longer described him. He paced across the floor so wildly that I thought the click of his shoes might wake up the boys. His hands became fists and his face grew patchy spots the color of his sweater. I wondered if flames might fly out of his ears until he pounded his way into the kitchen, poured some water, and devoured it. He emerged only slightly cooler, his face still splotchy and his fists still firm. We froze.

I stuttered, "I didn't mean to—"

"It's not you, Jonna. It's the administration. It's the injustice of it all, especially because . . ." His expression was still angry, but the kindness returned to his eyes. He continued to pace and click and gesture.

"Because what, David?" Luke asked.

"Because from what I can tell, there's no one who's still alive to speak up, to challenge what's happened."

All three of us blinked. Sarah leaned into my brother, who put out the solitary question: "Alive?"

"Let me explain." David sat down as he recounted how that first letter he'd discovered was from a Mr. and Mrs. Frank Cherrinard. It'd been clipped to a legal document that, in turn, took him to other financial records and letters. Apparently, Frank had been a successful and sincere alumni who'd worried that the university might wander from its original mission. So he and his wife had instructed Regal's officials to establish a fund in their name and had provided specific instructions for administering it.

David pulled another piece of paper from his pocket and unfolded it in front of us.

"This is a copy of the original letter from Frank himself, dated July 21, 1833, asking the university to . . ." He held it out in front of him and read, " . . . 'to ensure the integrative scholarship of biblical education into all academic departments at Regal and provide for good charitable works throughout the city so students can extend their faith in godly service.'" David glanced up from the paper, the light from the lamp beside him casting a circular pattern across his face as he continued. "The Cherrinards never had children, and it looks as if this was their way to carry on their legacy." He paused as he handed the letter to Luke. "Think about it: Their endowment, which would have accumulated a lot of interest by now, was established for the specific purpose of funding things like special lectures or curriculum resources, as well as salaries for theology professors and scholarships for ministry students."

"Well, who knew?" Luke said reading over the letter. "I had no idea Regal was so . . . religious."

"Exactly." David leaned back in his chair and stretched. Luke passed the letter to Sarah and finally to me. I read over the intentions of the Cherrinards and tripped when I came to one small sentence at the end, right before "Respectfully Yours." I read it aloud:

" . . . 'that our beloved Regal, a light set on a hill, might beckon all of New York to look on it with gladdened heart.'" I reread it silently and handed the letter back to David. "With gladdened heart?"

"It was a great vision," he said, returning the letter to his pocket. "See, the Cherrinards believed the college had a mission to the city, not just its students. They'd become convinced—and wrote about it in their journals—that the highest form of learning came in service to the poor and marginalized, so they'd come to expect that from Regal. When they established their fund, they included a clause that hoped it would help new immigrants and poor families; hospitals, as well as theology students and professors."

"And that would make everyone glad they were there," Luke said. He shook his head at the idea as if he were amazed by the sound of his voice uttering such a possibility. David nodded silently. I didn't know what to think.

Finally, David walked slowly toward the bookshelf at the end of the couch like he'd spotted a title he'd been searching for. But he didn't reach for one. Instead, he glanced at his watch and turned to us. "I know it's getting late, so let me just cut to the quick: Regal's trustees eagerly accepted the Cherrinard gift over 150 years ago, and to be blunt, they have gotten fat off it all these years. I've found letters from Regal's administrative leaders assuring the Cherrinard estate that the funds would be well served. But I've also come across statements dating back at least sixty years that justified the diversion of the Cherrinard donation into personal accounts, office updates, stock investments, and academic departments that explored everything but Christian theology, let alone missions to the city." David returned to his chair and leaned back as though he were grateful for the support it offered. He was tired.

No one said a thing. Aside from the refrigerator's hum, we sat still in the silence, sorting through the information David had just revealed. My brain flashed back to the morning, stepping through the cold at the edge of the Regal campus to cover a group of witches rallying for their rights. Students had wandered past us, busy, focused, and hectic, and the university seemed alive in the way most did. It was far from the quaint picture David had painted of it at the time Mr. Cherrinard attended. I had to be honest; I wasn't so sure that was bad.

"Don't these things happen all the time?" Luke asked. "I mean, money gets donated for one reason and something else comes up that they need it for. You know, tyranny of the urgent, that sort of thing."

David looked away and toward the bookshelf again as if he didn't like either the question he'd just heard or the answer he was about to give. "In the criminal world, Luke, that's called money laundering. Or fraud. You can't take money donated for one thing and divert it into personal accounts or real estate acquisition or other pressing needs. It's not legal."

I scratched my head and scrunched my hair, hoping some revelation might drop into my brain so I'd understand what he was talking about. Nothing. I pushed the point: "So you think an Ivy League school stole a bunch of money from a rich religious guy who lived a couple hundred years ago? And we should care because . . . ?"

My brother tossed a pillow at me, chastising me for being so crass. He looked at David, his eyes full of apology. "My sister doesn't—"

"She's right. It sounds crazy. And obviously, the school has changed over the years," he said. "I get that. We live in a very different world today than when Frank Cherrinard attended Regal."

He drank the last of his coffee, which was probably cold, and took his mug along with ours to the kitchen sink. Luke glared at me. When David returned to his seat, he breathed deeply and narrowed his vision.

"But the letters and the endowment were very, very specific, regardless of what happened around the campus or the city, so I've been worried, thinking how I should go about exposing this crime," he said, his voice quiet.

"Are you sure you should do anything?" I asked. "I mean, it'd be hard for you to —"

"But who else will?" He took off his glasses and rubbed his eyes. "I guess if it were my money, I'd want someone to do something about it."

"And someone . . . else . . . could," I said.

He shook his head. "Not so far. In fact, once, a few years ago, a member of the Baptist Student Union on campus wrote the administration about the Cherrinards, asking if there were scholarships available for students like him . . ."

"See?"

" . . . and he was reassigned. To Tennessee College."

"Sounds like a job for Lois Lane." My brother gazed straight at me when he spoke, his face pudgy. It was the last thing I'd been thinking.

"No thanks. I've got my share of bad news already — witches, remember?"

"Right," Luke said. "They're your ticket to the campus."

"I don't think so."

"You can use them as an excuse to snoop around campus." I glared at him, but my brother continued being a brother. "Jon, you know as well as I do that this is why you became a reporter: to expose stories like this. To win back some of the good in religion. This sounds like as good a time as any."

It was my turn to pace. I walked toward the table in case any brownies were left, and when I didn't find even a crumb, I considered reaching for a cigarette.

"Don't worry about it, Jonna," David said. "After all, I'm not supposed to know about these documents. That was the official word from President Coen when I met with him about them."

"You met with the president?" Luke and I now were in stereo.

"Wouldn't you?"

Luke nodded. I didn't.

"He wasn't very happy with me for 'wasting' his time on such 'trivial' matters." David punctuated the terms, forming imaginary quotation marks in the air with his fingers. "But I think I got his attention, especially when I told him I was fairly sure these were legally binding documents and it seemed as if Regal—under his leadership—could be guilty of money laundering, for starters."

"What did he say then?" I asked, astonished at the nice man's nerve.

"That I might want to start looking for another job . . . and I have."

The room went quiet again. And as if the severity of the situation had just stolen the last of any energy we had, we all rose from our seats at the same time. Luke handed David his backpack and coat while I pulled mine from the closet. My brother charged us to meet here again Sunday after church with the following directives: David was to bring copies of some of the documents he'd shown us, I was to snoop around the newsroom to see if anyone else might know anything, and Sarah would call her father, who was a lawyer, for advice on how to handle the situation. Luke remembered that some of his students' parents were

Regal alumni, so he, too, would see what he could find out. I felt sort of queasy about his plan but knew better than to take on my brother this late in the day.

Instead, I put off thinking about it until tomorrow and left the Hoboken apartment — at the same time David did. Because he lived on the Upper West Side of Manhattan, not far from Harlem, he offered to make sure I got home safely. It was after eleven and I was too tired and too cold to argue. But when we turned the corner, he paused.

"Um, this is going to sound crazy, Jonna, but would you mind if we took the ferry across the river instead? I have this thing about tunnels in the water. They sort of make me nervous."

I blinked at him. Maybe it was the moon, or the discussion we'd just had, but David Rockley didn't look quite the same.

::Chapter Four

Anyone else might have called it romantic—a ferry ride across the Hudson River, the moonlight glowing on the water, and the lights of the Manhattan skyline beaming in front of us—but I found the boat both freezing and annoying. It was packed with high school students apparently away from their parents for the first time and making sure all the other passengers knew it.

Inside the cabin, the heaters kicked and fussed and gave off little heat. I sat shivering in my red parka, my earflaps pulled down as far as they'd go and my hands stuffed in my pockets. I was feeling my age, watching these teenagers act like, well, teenagers, swearing and racing and tossing balled-up gum wrappers at each other. Impatience nudged my insides like a sharp elbow.

David, however, who sat across from me as if he were enjoying a tropical day, was fixed on the lights of the city. He smiled at the delinquents running by us.

"I remember when I first made this ride," David said, sitting back on the hard bench, his arms crossed in front of him. "I was thirteen, and it was a humid June Saturday, temperatures reaching into the nineties, but I didn't care. I was with my dad. He'd promised me a month before that he'd bring me to the city. It was one of those days . . ." He shook his head, his eyes alive with memories. "Dad took me on the ferry and pointed out each of the buildings we saw from the river. Of course, it looks a lot different now."

I looked toward the lights in front of us as he spoke. The Manhattan skyline had always been a picture to me, so it wasn't hard to imagine how much more spectacular it would have been for a boy with his dad. As he continued, David's face seemed to relax and his eyes sparkled at the memories. I liked that look. Even as he chattered quaintly about growing up on Long Island, about his father's work as a minister of a small church, peace pulled over him like a magnet. I wasn't sure what was happening, but I couldn't stop staring at him as he spoke: his long nose, his round glasses, his scruffy eyebrows. I even watched his lips move and only realized I'd lost track of the words when he grinned suddenly at the idea of someday showing his own son the same experience.

"But I'm in no hurry," he said, looking thoughtfully at me, his voice a soft blend of nostalgia and hope. I shoved my hands further into my parka and glanced away.

When we docked a few minutes later, I was relieved. We caught the local uptown subway, which was quiet and warmer than the ferry had been. I found two empty seats under an ad for Fairway Grocery. David sat down beside me.

"Okay, enough of my rambling. Tell me how the move's been for you," he said. I pulled off my cap and could only imagine how my hair looked. Maybe that would deter the guy. Instead, he followed up his question with another: "And how are our friends in New Orleans?"

His probe unexpectedly took me to a dozen or so faces of women and men who were elderly but who were not old in spirit. I'd met them for a story I'd thought would have been a beautiful profile of good news; instead it turned into a tragedy I wanted to forget. Then headlines of Hurricane Katrina had only pierced the wound. I'd forgotten that David had met these same seniors when he'd come to town for a conference. Now that he asked, though, I realized I really had missed them since I'd come here. But every time their memory popped up, I'd pushed them out of my head. I'd failed to help them keep their community, after all, and that was a reality I wanted to avoid.

"Fine. Everyone's fine," I answered, hoping the solitary word would answer each part of his question. The truth was, I hadn't spoken to any of my friends in New Orleans since I'd joined the *Clarion*. I'd been too busy.

He smiled. And we sat in silence until we approached the Ninety-sixth Street stop.

"This is my usual stop, Jonna, but I'm going to stay on to make sure you get home."

"I'll be fine," I said. "You're tired. Don't worry."

He looked at me with the same look he'd had on his face when he first came into Luke's apartment, though a tinge of disappointment emerged on his face.

"Really? No, I'd feel better knowing—"

"I'll be fine," I said again. Louder. He nodded, collected his backpack, and stood up as the train slowed to a stop.

"Okay, then. It was great seeing you." The doors slid apart. He looked conflicted, but added, "I'd like to see you again."

"Sunday," I said, waving him off. He stepped off, and within seconds the doors closed. But David stood on the platform and looked back toward me even as the train began to move. He stayed there, waving, until the subway was out of the station.

What was so wrong with a nice guy? I was too tired to think of an answer.

The 110th Street platform was virtually empty when I got off at my stop. I glanced at the clock in the ticket booth — 12:36 — and realized it was the latest I'd come home alone since I moved here. If I had to work late or stay out after eleven, I was usually with Hannah. Or I'd take a cab. Tonight, though, I'd been too tired to sort through the emotional tension that had surfaced with David and his stories, first about Regal, then his dad, and finally his questions of me.

Instinctively, I lit a cigarette, glanced back and forth, and felt a chill in my spine at the cold emptiness of the underground world. I put on my cap and hurried up the steps into the midnight street. As I did, I almost ran straight into a homeless man who was coming down into the subway.

"Sorry, lady," he mumbled. "Hey, can you spare a —?"

"Sorry, sir." Usually, I didn't mind giving a buck or two to someone who seemed to be living on the streets. But I also knew if I gave to every person asking for change, I'd go broke soon. It was never easy knowing the right thing to do, so tonight I opted simply to keep walking.

On the sidewalk, I picked up the pace and inhaled my cigarette as if it were my last. As I walked, I scrounged through my bag for the keys to my apartment and held them between my fingers. A few women walked past me, and a couple of teenagers leaned against a building laughing. I smoked and shivered in the cold.

I heard someone behind me, a clacking sound on the sidewalk not far away. I walked under the streetlights and around the corner. The clacking kept pace — or was I just hearing things? A yellow taxi sped by. Somewhere not far away, a siren bellowed.

I breathed harder, determined to quit smoking and start

exercising, tomorrow. Then I was sure of it: The clacking seemed closer just as I came within sight of the brownstone apartment building where Hannah and I lived. I climbed the steps and tossed the cigarette over my shoulder at the same time I thrust my key in the door. It didn't turn. This lock had always been belligerent, and I jiggled the key. Finally, it caught, and just as I was shoving open the door, I heard a man's voice, low and gravelly, deliver the strangest sound I'd heard all day:

"Thanks, lady."

I spun around. The homeless man I'd almost clobbered in the subway stood calmly on the sidewalk.

"Didn't mean to scare ya, just wanted a smoke," he said, picking up my half-smoked cigarette and inhaling it with as much satisfaction as I had. As he looked up at me, the streetlight revealed a grin the size of Central Park, but I also saw that he was wearing a couple of coats, several pairs of pants, and a baseball cap. A plastic bag hung under his elbow, bulging with cans and bottles — hence the clack — and a Mexican-looking blanket hung over his shoulder like a poncho.

"Yeah, thanks," he repeated. "You know, for this." He held up the cigarette as he spoke, and I saw his breath in the cold. Which made me wonder where he would sleep on a frigid night like this.

I asked him.

"On the train," he answered. "It's not bad." He shrugged and turned back toward the subway.

I hurried back down the steps, handed him my entire pack of organic cigarettes, and breathed out some pathetic prayer that the man would stay warm.

"Thanks, lady," he said, shuffling down the street, smoking

the life out of that cigarette. I waved and wandered upstairs.
That night I dreamt of blankets and elderly people, boats and
cauldrons, old letters and fresh brownies — all of which paraded
around a noisy newsroom like a mini-hurricane.

When I woke up, it was to the smell of hazelnut. Hannah
had set a cup of coffee on the table beside my bed. Light streamed
through the window as I opened an eye and saw my clock read
7:21.

"Rough night, eh, girl?" she said. She was already dressed for
work, perfectly, of course.

"Ah, the usual," I muttered as I reached for the java. "Thanks,
Hannah. What would I do without you?"

"Oversleep," she said, hurrying into the living room, a scent
of some Macy's perfume lingering behind her. "I'm leaving now
for a press conference at city hall, and remember this weekend I'm
going upstate with the senator's reelection campaign. But save me
a seat at the staff meeting, okay?"

"Staff meeting?"

The door slammed and I staggered through the apartment,
which this morning had turned into an oven because the landlord
had finally decided to turn up the heat, full blast. I tried waking
up with more coffee, a lukewarm shower, and Cheerios. But by
the time I'd walked outside into the winter, I felt only mildly
alive, my head still cobwebby from the whirlwind in my dreams.
Even the frigid air couldn't kick my gears into full speed.

Emma, my new subway worker friend, was singing a gospel
hymn when I dropped a ten-dollar bill into the tray.

"Hey there! It's Miss Jonna, right?" She paused from the
song, taking my money and exchanging it for a new MetroCard.
I yawned.

"Glad it's Friday?" she asked. Her eyes were bright, as if this were the best day she'd ever had, though I suspected that was how she felt about most mornings.

"Friday? Oh yeah," I said. "You?"

"Blessed to be here!" A rich, full laugh formed in her belly and spilled onto her face and shoulders, pulling both a grin and a chuckle from my sleepy soul. She winked her affirmation and returned to her song, and I went to wait for my train. When it pulled into the station, I glanced back at Emma, who was still singing. She waved at me, and I decided if she could be happy that it was Friday, I could at least try.

But the subway was crowded with rush-hour commuters in baggy jeans or hotel uniforms, and I couldn't find a seat. I leaned in close to a cold metal pole, wrapped my arms around it to hold me up, and closed my eyes for a mini-nap. Instantly, I was on the water, city lights in front of me, David's voice whispering gently in my ear. But instead of the stories of his father, I was listening again to the accusations he was making of Regal officials. I sifted through the details in my head: the centuries-old letters he'd discovered, the Cherrinard endowment for religious training and services to the city, even the threat from President Coen. A sting slid down my throat and into my stomach. Would a world-class university intentionally ignore the wishes of a generous alum and divert his funds to other causes? Was David just being paranoid? After all, hadn't Regal always supported the folks on the fringe of the culture, like Wiccans, as Skip had told me? Surely they would honor a donor's request for something as mild-mannered as Christian scholarship.

I opened my eyes. The people around me had shifted in class and culture as the stops came and went. Most who got on the train on the Upper West Side around Seventy-second Street wore business suits, ties, and shiny shoes. Many were reading the *Financial Times* newspaper or the stock market pages in the *Clarion's* business section, which might as well have been a foreign language to me. I couldn't make sense of any of it. Money matters had never been high on the priority list for MacLaughlins, so I had to concentrate extra hard whenever anyone brought up mysterious terms like the New York Stock Exchange, NASDAQ, security bonds, and hedge funds. I didn't even know what the NASDAQ acronym stood for.

Which reminded me of Lee Cheung, our new office mail worker Hannah had introduced me to. By Fifty-ninth Street, Columbus Circle, I found myself wondering what Chinatown would be like on a Friday night, and by Forty-second Street, after I stared at two blond Mormon missionaries—I couldn't help it—I was listening again to a Catholic priest ask for money. This morning I pretended I didn't speak English.

At Thirty-fourth Street, I emerged from the subway wide awake, thoughts and questions popping around my brain like popcorn: *East Coast winters felt much colder than Colorado's; how did Lee's parents accept his conversion so easily? Someone should make a law for teenagers riding ferries late at night. Why did Griffin Lewis get so defensive about the Wiccan symbol? I'll have hot dogs for lunch today. David Rockley looked nice. How could an Ivy League school wander so far from its mission?*

"Easy. They need students," Skip answered the last question when I found him at his desk in his office, alone, sipping tea, reading the morning papers, calm as always. My face stung from the change of outside to inside temperatures.

"Well, yes, but—"

"Aren't colleges sort of a microcosm of the country, a mini-society within the bigger one?" He folded his fingers under his chin and propped his elbows on the desk. "They reflect what the people want, but they also help define them. Humans change; so do our institutions, I guess."

I stood in his doorway, one foot in the hall, the other in his office, still in my parka with my bag on my shoulder. My parents had gone through so many conversions so many times in my life, according to whichever religious institutions they'd joined, that I knew I couldn't argue with Skip's point.

"Why?" Skip said.

"Why what?" I asked.

"Why the question about Regal? The Wiccans? How's that story coming, anyway?" Skip licked his thumb and index finger and turned a page in the newspaper.

"No, not about the Wiccans. Well, sort of."

"Sort of?"

"I mean, a friend told me last night, well, sort of a friend, anyway, that he thinks Regal isn't very tolerant of all religions." I set down my bag. Skip pulled his shoulders back against his chair. His tie this morning was a frosty gray-green, which oddly matched the color of the mug on his desk.

"Hmmm. Well, that hasn't been my experience, Jonna." The only shift in his facial expression was a slightly raised eyebrow. His phone rang. "Anything else?"

I shook my head and hurried toward my cubicle by way of the employees' lounge. The stars had miraculously aligned them-selves: There was an entire pot of coffee and an opened box of donuts on the counter beside the pot. I helped myself to a chocolate donut, poured myself a cup, adding a little extra sugar, and

Jo Kadlecek

wove in and out of the newsroom desks wondering what gospel song Emma had been singing in the subway. I made one up.

My phone was ringing.

"Jonna Lightfoot MacLa—"

"Yes, Joan. This is Professor Evan Hartman. I believe you left me a message yesterday."

"I sure did. Um, could you hang on one second?"

"Certainly," he answered. He cleared his throat while I scrambled for my notebook and turned on my computer. I clicked on the Regal Web site and scrolled my way into the religion department. Dr. Evan Hartman was a professor of neo-pagan ancient religions, with scads of articles and books and honors listed beside his name. His faculty photo revealed a middle-aged man with gray untidy hair, not on his head but on his jaw. His upper lip—like his head—was shaved, and his mouth was half-open in the picture, as if the photographer had caught him mid-sentence. He wore a denim shirt, no tie, and black-framed glasses.

"Sorry about that, Professor Hartman. Just got into the office. Anyway, thanks for calling back. It's about the Wiccans who rallied yesterday morning on campus. I'm wondering if you could help me make sense of who—"

"Of course. Perhaps you don't know that the number of people who identify themselves as Wiccans has grown from 8,000 to 250,000 in the past fifteen years—a growth rate of 1,575 percent."

"Really? I wonder why they—"

"Many scholars believe—and I happen to be one of them—that the numbers are actually much larger. For instance, Dr. Eileen Saxelby, who recently authored an excellent study called *Pagans Talk: A National Study of Witches and Neo-Pagans,* suggests the number of serious practitioners is growing all the time. Granted, some are what she calls 'dabblers.' You know the kind: people who take a little Wicca with their Christianity, Judaism, or other traditions."

I scribbled the numbers and the book title across my notebook, though neither was exactly what I was after. "Hmmm. Well, what exactly do — "

"I suppose many would see this as a progressive shift in our modern values, taking us back to where we should have been all along, with pre-Christian gods and, of course, goddesses. When you get right down to it, Joan, Wicca is an eclectic modern belief system, a new form of spirituality that re-creates older practices and ideas, drawing on inspiration from many sources, both ancient and modern."

I devoured my coffee. "Um, it's Jonna." I heard breathing. "Excuse me?"

"My name. I'm Jonna, not Joan. Anyway, you're saying that Wicca is sort of a prehistoric religion with a modern flavor?"

There was a garbled sound, as if he'd heard something really funny and put his hand over the phone so I couldn't hear him laugh.

"Well, that's a simple way to put it, but yes, I suppose that'd be correct. What you conclude about Wicca and witchcraft really comes down to how you define terms and whom you believe. "

Professor Hartman continued to provide more material than I would ever need, as though I were hearing a lecture, but whether this information would be on the test was anyone's guess. At its core, Wicca was a continuation of a very old set of rites passed down through families or covens before the birth of Christ. In recent centuries, outsiders relegated it mostly to the infamous witch hunts, though, according to the professor, most who were accused of witchcraft and subsequently burned were not witches at all; they were Christians or Catholics who'd said or done something few others understood. They might have practiced herbalism, healing, or Celtic traditions, some even performed miracles like the apostles of Jesus, but rarely did they exercise real witchcraft. Authentic witches throughout history attended agricultural and fertility celebrations or festivals that were timed to the cycles of nature. That's why some people today still defined Wicca as a natural way of life, while others considered it an organized religion with rituals and chants.

"Would you call it a religion?" I asked, glancing occasionally at the photograph of the professor on my computer screen, his beard and his head a peculiar contrast.

"Wiccans worship many gods and goddesses, so yes, I have no problem saying that it would qualify as a religion. Besides, everyone's got some religion, don't you think? All humans believe something, though they might not call it a religion. Even atheists are religious about their convictions, aren't they?"

"Uh-huh," I said, pausing as the words reverberated through my ears and into my brain. I remembered the Department of Veterans Affairs Web site. They did indeed consider atheists religious, adding theirs to the official DVA list of approved religious signs. I repeated his sentence silently, writing it down in my notes: "All . . . humans . . . believe . . . something; everyone's . . . got . . . some . . . religion."

It was probably not a new concept to him or other scholars, but for me, the professor's observation might as well have been a light that had just been switched on. I read the sentence again, and a third time. I looked around the newsroom at the reporters and editors scurrying back and forth. What did *they* believe? Few of them would have claimed any specific religion, yet they couldn't have gotten to this point in their careers without believing passionately in some truth, some sense of right and wrong. After all, that was what drove breaking news. Some truth emerging from a scandal, some injustice exposed—*that* was what motivated journalists. But religion?

I pulled out the dictionary and was intrigued by the definition's evolution: *"religion: the service and worship of God or the supernatural; commitment or devotion to religious faith or observance; a personal set or an institutionalized system of attitudes, beliefs, and practices; a cause, principle, or system of beliefs held to with ardor and faith."* I'd always assumed God would be at the center of religion, but I'd never considered the possibility that someone could be religious without God.

Wasn't that missing the point?

The professor cleared his throat and was about to launch into another academic perspective when I cut him off.

"Why, then, do you suppose the government won't allow Wiccan symbols on tombstones of fallen soldiers?" I tapped my pen against the notebook, underlining the words *all* and *believe* while I waited for the nugget I needed for my article.

He sighed and sounded faintly sympathetic. "I suppose it's because Wiccans have always had so many things stacked against them, from the biblical passages about the practice of magic to witch trials in history to deliberate plots by churches or Satanists or political leaders to persecute them that, well, if I may be so frank, they've suffered an ongoing image problem."

"So it wasn't what they believed, just how they were perceived in the culture?"

"That's correct. All religions are basically the same, Joan, providing comfort for the weak, direction for the lost, friendship for the lonely, that sort of thing. Each neo-pagan ceremony wasn't much different from early Christian acts of worship, when you think about it, where . . ."

The professor lost me. Though he continued explaining point after point, his voice began to drone into a line of sounds in my ear. Not words, really, or meaning, just noise. I picked off part of my donut. And for some reason, I thought about those guys in Times Square I'd seen last week with the overturned buckets that they whacked and railed like drums. At first I found it enjoyable, but it took only about five drumbeats for me to lose interest.

I scrolled up and down Hartman's Web site page while he talked. The movement made his picture look like the kind I'd see in an amusement park mirror: stretched and wobbly and distorted. I scrolled; he kept talking. I scrolled some more; he rattled off another list of factoids and theories. I scrolled and fiddled but then stopped in a heartbeat when a tiny detail at the bottom of his faculty bio jumped out on the screen:

Professor Evan Hartman was the 1993 recipient of the Mr. and Mrs. Frank Cherrinard Endowment for Religious Training.

I interrupted. "Tell me about the Cherrinard endowment."

It was the first time the professor seemed stumped. I started to sweat. He cleared his throat. Beads formed on my neck. He coughed. I looked down and saw that I was still wearing my red parka. I shook myself free of it, pinching the phone between my ear and shoulder as I waited for Dr. Hartman's response.

Finally, he said, "Oh my, is it 8:50? I'll need to get to class, so—"

"But the endowment—I mean, real quick—do you think Regal University respects all religions in its study, including Christianity?"

"Ah, I'm afraid that'd be another conversation. But suffice it to say, it'd depend on how you defined *religions* and *Christianity*." From his tone, I thought he might roll into another lecture, even if he didn't have time, but he caught himself. "Let me conclude by offering this: I believe the University is actually a lot like the Wiccans who gathered the other day; it's a very open place, and Wicca is a very open religion. It allows you to be the ultimate authority of your own experience."

"But what if—"

"I . . . I hope this has proven helpful for your story. Please, give my regards to Skip."

He hung up. I put down the receiver and tried to imagine Skip sitting next to an early version of this man in some English class at Regal twenty years ago. It wasn't easy. They'd probably been typical college students, sharing notes and cramming for exams, but they seemed so different now. Skip always appeared so relaxed in his office or as he ran staff meetings or when he—I realized I was late for my morning staff meeting.

I raced down the hall in time to find the last free seat in the back of the conference room, in between a young intern who must have been new and a sports reporter name Fred Kordowicz. Fred wore black jeans with a Donald Duck necktie that hung down the middle of his golf shirt. He was picking two glazed donuts from the box when I sat down. He passed the box to me; I obliged and passed it to the intern, who handed it to a copy editor beside her whom I knew only as Lila.

Skip quieted his staff and began reviewing assignments alphabetically and according to beat. The arts critic updated him first on an opening exhibit at a SoHo gallery and an Irish music festival at Carnegie Hall. Two business reporters next cited a few changeovers on Wall Street and stock-option trends. Then came dining — a beat I secretly coveted — followed by prospective education, fashion, and health stories. When he'd reached the New York region, Skip scribbled something on his yellow tablet and sat down.

Walter Wood stood up, his bow tie as neatly arranged as his gelled white hair. He waited for silence in the room, resting one hand in the pocket of his black slacks and the other on the podium. His eyes were small, but his gaze firm and piercing. Once he had our attention, he picked up a blue marker and wrote on the white board behind him, "Med-USA."

"Good morning. Some of you might not know who I am, but my media firm" — he pointed at the name he'd just written — "is very interested in the *Clarion*. Unfortunately, New Yorkers are not as interested in your traditional newspaper as we are. In fact, they're turning to other sources for their news. Which makes your job a little trickier." He tilted his head and raised his hand like a traffic cop. "The stories you've just provided your editor are good, but they won't sell newspapers. We'd like you to find the kind that will." He paused and grinned. "Any questions?"

I scratched my head. Hannah, who was standing near the front wall about ten yards from Mr. Wood in the crowded room, glared first at me, then at the man who'd just addressed us. She shot up her hand but didn't wait for him to acknowledge her.

"What did you say your name was?" she asked, her notebook

open as if she were at a press conference.

"I didn't." He turned his shoulders toward Hannah as she clicked her pen. "But now that you ask, I'm Walter Wood."

She dropped her pen to her side as if she suddenly weren't interested. "Well, that explains lots of things," she said. I was perpetually amazed at Hannah's ability to keep up on so much, because I had no idea what his name explained. "You've had your hand in a few media takeovers, haven't you?"

He chuckled. "My firm has helped numerous news outlets stay alive, if that's what you mean."

"No, it's not what I meant, but thanks for clarifying."

"Miss Hensley, isn't it?" She nodded. He continued, "You're a political reporter, I believe. Your reporting is good, but let me just say this: The more colorful your stories become, the more likely New Yorkers will pick up the *Clarion*. This is part of our new strategy."

"Our strategy?" She looked at Skip.

"Yes, Hannah, our strategy," Skip said, turning from her to the rest of us. "It's a business reality, folks. I don't need to remind you all how stiff the competition is, especially now with the Internet winning over audiences who used to buy a paper to get their news. We have to start asking the question, Why should New Yorkers pick up the *Clarion*? The answer is because you're writing the stories that make these others look boring. And the more we do, the more we can guarantee salaries, even raises."

Hannah huffed. "I don't write entertainment. I write hard news."

"Of course you do," Walter intervened. "But why can't it be a little of both? Like, say, the story that's running tomorrow on the Wiccans at Regal University? Now *that's* a story!"

I was licking the chocolate off of my fingers when every eye in the room fell on me. Fire formed in my cheeks as Walter Wood nodded my direction. "Right, Joanie? Witches rallying at an esteemed institution is exactly the type of piece we believe will get people's attention."

"It will?" I mumbled.

"But it's a religion story, for Christ's sake," Fred exclaimed, spitting little globs of wet sugar from his mouth and onto my sweater. "It doesn't hold a candle to what the Yankees have got cooking for—"

"Are you kidding? The mayor's announcement this morning is much more important than a baseball—" Hannah tried to sound diplomatic, but soon the entire room exploded in an uproar, each reporter fighting for his or her beat, hoping it would be just what Med-USA was looking for. Skip stood up, waved his arms in front of him, and regained control. He insisted on politeness in the exchange, and for the next fifteen minutes, as he finished running through the story updates, beat by beat, politeness was what he got, give or take a lot passion here and there.

When Walter Wood sat down, a tiny corner of his mouth curved upward.

Back at my cubicle, Hannah slapped my back.

"What the heck was that?" she fumed.

"A reality check?"

"And you didn't even save me a seat." She shook her head and got to work. I picked up where I'd left off with the story I now knew was expected to run in tomorrow's paper:

> *. . . the decision cast a bad spell on a local group*
> *who protested this morning at the steps of Regal*

*University. Leaders of the witches say they're tired
of the discrimination and just want to be included
with . . .*

I scratched out *included with* and rewrote:

*. . . and just want to be given the same recognition
as other religions. That won't be easy, though,
since Wiccan symbols and practices have always
elicited suspicion from outsiders for a variety of
reasons, according to neo-pagan religion scholar
Dr. Evan Hartman of Regal University. Hartman
says that Wiccans have "suffered an ongoing image
problem" . . .*

I spent the rest of the day tweaking the story, alternating
between shifting sentences and reading snippets from the latest
edition of *ChocoLatte* magazine. By 4:03, I dropped the story into
Skip's box. Then I grabbed my bag and found Lee Cheung in the
Clarion mail room. We were on our way to Chinatown, where I
was about to find out what a Friday night looked like with former
gang members who now thought Jesus rocked.

And as curious as I was about where we were going, something about Walter Wood's demeanor stayed with me even as we
left the office. For some reason, I was curious what religion he
believed.

::Chapter Five

Though the sun had already set over the rest of Manhattan, there was not a spot of darkness that I could see at the Chinatown Jesus Center. Two blocks east of Canal Street, Lee led me up the steps to the seventy-five-year-old converted elementary school and into an enormous auditorium that looked as if it had once been a gymnasium or cafeteria. Or both. Rows and rows of wooden folding chairs covered forest green carpet. The walls surrounding them were more window than concrete, and although it was 7:35 p.m., it might as well have been noon.

It could have been the fluorescent lights that lined the ceiling. Or it might have been the two towers of fixtures on either side of the stage, directly across from the spotlights in the back corners of the room. But it wasn't the electrical wiring illuminating the center that got my attention.

Every direction I turned—whether in the hallway or the rows of chairs; around the book tables, the windows, or the stage—I saw faces somehow different from any I'd seen since I'd moved here. These were unhurried. Soft. Hopeful. Content. As if they'd been nudged awake after years of living with their eyes closed.

"Yo, that's what Jesus does," Lee said when I asked him to explain what all the excitement was about. Most of the people who'd come tonight were—like Lee—young, Asian, and fluent in at least three languages: Mandarin, English, and hip-hop. They wore baggy sweaters and jeans with rips in the knees; some had baseball caps on or leather packs hanging off their shoulders. Most had probably gone to a million other places not many Friday nights ago, but now they were in church—to rock with God, the One that Lee said had pulled them out of their "sorry old excuse of a life."

And rock they did. A ten-member band of twentysomething men and women took the stage, complete with electric guitars, basses, drums, and keyboards. Two members played saxophones into microphones while one young man—whose green-black hair shot straight off his head—held a harmonica in one hand and snapped his fingers with the other as he directed the band. As he did, a loud, perfectly blended melody echoed around the auditorium, an upbeat version of an old Christian hymn I recognized from the Southern Baptist Convention I'd covered in Denver. Only this one included screaming guitar licks harkening to an era far removed from these musicians. No matter. They made the music theirs.

Next, they slid into urban sounds that included rap, beat-boxed verses from the Bible, and hip-hop, though I was never quite sure when one style ended and the next began. The words to each were projected on a movie screen beside the stage so that the six hundred or so young worshippers who'd come tonight could sing and rap and beat-box too. And with each song, they moved. They clapped or raised their hands; they bobbed heads or shoulders. And when they weren't smiling, the expressions on their faces were serious but satisfied, as if they were sharing personal secrets with a friend.

Forty-five minutes later, the green-haired singer/director rapped out the last of the hymns, and the musicians took their seats, leaving their instruments onstage. A woman stepped to the microphone, read a passage from the gospel of Mark, and closed her eyes as she invited the congregation to join her in a prayer of thanksgiving. When she finished, the oldest person I'd seen yet that evening — who was probably only my brother's age — crossed the stage and placed a thick black book and a yellow legal pad on the pulpit.

The Reverend Daniel Cho — or Danny Bro, as the crowd called him — jumped passionately into his sermon. He was a tall thin man who didn't wear jeans like his charges but tan corduroy pants and a solid navy sweater. His hair hung just above his collar in the back, and his hands did not stay still as he spoke. Mixing stories from his own experiences as a gang leader with Christ's words from the gospel of Mark, the reverend again and again drove home the point that "the streets of Christ's kingdom are far better than the streets of New York."

When he finished, the band members resumed their places on the stage and broke into three more songs before Danny Bro sent off the crowd with the hippest benediction I'd ever heard. And with hippie parents, I'd heard some hip send-offs. Still, not many at the Chinatown Jesus Center left once the Friday night service officially ended; instead, they turned and talked with friends, laughing and hugging and forming dozens of small huddles across the auditorium. The buzz of joy grew. And when some-one announced something about an after-church party upstairs with desserts and coffees, the huddles connected with others and formed a patchwork line into the hall and up the stairs.

Lee took me up toward the stage to meet Danny Bro, but so

many young people had surrounded him that I knew it wasn't a good time for an interview. I'd call him next week. I did manage to slip a business card into his hand just to let him know I was there. And because Lee wasn't in any great hurry, he was willing to talk with me over coffee at the party. I scribbled more notes about what he called his "BC days," his parents' ongoing support—though they showed no interest in coming to the Jesus Center—and his hope to someday do what Danny Bro was doing. Lee considered his mail-room job at the *Clarion* the first step toward his dream; he was saving for college tuition.

I left Lee at the church party at 10:12, determined to make it home before eleven, and caught an unusually empty Friday night uptown train. By 11:02, I was on my block. Hannah was traveling with a senator's reelection campaign for the weekend, so the apartment was as dark as it was quiet when I got home. I flipped on the lights, dropped my parka and bag on the couch, and noticed the light on the answering machine blinking as I wandered instinctively to the kitchen. The Chunky Monkey ice cream in the freezer distracted me. And when I set the empty, sticky bowl on top of the others that had been accumulating in the sink for the last two days, I got distracted again.

I squirted Lemon Sun liquid soap and filled up the sink. My dad used to tell me about an old monk named Brother Lawrence who always felt closer to God when he was in the kitchen washing dishes. For a while, the strategy worked in motivating me to do my chores. It even carried over after college and especially when I'd lived in New Orleans. I supposed the warm suds on my hands relaxed me—and kept me from smoking—so much so that I'd occasionally chat with the Almighty until the water drained. I'd feel better—and cleaner—for both.

But that seemed a long time ago. Considering what had happened with my friends in the Crescent City, I had to be honest: I wasn't sure how much God had been listening. So the dishes tended to pile up, and when I did get to them—like tonight—I just scrubbed.

By the time I'd set the last bowl in the dish rack and collapsed on the bed, it was a minute before the end of Friday, signaling the official completion of another week I'd survived in the city. I'd been counting the weeks that I'd lived and worked in the Big Apple, and I secretly celebrated each time I made it to Saturday, as if it were an accomplishment that deserved a medal, or at least a beer. Though there was so much to love about this city—the pace and diversity, the stories and sounds, the history and food—it could also be those very things that could wring me out like a dishrag. I closed my eyes, and the image of last night's homeless man, for some reason, ran slow-motion-like across my mind. The weight of weariness pulled at me. And the last thing I remembered before falling asleep was that I felt glad I was sleeping in a bed, not a subway car.

I was not so glad to wake up to the doorbell buzzing obnoxiously the next morning. My one chance to sleep in, I savored Saturdays as a pretend retreat. When she wasn't out of town, Hannah was usually at the gym for kickboxing class by 8:30 a.m. on Saturdays, so when I'd hear her leave, I'd imagine the evergreen trees of the Rocky Mountains or a Gulf Coast breeze, breathe deeply in a very spiritual way, and then roll over. I'd drool little bits of slobber on my chin that would wake me up, and I'd do my spiritual exercise all over again. Until around eleven, when I'd decide it was time to move. So I'd walk into the living room, plop on the couch, and read the paper or Gideon, my little Bible, or a

Dorothy Sayers mystery, depending on the week. Eventually, I'd make breakfast, maybe even walk around the block. This morning, though, I'd have to break routine and move before nine.

By the third buzz, I threw on my jeans, slippers, and sweatshirt and rolled down the stairs, which were at Antarctica temperatures compared to our apartment's Florida climate.

I shivered. Especially when I opened the door and was surprised by both the February chill and David Rockley. He stood at the top of our stoop with a bag of H&H bagels in one hand and a blue paper coffee cup in the other. He was buried in his brown ski parka and Yankees baseball cap. I rubbed the sleep from my eyes and debated over which I was happier to see: the coffee or the bagels.

"Morning, Jonna. I left you a message last night—don't know if you heard it."

"No, I, um. No."

"No problem. It's just that I felt guilty for not seeing you home Thursday night, so I wanted to redeem myself. Hope you don't mind."

"Well . . ."

David slipped the goods carefully into my hands and smiled. His teeth sparkled and his cheeks were pink from the cold. He crammed his hands into his coat pockets so that they poked out in front of him just a few inches from me.

"I hope you like them. They're my favorite," he said, turning toward the steps. "Now, I don't want to interrupt your morning—just wanted to bring you breakfast. See you tomorrow." He'd reached the sidewalk in front of our neighbor's building when he looked up at the frigid white sky as if he saw something bright. He twirled back toward me. "I'll see you tomorrow—that is, unless you'd like to join me tonight for dinner?"

The smell of coffee floated up to my nose, and the caffeine must have triggered some brain activity because I heard words come out of my mouth: "Dinner? You mean like pizza or hot dogs?"

"Either one. Or hey, I know this great organic sushi place."

"You do?" I didn't know why it surprised me that a nice guy like David would like sushi or organic, but it did.

"Yup, the Wet Fish Café. It's on the southwest corner of Broadway and 107th. How does that sound?"

"What?"

"Wet Fish? I could meet you there tonight at around seven?" He looked up from the sidewalk, waiting in the cold, moving his boots back and forth like he was getting ready to do jumping jacks. "If you don't already have plans." That's when his question registered in my sleepy head.

"You mean, like a date?"

He laughed and his cheeks seemed pinker than they had a minute ago. "We could just call it dinner."

The sun broke onto the street from behind a cloud and I scrolled ahead on my mental calendar for the events of the day. Aside from the Laundromat, I had a big fat nothing planned. I didn't even have dishes to do, so I couldn't use that as an excuse.

"I like dinner," I said.

"Me too. Actually, I like food in general. So dinner, breakfast, you know, it's all good."

I couldn't have agreed more, but not now. It was freezing. "Okay, well, thanks for this." I held up my breakfast. David shrugged and tipped the bill of his baseball cap.

"The least I could do. See you tonight!" He threw his hand

in the air to wave. Then he turned and began to jog down the street, though I never really saw his boots touch the sidewalk.

I climbed back into bed, licking poppy seeds off my fingers and setting the coffee on the table beside me. I was still shivering from the cold, but my palms felt clammy. Had I really just agreed to my first date in New York City? With David Rockley, of all people? I felt strange and tired and cautious all at once, especially as the pictures surfaced in my head of evil men in the past who'd called themselves dates. Maybe I'd stop by Saint Helena's convent on the way to the Wet Fish to fortify my resolve.

Of course, David had said it was only dinner.

It was too much to think about for a Saturday morning, so I finished a bagel and the coffee, napped a little more, and shoved my dirty clothes into a pillowcase. I picked up my notebook on the way out the door to Charlie's Wash-O-Rama around the corner. It was a narrow but busy storefront space, with about twenty mammoth washing machines stacked on one side and rows of dryers on the other. Half a dozen African and African-American women were folding clothes by the door, while white, Asian, and Latino men and women at various stages in their washing or drying cycles stood staring blankly. My mom and pop had always seen Laundromats as the great human equalizer—regardless of who you were, they'd say, your clothes still got dirty—so it was a natural part of my week. I found an empty washer, put in all my clothes and quarters, and sat on a long white bench.

A copy of today's *New York Clarion* lay beside me. I glanced at the headlines on page one and silently applauded Hannah for her front-and-center story on the mayor. As I folded it over, I saw my story on the Wiccans beneath hers, in a box by itself with the headline in bold letters: "Witches Can't Bury Their Dead." A small photo of Griffin Lewis standing with Lady Crystal beside the entrance of Regal was featured next to it.

"What?!" I said aloud. Since when did religion go page one in this city?

I read the first several paragraphs and shook it as if bugs had infested it. Though my byline was placed beneath the headline, the story wasn't exactly mine. It had been edited and given a spookier tone to make it sound as if witches were the next victims of civil oppression. I kept reading. Professor Hartman's quotes appeared closer to the lede than in my original and a chart had been inserted that listed all the DVA's approved religious symbols, putting a line through the word *Wicca*. True, the information was accurate, but the mood of the article had a slant that seemed more interested in marketing than in reporting.

I dumped the paper back where I'd found it. Walter Wood's speech must have inspired the night editors. And it might as well have been a slap on the knuckles. I'd always expected Skip to edit my writing, but usually that was a process that would make a story better to read, not simply easier to market. No, today's spooky tone was clearly not his work. I reached for a smoke and then remembered. I'd given away my last pack. It was turning into a bad morning. So I pulled out my notebook instead, looked around the Wash-O-Rama at the unique sizes and features of my fellow washers, and wrote while I waited.

Some people did their meditating at the sea or in the woods; I seemed to do mine Saturdays at Charlie's. At least people were honest here. Everyone had dirty laundry and wanted to get it clean. That's why they came. It was the stuff of life—not death—that mattered more in this place; the grimy little spots could come out brighter than ever with the right amount of detergent and quarters. Why would folks here care what symbols the government would or wouldn't allow on a military tombstone?

I felt better when I got home and tucked my clothes into the dresser. I puttered through the afternoon, baking chocolate chip cookies, reading a novel, and eating the cookies. At six thirty, as primped and ready as I could be, I left the apartment for the Wet Fish Café. For dinner, not a date, I reminded myself. Dinner I could do. Dates were, well, bad karma.

I was strangely relieved to find David waiting for me in the entrance. That was the first good sign: At least I hadn't been stood up. The second was that when he saw me come in from the cold at 7:05, he bounced from his seat. Maybe he was as hungry as I was.

We sat at a table not far from the sushi chef. We watched him chop a long strip of raw tuna with what looked like a miniature machete. Next, he placed the thin piece across a bamboo mat covered with white rice and dried seaweed. He rolled it carefully, squeezed it hard, and then unrolled the mat, leaving a small log-shaped roll. Next, he sliced it with his machete and dropped it onto a plate, plopping a tiny blob of wasabi beside it. He topped it off with a pinch of pickled ginger.

I had asked David to order first so I could simply get what he was having: a deluxe combo. When the waiter set down our Japanese beers and Edamame, David sprinkled salt across the soybeans and picked up his beer.

"I read your story this morning, Jonna, on the witches," he said, toasting. "To page-one stories!"

I clinked his glass and guzzled.

"You're not happy about it?"

"It wasn't exactly my story."

"You know, I did wonder when I was reading. It didn't have your usual . . . touch."

"That's because the *Clarion* apparently thinks more drama will sell newspapers."

He squeezed a soybean pod and popped the pea-shaped beans into his mouth. I copied him. "But your stuff's always been so good. Why would they edit you?"

"It has?"

"It's one of the great advantages of working at a library. I can access every newspaper in the world. And read stories by reporters I'm interested in — like you." He cleared his throat. "I mean your stories."

The chef chopped another fish and set a plate up on his counter for a waiter to deliver. I concentrated on the green pods. So did David. An older couple sat down at a table beside ours.

"Nice of you to say so," I said, "but it's not like they're making much difference."

He sat up. "What do you mean? Remember that story you wrote on the Buddhists in Denver? Or on that scumbag who ripped off his immigrant congregation? You can be sure those made a difference, Jonna."

I gripped my glass. "Yeah, maybe."

"Maybe? Of course they did. And how about the story of that Catholic charity center for the kids, or the hate crime at the synagogue, or our amazing friends at the senior center in New Orleans? You know your reporting mattered to all of them, right?"

"A lot of good it did." I remembered the monstrous bulldozer plowing over their dreams, and leaned back so hard in my chair I thought I might break it. I pushed my hair around and pulled it tighter in its clip.

David reached across the table. "But you tried! That's what I've always thought was so amazing about you and your journalism. It matters to you. Really matters. In here." He tapped his heart with his thumb. "You don't find that everywhere."

"You don't?"

Our combos arrived. Tuna, salmon, shrimp, and California rolls. I picked up the chopsticks and pinched a shrimp, but it tumbled off the rice and back onto the plate. David held up his hand.

"Mind if I say a quick word of thanks?"

Chopsticks midair, I shook my head. He smiled and shut his eyes.

"We're thankful, God, for good fish and good friends. Please bless both now. Amen."

"Amen," I whispered. David broke apart his chopsticks and slid them against each other as if he were sharpening them. I succeeded in dropping a California roll into my mouth. It melted. I grunted.

"I knew you'd like it." He picked up a raw piece of tuna and had the same reaction. We were both quietly reverent through the next few bites. Each melted and delighted and awed. No wonder the Wet Fish Café was filling up with more customers, until there was a line at the door waiting for a table. Even the ginger was fresh and sweet. David broke the culinary spell and returned to the conversation.

"I don't mean to sound, well, gushy, but ever since I met you, I've read your stories. And you know what?" He set down his chopsticks and leaned toward me. I thought of Saint Helena's convent.

"What?"

"Well, it's made me, uh, care more about my own work." He looked firmly at me, the café light reflecting little sparkles in the lenses of his glasses. "Do you see what I'm saying? You've had a good influence on me, Jonna Lightfoot MacLaughlin, even if you don't think you've made a difference."

A tiny flame from the wasabi jumped up my nose and caught fire in my sinuses. I wiggled my head and let out a nasal scream. The couple beside us laughed. The chef glanced over and grinned before slicing off the tail of some fish.

"Well, I was hoping you'd have that kind of a response." David smirked. I guzzled the rest of my beer to put out the fire. And when he asked if I wanted another, I shook my head and changed the subject.

"So, tell me about the Cherrinard endowment," I said.

His face fell.

David talked softly about the documents he'd found that he claimed linked a litany of Regal officials — past and present — to what he called "stolen funds." He could now prove that for at least sixty years and at least four college presidents, the Cherrinard funds had been diverted into personal accounts, funding specific departmental research, stock options, and property acquisitions. Some of those funds now would have accumulated into land and stock worth millions of dollars. David spoke barely above a whisper, and he leaned in over his deluxe combo as if he couldn't afford to have anyone else hear him.

"It really is money laundering, Jonna. Fraud and embezzlement, plain and simple."

He drank some of his beer as if the words had dried his throat but not his resolve. Again he explained both Regal's original mission to train Protestant ministers by the "Light of Scripture" so they could serve the city, and Frank Cherrinard's endowment to do the same. Though President Coen had dismissed his claims, David kept poking around. But no one would take his phone calls, so he wrote a four-page, single-spaced letter to all of the members of the board of trustees, chronicling his findings about the misuse and misappropriation of the Cherrinard funds, dating back to the original letter from the Cherrinards. No one seemed interested.

The only response he'd gotten so far was a single letter, which he pulled from his pocket. He unfolded it and handed it to me. It included only two sentences. I read it aloud, but not loudly:

> *Dear Mr. Rockley,*
> *The endowment about which you have*
> *inquired is indeed being allocated correctly.*
> *Detailed information to confirm this would be*
> *extremely burdensome for the University to produce*
> *and will not be provided for you.*
> *Respectfully,*
> *The Office of the General Counsel, Regal*
> *University,*
> *President Dale M. Coen and the Board of*
> *Trustees*

I read it again silently before handing it back to him. But he didn't touch it. He just left it on the table, leaned back in his chair, and took off his glasses. He breathed on them and dabbed his napkin across the lenses. I slid the last soybean through my teeth and plopped the empty shell with the others.

I didn't know what to say. It wasn't exactly a warm and fuzzy letter, especially when I considered that it was from the office of the general counsel—which translated into scads of attorneys who worked for one of the most prestigious universities in the world.

"It gets worse." David stopped cleaning and pulled out another piece of paper. It was a memo his boss had recently been sent from Regal's records management office about its newest policy, detailing exactly how records were to be authorized for destruction. David held the memo close to his face and read: "First, documents will be destroyed by the custodial office as a part of their normal business practices. Second, documents will be destroyed by the RMO once all retention periods have expired, all audit requirements have been satisfied with no pending requests for information, and no reasonably foreseeable litigation involving the records."

He resumed cleaning. "Do you know what this means?"

"Not really."

"It means they can't provide the documentation for the original endowment, not because it's burdensome but because they don't have it. All the letters, forms, and documents from the Cherrinards have been destroyed because there were no pending requests for them and certainly no foreseeable litigation. Until now."

I gulped the rest of my water and realized what he'd just said. "But I thought you had the documentation? Which would mean it hasn't been destroyed, right?"

He slid his glasses back up his nose and smiled. "I've got copies. I'll bring them tomorrow to Luke and Sarah's."

David tucked the letters back in his pocket. As he did, I

picked up the last California roll, but I felt slightly queasy, not at all because of the sushi — it was heavenly — but because David's revelation suggested that he was about to take on one of the biggest institutions in the city. And for what? A few religious terms in a bunch of old records? I couldn't keep going with this, even if he was my brother's friend.

"But is it really worth all this trouble, David?"

He looked around the room, which was alive with Saturday night busyness. "For instance, are you sure the original documents were for Christian training? Not religious? That matters, you know."

He dropped his napkin on his plate. I went on.

"Yesterday I interviewed a religion professor who'd been a recipient of the endowment, and he seemed to think there wasn't much difference in —"

"Ah, yes, Professor Evan Hartman is quite the evangelist for all things religious being equal, as if all truth is man's truth and we can do with it what we want."

The waiter appeared, took our empty plates, and set down freshly sliced oranges in a bowl. I sucked on one and thought of my phone conversation with the professor, the time he took to explain so much of his perspective. David might have a point about —

"How did you know it was Hartman I'd talked to?" I said before I discarded the orange peel and grabbed another.

"Because I read today's paper, remember, where you quoted him in your story on the witches. That guy loves the press, with all due respect." David stripped the peel from his piece of fruit and plopped it in his mouth.

"But my editor told me Hartman was an expert on ancient

pagan religions. That's why I called him." I knew Skip wouldn't lead me to an expert source he couldn't trust or that would be using the *Clarion* for his own purposes. Skip cared too much about the integrity of the profession. There was too much at stake.

When the waiter handed the bill to David, I pulled my wallet from my bag and held out a twenty-dollar bill. "Just dinner, right?"

"Right." He accepted the money and paid the check, but we sat a few minutes longer trying to work out what had just transpired. He said that as long as he'd been an archivist at Regal, Professor Hartman had been eager to push his agenda, to equalize religions so that no one would feel left out, as if that would create a more peaceful community and, consequently, a more cooperative city and world. But after a few years had passed, David began to hear about campus groups or churches that Hartman and others at Regal hadn't included in their dialogue, though they'd been supporting students there for years. He said they even asked some of these same campus Christians to keep their religion to themselves. Granted, David confessed, they had good reason to at times, since Christians could be more dogmatic than inviting about their convictions.

I remembered the skinny man who'd screamed his condemnations at the Wiccans' rally, as well as the dozens of other bad-news characters I'd met since I'd started this job who'd called themselves Christians. David was right about that.

But that, he exclaimed, did not mean all Christians were the same any more than all religions were like Wicca or all religion professors—or reporters for that matter—were alike.

"Well, duh." Of course we weren't all exactly the same. But we did have a lot in common—like laundry. Then again, what my parents and brothers believed now as Presbyterians was very different from what Muslims in Harlem believed or psychics in New Orleans. The professor had said the purpose of all faith traditions was essentially to comfort the weak no matter what other duties were required of them. But I knew my parents and my neighbors would say it was about much more than comfort.

Why did religion have to be so complicated?

"What if there is a standard all these other religions point to?" David said. "A Truth that's behind all the others? What if he's a person who came to earth? And what if history confirms it, Jonna?"

"You're an archivist. You're supposed to think that," I poked.

A small Japanese man appeared suddenly at our table and pointed to the line at the door of the café. We pulled on our parkas and got up to leave. David glanced at his watch.

"If it's not too late, could I show you something?"

Within a half hour, we'd bundled up and walked north on Broadway, down 110th until we came to the edge of a small park. I thought maybe he was seeing me home, but instead, in what seemed to come out of nowhere, David pulled me up the steps to the Cathedral of Saint John the Divine, a structure that seemed almost as big as our block in Harlem. As we approached the tall elegant doors, we heard music floating from inside. David pushed open the wooden frame as if it were an entrance to a castle, and we hurried through the foyer to the gap in the back. Up near the nave of the church, I saw a string quartet. Between us, rows and rows of chairs were filled with hundreds of people who had come to hear the concert. Stained glass windows with small lights positioned around them glowed above the rows, and candles on long tables flickered softly beside them.

I stood breathless, not from the walk or the cold but from the beauty that resounded throughout the space.

For all their dabbling in world religions, my parents never ventured into a cathedral like this, at least that I could remember. At one point in their journey, they'd gone so far as to call cathedrals 'ostentatious' and a 'monumental waste' of energy, emotion, and money when God's natural cathedrals—the Rocky Mountains—were free for all to enjoy. And so we rarely set foot in a structure such as Saint John's, because, after all, with all the people starving in the world, they'd said, spirituality was at its best when it was simple and pure and free.

I doubted they would have said that, though, if they'd heard the music echoing off the walls of this sacred space.

:: Chapter Six

I t was the cross that made the difference. Positioned perfectly at the middle of the cathedral, a simple wooden cross resting on top of an altar brought all points of vision to its center. Streaming from beneath the windows, flickering from the sides, the evening lights upon it were vivid and magnetic; there was no place I could stand in the sanctuary that didn't fix my eyes on the Christian symbol. Maybe it was the juxtaposition of the small altar up front against the seemingly endless height, the arched columns that towered toward the sky, or the magnificent colors stretched across stained glass images, but the Cathedral of Saint John the Divine was a place unlike any I'd seen.

Or heard. The stringed instruments sent out soothing melodies around the columns and over the chairs. Each note reverberated in the air and lingered like birds whistling praises, it seemed to me, fluttering gently past our ears and floating through the space. I trembled as I listened and looked.

David cupped my elbow and led me to a seat. We sat still, breathing in the sacredness of the cathedral and the music for an amount of time that seemed somehow like both an hour and a second. And then as if I were being nudged from a dream, the sounds faded and the people who had gathered shifted slowly as if they, too, were emerging from a dream. The concert had ended.

I felt empty and full at the same time. David stretched back against his chair and looked forward at the church nave. He spoke quietly as he stared.

"This is the second largest Gothic cathedral in the world, Jonna, and it's not even finished. I love that such beauty could still be in process, you know?" He sighed before he continued. "Anyway, they have these free concerts all year long. I couldn't live without them." He lifted his arms high above him as if to express his gratitude, and rose from his chair. "Let me show you something else."

We walked the opposite direction of the people as they were leaving and came to the edge of the nave while the musicians put away their instruments. In the bays on either side, stained glass images of prominent biblical figures were surrounded by scenes that included—of all things—football, soccer, and base-ball players. David pointed to each before directing me to others with themes from American history, the military, even medicine. Above them were small whitish-gray statues that filled the front of the high altar. Most were of religious icons, beginning with the apostle Paul. But I was surprised when I saw Christopher Columbus, William Shakespeare, George Washington, and Abraham Lincoln also represented.

Above them, a set of larger, more colorful windows told the story of Jesus.

David stared at those windows for a few minutes as if he were reading his favorite book. Then he turned around and started for the back of the cathedral to a place, I noticed once I caught up, that was called The Poet's Corner. The names of famous American authors lay on the floor with a quote from each underneath. On the wall above the quotes was a montage of children's poems.

Finally, David spoke. "So now do you see?"

My eyes shot around the majesty of the place. "There's a lot to see, David."

"Exactly. Common human efforts—like baseball or poetry— by great and flawed human beings, all honored in a sacred space like this. And what's at the center?" He shifted his vision. "The cross, just as it has been throughout history. A lot of brilliant people throughout the ages have said so; some have even died because of it. But it's like that's his invitation to all humanity, and it's not a religion."

David's eyes moved from the altar up to the ceiling as he spoke, as if he were still hearing the string quartet and watching the notes rise. His jaw jetted from side to side, his shoulders bent slightly back as he stared upward. He brushed his hand over his face, and I got the impression as he did that what he saw both inspired and burdened him. He breathed deeply and faced me, latching on to my wrists like a man convinced of justice.

"This is why I've got to do it, Jonna. Him. Imagine how different the city, even the world, would be if the endowment had been used as it was intended." His voice faded, and he squeezed my hands before dropping his to his sides. But just as he let go, David Rockley no longer seemed like merely a nice guy my brothers would call a friend.

Somehow he'd changed into a man I'd never before seen. Really seen. Until this second. In this holy place. I swallowed.

Outside, he hailed a cab and directed the driver to my street. We sat wordlessly in the backseat, watching the meter on the dashboard tick off as the blocks spiraled by, glancing occasionally at the cars beside us. Though the cabdriver was weaving in and out of various lanes, dodging through traffic as though he were playing a game, I couldn't quite explain why I felt safe. But I did. Twenty minutes later, we pulled to a stop in front of my building. David jumped out of his side to circle around the taxi and open my door. I climbed from the taxi and we stood in the cold, still not sure what to say.

The cabdriver hollered for him to get in or pay the fare. David motioned for him to wait.

"Thanks for coming tonight, Jonna. I've wanted to have dinner with you for a long time," he said. He leaned over and put his lips to my frozen cheek. "See you tomorrow."

He slid back into the taxi. I stood watching it drive off, my hands pressed into my coat pockets. When it was out of sight, I turned toward the stoop and took out my keys. The air was cold as I unlocked the front door, but for the first time this winter, my cheeks felt warm, not icy. And I felt a funny little tickle in my throat because of it.

I slept soundly that night.

The organist had already started the first song at Second Presbyterian Church of Hoboken the next morning when I hurried into the back of the sanctuary. My subway had been late. So had the PATH. It didn't help that I still hadn't mastered the art of gauging the amount of time it'd take to get from one part of the city to another on public transportation, let alone weekends with the transit system's limited schedules and traveling to another state altogether. Even if New Jersey were just across the river. So on the Sunday mornings I joined my brother's family at their church, they could count on me to be late.

Like now. I found Luke and Sarah with the boys in a middle pew and scooted past a white-haired man in a green sweater to join them. They waved as they sang. I pulled up the hymnal from the back of the pew and flipped the pages until I found "Rock of Ages." They'd just finished the second verse and were moving into the next. But all I could do was read:

> *Nothing in my hand I bring,*
> *Simply to the cross I cling;*
> *Naked, come to Thee for dress;*
> *Helpless, look to Thee for grace;*
> *Foul, I to the fountain fly;*
> *Wash me, Savior, or I die.*

I found myself surprised by the words, in the same way I had been with the violins last night. There was a force, a fountain even, I realized, greater than all human efforts combined, one that established right from wrong, peace from chaos. Apart from it, we were "foul." David's need to make right the Cherrinard's wish made a little more sense this morning.

When we finished, I glanced behind our row to see if he was here. I looked past my nephews, who were coloring on the bulletin, to see if David had found a seat on the other side of the sanctuary, but I didn't see him there either. He'd probably had subway trouble as well. Though we spent the next hour singing two more hymns, offering a confession, reciting the Lord's Prayer, and hearing the middle-aged minister's sermon about the parable of the Good Samaritan, I felt as if I were eavesdropping. As much as I tried to engage in each aspect of the worship service, I couldn't stop thinking about raw fish and stained glass.

We stood in the sanctuary's center aisle as the organist played the final benedictory hymn, and inched our way down to the hospitality center for coffee. My nephews elbowed a path to the table and retrieved a handful of mini-muffins to share with me. Luke and Sarah stopped to talk with another couple, then with their pastor, while I tried to keep Jesse and Garrett from playing catch with a poppy seed muffin. After a few more snacks and conversations, we bundled into our coats and caps and walked the three blocks to Sinatra Street.

Without David.

"He'll show up," Luke said, dropping his coat on a hanger and helping Garrett with his. Sarah pulled Jesse out of his jacket and hurried to the kitchen to stir something in the Crock-Pot.

"Do you think we should try him on his cell phone?" she called out.

No sooner had they untied their boots than the boys grabbed handheld video games and began to punch the buttons wildly with their thumbs. "He's a dependable guy. If he says he'll be here, he will," Luke answered, pinching the games from his sons' hands. "Not on Sunday, guys. Let's help your mom instead."

In the kitchen, we joined Sarah, who was shaping bread rolls on a cookie sheet. We pulled glasses and silverware from cupboards and prepared the table for Sunday afternoon dinner. Jesse and I folded napkins, Garrett told knock-knock jokes, and Luke poured water. I glanced at the clock—1:02—and tapped my fingers against the counter.

"Well, while we're waiting, let me tell you what I found out," Luke said.

"What about David?" Sarah asked.

"I'll tell him, too, when he gets here." Luke took a gulp of water, leaned against the sink, and folded his arms across his chest as if he were preparing for a whopper of a story. Two parents from the private school where he taught graduated from Regal fifteen years ago, but when Luke asked them about the Cherrinard endowment, they told him they'd never heard of it. That didn't mean much, though, since they were both English majors and couldn't remember taking any religion classes. They also were quick to defend the climate at the university as one that had always been open to unique perspectives, sometimes even zany ones, and that's what made it such a good education. Because they'd been exposed to a variety of philosophies and beliefs from throughout the world, they were convinced they were better prepared to tackle their careers.

Luke combed his fingers through his thick head of hair, though it didn't really make much difference. It was still frizzy and wild, like mine.

He continued the story. "When I asked these parents whether they'd heard much Christian theology in any of their classes, they looked as if I'd just stepped out of a spaceship."

That got the boys' attention. They moved in front of their dad, their eyes wide. Luke milked it for more. "And do you know what they said then?"

"What?" the boys said in unison.

"What's that got to do with literature?" He shook his head and remained silent in what I imagined directors would have called a dramatic pause. It worked.

"Then what, Dad?" Jesse asked.

Luke couldn't help himself. The ham in our family kicked into full gear and re-enacted the conversation like a stand-up comic: "So I said to them, 'Right. Good point. There's not a trace of Christian theology in Shakespeare or Dostoyevski, Milton or Tolstoy. Forget about it. I mean, what could Melville possibly have known about the Bible? That whale story was ridiculous.

Not to mention Austen or Kierkegaard or Stowe—where'd they get those zany ideas, anyway? You know, come to think of it, Western literature and Christianity are about as unrelated as tubas and drums.'"

Sarah and I couldn't hold back the laughter. The boys snorted too. Seeing their mom and their aunt laugh always made them do the same, even if they had no idea why we were laughing. I had to admit that it was at moments like these that I was grateful my parents never bought us a television growing up; we'd cooked up many a theatrical moment as kids to entertain ourselves then . . . and now.

We settled down when the bell on the oven dinged. Sarah pulled out the rolls, I dished the soup, and we sat around the table set for six. The empty chair was glaring.

"I don't get it," I said, buttering a roll. "David told me last night in the cab that he'd see—"

"You were with David last night in a cab?" Luke and Sarah traded glances. My cheeks burned.

"No big deal, guys. It was just dinner."

"Dinner?"

"Sushi, to be exact." I drank some water. My brother folded his hands above his soup.

"You mean, like raw fish—that kind of sushi?" he asked. "Since when did you start eating sushi?"

"Since last night. Living in New York has given me a little more culture."

"Yogurt has culture," Jesse exclaimed. "My teacher said that's kind of like mold. We're growing some in science."

"Cool, Jesse." I studied my bowl and pushed around carrots, celery, and chicken chunks. "This looks delicious, Sarah."

"Don't change the subject, Jonna Lightfoot." Luke glanced at the bowl beneath his hands. "So?"

"So what? It does look delicious, and David and I had dinner. So what? It wasn't a date or anything. I was hungry."

"That's great!" He grinned. When he bowed his head for grace, his sons imitated him and shouted, "Amen!" once he'd finished. Aside from the slurps and the clinks of silverware on ceramic, we spent the next ten minutes at the table discussing little besides how delicious the soup tasted or what else Jesse's class was growing in petri dishes.

The worst thing about having brothers who cared about my love life was that I had brothers who cared about my love life. Every detail. And considering mine had never been stellar, it was hardly the time to divulge much of anything but that I'd had dinner with David Rockley, friend to all MacLaughlin brothers. Forget about the cathedral.

Instead, I slurped. As I did, a tiny piece of onion slipped from the spoon down my chest. I was wiping it off when Sarah looked up from her soup.

"I couldn't reach my father yet, Jonna." He was a lawyer at a firm in Denver, a good-humored man I'd only seen twice since he'd married off his daughter to my brother. Sarah said that although he was on the verge of retirement, he was always willing to offer legal advice to family members for free. "I left him a message, but I'm not sure he's done cases like this. He'll probably know someone who has."

"Cases like detectives take?" Jesse asked, reaching for another roll.

"Not really, hon. Cases involving major universities."

I thought of some of the details David had revealed last

night: the memo to his boss about destroying documents, the original intentions from the Cherrinards, even the examples of bias directed at certain campus groups. And especially the letter from the office of the general counsel. It was hardly good news. In fact, the new details only revealed how serious his accusation was.

"You know he was right about the college's history, right?" Luke said. "I decided to do a little of my own research yesterday. Apparently, when it first started, Regal—like Yale and Princeton—required students not only to participate in daily Scripture readings but also to be ready to explain what they meant. It's documented everywhere—if you look in the right places." He helped himself to more soup. "That's pretty serious evidence if you ask me and—"

The phone rang. Sarah reached for it and nodded to us. It was David. She listened as he talked. Whatever he said made her gasp. We set down our spoons.

"Are you all right?" she asked. Sarah pressed the phone close to her ear, nodded some more, and offered David a series of yes's before she hung up abruptly.

"I can't believe it. He said his apartment got broken into last night. He's been filing police reports all morning and wanted to apologize for missing our lunch."

"His apartment got broken into? What? How?" I asked. I gripped my napkin.

"He wasn't sure. He said he'd gotten home late last night"—she raised an eyebrow my direction—"and when he did, the place was a mess. Books were all over the floor, papers and clothes and newspaper clippings he'd been saving were strewn across his living room and bedroom. He said they took his television and DVD player, but he was sure that was not what they were looking for."

"Is Uncle David okay?" Jesse asked.

"Fine, baby. He just feels a little . . . weird." She looked worried when she saw the expression on her boys' faces. "He's fine, guys. Really. Says he's going to take you to a game next week. And, Jonna, he asked if you could come by his office at Regal tomorrow at one so you could get, uh, a tour of the campus."

"I could do that," I said.

Luke nodded his affirmation at me, then turned to Sarah. "So where is he now?"

"He had to get off his cell phone. He was at the police station and apparently about to—" She stopped herself when she saw Garrett's eyes fill up. "He'll be finished in no time."

"When's he coming over?" Jesse asked.

"Probably not today, hon. He needs to clean up some things." Sarah smiled at her sons. "Now, how about some chocolate cake?" I wasn't sure who her suggestion helped more: the boys or me. But because chocolate in any form was always the next-best thing to do in troubling moments, Sarah began to clear the table. Luke pulled Garrett to his lap, and Jesse and I followed Sarah into the kitchen. We grabbed five plates with slices of double-layer fudge cake and carried them into the living room. Luke switched on the radio and found *A Prairie Home Companion* on the local public station. It was the perfect combination of distraction from worry: listening to good stories while eating dessert with family.

After I licked the last bit of frosting off my fork, and as the radio actors finished the segment "Guy Noir: Private Eye," I gathered the plates and went back into the kitchen alone.

It was a good time to soak my hands in dishwater.

By the time I left for the train, the sun was starting to set. I remembered the last time I was here, Thursday night, and David asked if we could take the ferry. He'd been so honest and nostalgic; I'd been freezing and annoyed. Granted, I'd thawed slightly since then, but I hadn't been nearly as warm as he'd been. Now I worried about how he'd felt when he walked into his apartment and saw he'd been burglarized. It was hard to imagine something so awful would have happened to someone so . . . nice. I gulped. The sky turned dark just as I headed down into the station, not from the time of day but from a storm that had rolled over in a second. The clouds broke, and I didn't know which surprised me more: my feelings about David or the rain on my head.

Rain? In February?

I held my breath in the PATH tunnel and caught the uptown subway to Harlem. Hannah had come home from her trip, so I was glad to find lights on in the apartment. She was lying on the couch, reading a travel book on Paris and wearing a red Denver College T-shirt and shorts (Honolulu temperatures had not left our apartment). Jazz music spilled from the stereo.

"Look what the cat dragged in," she teased.

"Welcome home to you, too." I threw off my parka and was tempted to get out the suntan lotion. "So how was Senator What's-his-name?"

"Her name." She flipped a page in Paris. "The Honorable Senator Lillian G. Milton, to be exact, and only the second woman in the U.S. Senate from the fine state of New York. But all good things must come to an end."

"Sorry to hear—"

"As hard as she worked those crowds, Lightfoot—and you should have seen her—I'd bet real money she does not get reelected. Which would be a shame . . . though of course you never heard me say that." Hannah stretched out her legs and rotated her head in a circle as if she were rearranging the muscles in her neck. "I'll deny it through and through, hard-nosed journalist that I am. But between you and me, Senator Milton is good people, you know? New York's lucky to have her."

I sat down, took off my boots, and put my feet up on the coffee table. "Sounds like quite a weekend."

Hannah dropped Paris on her stomach and folded her arms behind her head. She pulled up her knees so that they leaned against the couch, and a series of tsks escaped from the sides of her mouth as she recounted each stop on the campaign trip: the crowds in the farm towns upstate, the patients at the cancer research hospital where Senator Milton gave a speech, even third graders at the charter school where she read books aloud during story time. In less than forty-eight hours, Hannah had covered over six hundred miles and met hundreds of people with the senator and her team, listening and watching, probing and reporting. Tonight, at the end of it all, she was more convinced than ever that the country needed public servants like Lillian Milton.

"But that doesn't mean the voters will think so," she said.

"It doesn't mean they won't."

She moved her head my direction, her face on the edge of a smile. "Lightfoot, you surprise me. You haven't let yesterday's page-one story go to your head, have you?"

With all that had happened since I'd read it at Charlie's Wash-O-Rama, the witches' story was the last thing I'd been thinking about. Now that Hannah reminded me of the new-and-improved story about pagans' rights, I felt as if someone had just squeezed a glob of sour lemons in my mouth and it was slowly sliding down my throat. Acidic. Raw. Harsh. I tried to push it away but I'd never been good at sorting through feelings of anger or disappointment or passion. Which of them was good? Which was healthy? Which to express or restrain or confess? Emotions were confusing, especially when they were wrapped up with work, so I picked a chocolate cake crumb from my sweater and sampled it.

"It wasn't exactly my story, but you know how it goes."

She grimaced. "What I know is that there's a reason that man's name is Wood: He has no feelings, and if he does, the only thing he cares about are dollars, not news." That was all the encouragement Hannah needed to climb onto her imaginary soapbox and spend the next ten minutes—almost without breathing—ranting about the current state of greed motivating media conglomerates and ruining the integrity of one of the most important professions in the world. After all, she exclaimed, her fist in the air, a journalist's first loyalty was not to profits but to citizens. It was the people that mattered most with news, and it was our job, Hannah raved, to provide them with the information they'd need to be free and self-governing. Wasn't that the point? To report the truth so they'd be good citizens, not mindless consumers?

If we'd been in church, this would have been the point to come to the altar. Instead, another series of tsks dropped from her mouth, and I could tell Hannah was winding down, like a preacher coming to the end of her sermon. She settled back onto the couch, breathed deeply like she was at yoga class, and dropped her hand so that it dangled above the floor. The silence reeled us in.

I went to the kitchen and brought back two small glasses

of Cabernet Sauvignon. After all, I'd read in the last issue of *ChocoLatte* magazine that the antioxidants in red wine had the same health effects as those in dark chocolate: They reduced stress while building up the immune system. At least it made sense right now. We clinked glasses.

"To reporting the truth," Hannah said calmly.

"To truth."

We sipped.

"Well, I guess a little of the senator got to me," she said. "Whew. Okay, since I got that out of my system—at least for now—what's happened to you since I last saw you?"

I swirled the wine around in the glass and watched it gather its color. "Hmmm. Action-packed. Let's see: I did my laundry, baked some cookies, ate some cookies, and went to New Jersey this morning."

She stretched again. "That's all?"

"Pretty much."

"That's not what I heard."

My face felt hot. I opened the window a crack and resettled in my chair. "No?"

"No. Word on the street is you've been a busy girl."

"I have?"

"Yup. I even heard a certain young man was very eager to spend time with you."

"Oh, for heaven's sake. It was just dinner."

She blinked. "That's funny. I didn't hear anything about dinner. I only heard about the interview."

"The interview?"

She sat up at the edge of the couch and set her glass on the table. She rubbed her eyes and then leaned toward me like a detective searching a crime scene. An eyebrow rose. She chewed lightly on her lower lip and moved her head back and forth, as if she'd just solved the case.

"Lightfoot, did you have a date?"

"I had dinner! It was only sushi, if you must know."

She yawned and picked up her wine before lying back down. "If you had sushi, you definitely had a date. Spill."

"You first."

Hannah chuckled as she told me she'd run into Lee Cheung at the *Clarion* this afternoon. She'd been collecting her mail after the senator's bus dropped her off, and Lee was alphabetizing a special shipment of marketing gadgets. He told her he'd felt *totally radical* that I came with him to the Chinatown Jesus Center Friday night. And when she asked him about it, he talked so much she finally had to excuse herself. She couldn't remember seeing him so excited.

"Oh. That."

"Skip will love that story," she said, catching herself. "That is, if Wood doesn't kill it. Don't let me go there again."

"Don't go there again."

"Okay, your turn."

I shifted in my chair, crossing my legs this way, then that. I swirled the glass again. When I noticed the dust on the table, I went into the kitchen for the dust rag and returned to the bookshelf opposite the stereo, which I turned down. I lifted the window another inch and straightened the magazines on the table. Then I started to organize them by month, dusting each as I did. Hannah's eyes followed me.

"Uh-oh. It must have been good."

I stopped dusting. "All right," I began. "I'd been minding

my own Saturday morning when the doorbell rang." I met her eyes, then adjusted. "Okay. I'd been sound asleep when the doorbell rang, and there was David Rockley with H&H bagels and coffee on the doorstep."

"David Rockley?" Hannah said.

I nodded, then cleared my throat. "He's actually nice. Anyway, after I finished my Saturday laundry, I found myself on the subway going to the Wet Fish Café."

She raised a suspicious eyebrow. "Dinner," she deadpanned.

"I ate raw tuna and liked it," I justified, "and just when I thought it was over, I heard music that floated high into the heavens."

"You heard music? This is not good."

"Violins. At the cathedral. They do free concerts there."

She sighed and waved me on. That was when I told her what David had discovered at Regal, the letter from their general counsel, and the determination he'd shown at Saint John's to pursue this — as the right thing to do. The *only* thing. I did not tell her how he took me home in a cab and warmed my cheek with his lips. That would have pushed us both off the cliff.

Hannah didn't say anything. Instead, she rose from the couch, went into her room, and returned with her reporter's notebook. She flipped back the pages until she found an empty sheet and clicked the end of her pen.

"I don't necessarily buy it. Could be another conspiracy theory — you know the kind, how liberal universities are always belittling some saintly ideology — but it might not be either. In any case, I'm going to bet you haven't written any of it down yet, right?"

"Well . . ."

"That's what I thought. Go back to the beginning."

"And I forgot to tell you that this afternoon we were supposed to have lunch at my brother's, but David called from the police station. His apartment had been broken into last night."

Her eyes widened. "Every detail. Now."

I spent the next half hour trying to remember each word David had told me, starting with Thursday night at Luke and Sarah's when he first educated us about the mission of the university. I explained the Cherrinards' original hope that their endowment would make the city a better place and the documents and letters David had discovered that he said linked so many key leaders to the funds, careful to use the words he did: money laundering, fraud, embezzlement.

She looked up for a second when she heard the charges, sipped her wine, and then waved me to continue. I told her how David had met with President Coen—who'd told him to consider looking for another job, which he had—and how no one from the board of trustees would take his calls. So David had written a letter to them, and that was when he received the two-sentence letter in response from the general counsel. It affirmed their position that it would be too burdensome for the university to produce the documents he'd requested. So as far as they were concerned, the matter was closed. But tomorrow I was supposed to meet David at his office at 1:00 p.m.

She scribbled in her unique Hensley shorthand. And when she dotted her last *i*, she reread her notes, narrowed her eyes, and sighed.

"I hate to say it, girl, but this could be the one."

Whenever Hannah mentioned *the one*, I knew what she meant. It was that solitary story that could move a journalist into

Pulitzer Prize–winning categories, the lone discovery that could shift the entire direction of a reporter's career from small-town to big-time. For as long as I'd known her, Hannah X. Hensley was always looking for that story—hunting for it, really. The one that would outdo her last, the piece of news so important and so fresh that not a single reporter knew about it yet, but every person on the planet needed to. And would—as soon as she covered it. It was that story that would change everything. And she was always challenging me to find it as well.

"I don't know, Hannah. Regal's mission is so different now. And this feels so big. It's such a serious accusation."

"Lightfoot, I wasn't talking about the story."

She caught me off guard.

"I was talking about David. He could be the one."

::Chapter Seven

I was thirteen years old, standing on top of a ski slope at Breckenridge, staring at a sign with a black diamond printed on it. Freshly fallen snow seemed stuck on branches nearby, and the blue of the Colorado sky was an endless sea across the Rockies. I knew most of the intermediate trails on this mountain by heart. But now as I studied the expert trail below—the moguls were high, the powder deep and therefore hard to navigate—I wondered simultaneously if I could do it and how I would.

It didn't help that this was the steepest slope I'd ever seen in my young life, at an angle more like a wall than a staircase. Little wonder some genius had christened the trail "High Anxiety." Matt and Luke were already halfway down, flying from mogul to mogul, undaunted by either the black diamond or the slope's name. Mark was skiing on the other side of the mountain, and Mom and Pop were cross-country skiing in the snowy meadow by our home. It was a typical winter Saturday for the MacLaughlins.

Except that I was alone. I peered down the slope, watching each pile of snow and mountain grow bigger the more I stared and the less I moved. Skiers zipped past me. The snow was up to their shins, wet but slightly groomed on the mountain so that they could maneuver each turn easier. Most tackled it as though it were a beginner's trail. I swallowed as I watched them and then gripped my ski poles so hard my fingers tingled. I wiggled my toes in my boots to keep them warm, slanting the edges of my skis inward, then outward. I watched another zipper—whom I thought was showing off—and in what felt like at least thirty minutes, though it was probably only three, I finally slid my skis over to the tip of the mountain and pointed them downward. My knees pressed in, my mouth dry.

A few minutes later and not far from where I'd begun, I realized this run was bigger and harder than I could have seen from the top. I was skiing like a beginner, traversing long and wide across the mountain and falling into the powder each time I began to pick up speed that was scarier than I could handle. I tried to avoid the moguls or, if they'd surprise me, I'd absorb them as though I were on a trampoline. If the snow was too deep or the angle too steep, I'd simply fall up into the mountain and lie there until I felt I could try again.

An hour and a half later, soaked and sore and still alone, I was at the bottom of High Anxiety, looking back up at the monster, trying to figure out if I was either the dumbest person in the world for having attempted it or the bravest because I'd lived to tell about it. I never could decide which, and sometimes I still wondered.

Like now. The subway platform was as cold as Breckenridge and the memory of High Anxiety as alive as if I were still standing at the top of the mountain. Or at the bottom marveling at its size and steepness, still terrified of its danger from either vantage point. As I waited for a train this Monday morning, it wasn't hard to figure out why. The mess David was suggesting about Regal seemed its own version of High Anxiety: moguls that seemed too difficult to maneuver, angles too steep for—

"Jonna . . . Lightfoot . . . MacLaughlin!" I heard my name over the subway intercom, bringing me back from Colorado to New York City. I turned to see the bright face of Emma, my subway friend. A huge grin wrapped across her cheeks when she saw that I was looking her way. She put up her hand and waved me over.

"What have I lost this morning?" Immediately, I began scouring through my bag for something I assumed I'd misplaced and Emma had found, though I had no idea what I was looking for.

"Something very important." Emma spoke into the little microphone on the other side of the booth's glass. "I saw you staring into space over there on the platform, Jonna, and I couldn't help but think, that girl's lost her smile."

I looked up from my bag and immediately felt my face fill out.

"That's better. Whatever you were thinking about, well, child, it can't be that bad. Nothin' a little grace and smilin' won't make better." She erupted into a rich, full laugh that moved through her shoulders and gleamed out of her eyes. I joined her.

"You're right, Emma."

"Just blessed, girl. That's all." She turned over her palms at the same time she raised her shoulders, as if she were expecting a gift to drop into the empty open hands at any second. A young couple came up to the booth window and I scooted to the side to let Emma sell them a MetroCard. They nodded excitedly at Emma when they heard her charge to "make it a great day," as if that were just what they needed to hear. Once they'd hurried off toward the platform, I was sure that whatever the New York City Transit Authority paid this woman for making sure people got to work with a smile and a card, it was not enough. She looked back at me.

"You've got a lot on your mind?"

I bent over into the little microphone.

"There are some big mountains to tackle, Emma."

She held up an old copy of the *Clarion*. "I know. But that's why you're there. I reckon you and God make a good team." She pointed to a story I'd written last week about the challenges women faced in leadership roles at megachurches. She set it down and came in close to the window, pulling in her joy for a serious affirmation. "This city needs you, Jonna. Now, go catch that train."

I didn't know how she knew the train was coming, because the only sounds I heard were the musical notes of her voice. I spun around when the subway screeched to a halt, tossed Emma a "thanks," and jumped onto the train as the doors were closing. I found a seat and took out my notebook. I wrote down her words, if for nothing else but to come back to them in case the slope got too scary and I needed motivation to get up again.

Skip was not in his office when I knocked, which was unusual for a Monday morning. I almost bumped into him instead as he was coming from the advertising vice president's office and I was heading for my desk. I asked for a few minutes with him; he offered three. And not in his office but in the hallway as the newsroom buzzed around us with the energy of another new week.

"Sorry, Jonna, on my way to another meeting with a financial team. But if it's about the Wiccans' story, I'm not happy either. I've already talked with Lila and the other Friday-night editor."

He was good, this editor of mine. He could read a reporter's demeanor as though it were a paragraph and find in a matter of seconds what mattered most.

"Well, great. I did want to ask you about a couple of other stories I'd like to —"

"Weird thing is, I've gotten lots of good calls on the piece. Who'd have thought witches were so popular with New Yorkers? So I want a follow-up for tomorrow, on the military dad, okay?"

"Griffin Lewis? A story on him?"

"Exactly. By four o'clock. That's the priority."

He was around the corner before I could respond.

I wasn't expecting it. Usually, Skip was quick to stop and listen whenever I was unsure about a story or disturbed by a subject. He'd chew over the details and then offer suggestions about who to talk to and how. But this morning, the crunch of dollar signs seemed loud, stealing his attention away from his reporters. Or at least this one.

I wandered toward the employee lounge, thinking that a chat with Griffin Lewis, resident pagan and angry, grieving father, was not exactly the pick-me-up I'd been hoping for. I dumped the dregs of the coffee into a mug and remade the pot. The Chinatown Jesus Center seemed like a better story, one I'd hoped to pitch to Skip first thing this morning. Then I would have eased into a conversation about Regal, to see what he might know about the Cherrinard endowment or even the college's attitudes toward diversity. But this new assignment from Skip meant the others would have to wait and that I'd have to figure out what else to report about this shadowy man. He'd already made himself clear that the Wiccans wouldn't let up in their protests until he could bury his son with dignity, or at least with a pentacle on his grave. What more could I write?

Then again, what did I really know about this father? Or his son?

Back at my desk, I found the Wiccan flyer flung across the top of a thick booklet that I—and apparently every other religion reporter in the city—had been sent from a think tank for religious freedom. It was a study on the steady rise in New York City cults and the increase in drug use by many during supposed acts of worship. One group, who called themselves Jonah and the Whales, believed they'd been mandated to re-create the experience of God's presence with Jonah in the belly of the whale—with a little spiritual and hallucinogenic help from magic mushrooms. Twice I'd seen the Jonah story covered in the other papers. I just hadn't gotten around to it yet. It hadn't quite piqued my interest. Then again, no one else had reported on the Wiccan rally, besides the *Clarion*.

I called the number on the flyer. Griffin Lewis answered. I asked him if I could take a few minutes of his time, and when I did, his tone surprisingly shifted from the chilly morning we first met.

"I'd be happy to talk to you, Ms. Lightfoot," he said.

"You would? Okay, um, could you hang on just a minute?" It was another thing I wasn't expecting. I clicked open a new document on my computer and began typing his name but then changed my mind and picked up a pen. I flipped back a page in my notebook. Something about pen on paper seemed to help my brain flow a little more directly. Maybe it slowed down the thought process as I listened, or sped up the insights as I tried to interpret the interview. But whatever it was, the task of note taking in my own handwriting rather than on a keyboard seemed a time-tested method for making sense of the job. As helpful as sugar in coffee.

"Okay. First, I'd like to—"

"Actually, Ms. Lightfoot, let me begin by thanking you for your excellent coverage of our plight. The story and the front-page attention to it was exactly what we had hoped would move our cause forward for—"

"It was?"

"Absolutely. I don't need to tell you how this gravestone issue is another example of how pagans have been treated through the ages. Your story gave us sympathy with the public. It hasn't ever been easy, you know. Take for instance the time when . . ."

Though his voice kept moving, I struggled to interpret his words, either in my ear or through my pen. I was stuck instead on two he'd already articulated: Sympathy? Plight? The story *I* had written simply reported on the rally and a small group of witches who'd gathered to protest the government's exclusion of them as an approved religion for military burials. It wasn't reporting I thought would elicit sympathy, of all things. Then again, the story I wrote and the story printed in the Saturday paper weren't the same. My antennae pricked up again when I recognized another word coming through the phone.

"Regal University was great in letting us rally there. But they've always been supportive of people like us—you know, the type usually ignored or marginalized by this hypocritical society. But our friends at Regal have been different from—"

"Friends like Professor Evan Hartman?" I interrupted.

He paused. I pushed the phone closer to my ear as I waited for his response: "I'm not sure I understand."

"Oh, I'm just curious how friendly Professor Hartman is with your group. Any idea? He sure seems to know a lot about your religion." I sipped my coffee.

"Well, he is a scholar on these things."

"So you do know him?" I doodled a big dark star across the top of the page as Griffin Lewis explained his friendship with Evan Hartman over the past fifteen years. Hartman had helped him manage a difficult divorce and gain custody of his then twelve-year-old son, Teddy, in the aftermath. Mr. Lewis began attending gatherings that, according to Hartman, would bring peace and unity to his feelings, getting him in touch with the spirits and goddesses who had been sent to help him through his grief. He'd been practicing Wiccan beliefs ever since, and he wasn't ashamed to say so this morning. He believed the ancient religion saved his life; it gave him a new purpose.

"This might seem like a strange question, Mr. Lewis, but were those gatherings also held on the campus of Regal?"

"Why? What would be so wrong with that? It's very hard to get people to rent space to a coven of witches, even in this city." His voice whimpered as he recounted a handful of rejections from landlords. Most, he said, had mocked them, ridiculing the coven and claiming they were Satanists—which they weren't. They'd told him they didn't want to find skeletons or bloody drinks in the closets after the witches had left. As hard as the Eastern Order of the Pagan Sanctuary had tried, there were few places in the city where they felt safe or accepted, and fewer that would offer them decent space to gather—that was, except Regal. The university always rented, sometimes donated, conference rooms so they could come together and practice their magic. Sometimes they allowed them to keep their shrines in the rooms so they wouldn't have to cart them all over the city. And Regal never questioned the Wiccans' right to gather.

"Are you saying Regal is sort of the unofficial location for the Eastern Order of the Pagan Sanctuary?"

"Unofficially."

"And that's where your son, Teddy, worshipped too before he joined the army?"

Mr. Lewis suddenly descended into silence. I remembered the scowl he gave me when I'd talked with him that wintry morning at the campus, and I wondered if that same expression was on the other end of the phone. Instead, I heard a sniffle, followed by a cough.

"Yes."

"Yes, Teddy worshipped alongside you at the Eastern Order of the Pagan Sanctuary, at Regal?"

"Yes. Before he . . ." He sniffled again, then blew his nose. If he began to cry, I knew our interview would be over, more from my end than his. Something about grown men sobbing — even if they were pagans — always did me in. I listened and braced myself. He sniffled, then, thankfully, seemed to collect his composure. "Yes, before Teddy was sent overseas."

I exhaled and glanced over my notes. I still needed more background to make this a genuine story. I'd always found that if I asked a few questions about a person's life — regardless of his religion — he willingly offered it. Pop always said everyone liked to tell his own story if someone offered to listen.

Which was how I discovered that Griffin Lewis grew up in Brooklyn and now worked as a manager at Mother Earth Grocery, not far from where he'd raised Teddy. They'd spent Saturdays at the Botanical Garden or the Central Park Zoo and tried to make as many Mets games as they could — when Teddy wasn't staying with his mother in Boston. When I asked him if he'd ever participated in any other religions, Griffin also told me that he'd been raised a nominal Lutheran before the pagans helped him through his crisis. He wanted me to know that his witch friends and their "magikcal draw of the moon"—he spelled it out—possessed a "healing power of the earth. Their prayer rituals to the higher and unknown deities kept me alive to this day," he said. Because of them, he'd do what he'd have to in order to get the government's approval of their beliefs, even if that meant taking the case to the courts. He said he felt indebted to the Wicca community.

"The Lutherans didn't offer you that kind of support?"

"Christians hardly ever get it right, do they?"

I took that as a "no" to my question. He kept talking.

"Lutherans, Methodists, Presbyterians, you know, they mean well. It's sad, but really they're all the same and interested in only one thing."

"What's that?"

"Themselves."

As a Presbyterian by default, I had to admit that I wasn't happy about being lumped into this list of self-centered hypocrites. I scribbled his comments down to balance out the story and threw out one last question: Did they have any more plans to rally?

"This Thursday. Just before midnight at the steps of the mayor's office in city hall. We want his attention too."

He thanked me again for helping the witches and told me he hoped to see me at city hall. When we hung up, I found myself thinking not about another protest, or even about his conversion from Lutheranism, but about his son. Certainly, I could understand hanging on to the shirttails of your parents' belief system. Lord knew my brothers and I had done that all our lives. But something about Teddy—or, really, about his father's comments—didn't settle well in my gut. It could have been the bad coffee, but I had the feeling Griffin Lewis's perspective on military tombstones had more to do with his own life and less to do with the death of his son.

I typed his name into the *Clarion*'s obituary archives. There were dozens of Lewis's who had died just since the time I'd moved from New Orleans to New York. I scrolled through most of them—still a sucker for the raw details of a person's life I'd find in these daily death announcements—until I came to the T's:

> *Teddy Griffin Lewis, Jr., of Brooklyn, NY, had been assigned to the 2nd Battalion, 508th Parachute Infantry Regiment, 4th Brigade Combat Team, 82nd Airborne Division, Fort Bragg, N.C., and died in Afghanistan of wounds sustained when an improvised explosive device detonated near his vehicle. He was 20 years old, the only child of Dr. Anna L. Kostas of Cambridge, MA, and T. Griffin Lewis, Sr., high priest of the Eastern Order of the Pagan Sanctuary in New York, NY. Memorial services will be held 10 a.m., Saturday, June 15, 2005, at Saint Constantine Greek Orthodox Church in Cambridge.*

I clicked on the public records for Cambridge, Massachusetts, and typed in Dr. Anna L. Kostas. I found her easily, listed as a research scientist in the school of public health at Harvard University. I picked up the phone. A woman answered and I introduced myself. She sighed like a hot breeze.

"What's he done now?"

I hadn't even grabbed my pen yet. "Excuse me?"

"I'm assuming this is about another of Griffin's pagan rituals. Which one this time? Worshipping the neighbor's cat? Casting spells on his boss? Picking flowers from the Botanical Garden for the vernal equinox?"

"Um. Actually . . . did he really pick flowers at the Botanical Garden?"

"That's what the police said. But he claimed he thanked the flowers first for their sacrifice and left behind an offering of milk and honey. That seemed to balance it out."

I tried to imagine this burly sour man picking flowers anywhere and suddenly felt a soft spot for him. Still, he'd had no problem reeling his anger at a reporter the other morning either. I refocused.

"No, this isn't about any of those; it's about Teddy. First let me say I'm really sorry for your loss." She said nothing in response. I clicked my pen, wrote Teddy's name, as well as her litany of Griffin's activities. I explained the story I'd done on the Wiccan rally and the DVA's role in approving religious symbols for military tombstones. I also told her I'd just talked with her ex-husband.

"So I'm curious about Teddy's involvement with the Wiccans before he left for Afghanistan."

"What? He was confirmed in the Greek Orthodox Church when he was a teenager and never left our faith tradition. He loved the history and orthodoxy of the Greek Church."

This was a morning full of surprises. I was about to ask her more, but I didn't need to.

"My son was given a Greek Orthodox burial in a cemetery here, if that's what you wanted to know. Come see for yourself. Besides, he'd always talked about how uncomfortable he'd been with his father's religion, if you could call it that."

Dr. Kostas excused herself for a meeting and said she hoped she'd been of help. She had. She'd essentially just killed the story I didn't want to write in the first place.

I jolted from my desk to Skip's office in seconds. It was still empty. My fingers had a sudden itch for a cigarette, but I was still smokeless. I'd forgotten to order a new pack from the organic cigs Web site. I opted instead for a cup of my newly brewed coffee, but by the time I was back in the lounge, the pot had only grounds on the bottom. And they'd started to crust because someone had left the burner on. Reporters could be a selfish lot.

So I brewed a new pot and waited. If his son had already been buried with a Greek cross, why would Griffin Lewis be pushing so hard for the Wiccan symbol? Surely, he wasn't hoping to erect another tombstone on the young man's grave. From what I'd just heard, I doubted his mother would allow it anyway, even if the DVA changed its mind and suddenly approved the pentacle. It didn't make sense, but that was beginning to feel normal.

"So you're the saint who makes the coffee?" Walter Wood was standing in the lounge, his hair neat, his bow tie slick, his eyes narrow. I stepped back.

"I should have known," he quipped, reaching for a mug. "How are things in the world of religion, Joanie? I'm told your Wiccan story was a big help with sales."

I slid closer toward the pot, feeling protective of my creation. "It wasn't exactly my story. It got quite the makeover after your, um, lecture on Friday."

He smirked and straightened his tie. "Nothing is easy in the business world these days. We're all having to make sacrifices, aren't we?" He pushed his mug my direction on the counter.

But the clock above his tidy head said 11:14, and I decided I did not have time for a friendly chat with the enemy. I poured my cup, set the pot back on the burner, and made my morning sacrifice—one sugar, instead of two. I nodded as respectfully as I could at the small man in the bow tie and hurried out of the employee lounge as if I were desperate for fresh air. I slurped my coffee, missed my mouth, and was wiping it off my sweater when I found Skip back in his office, finally. He was staring over a pile of papers, a water bottle in one hand and a pen in the other.

"Got a minute now?" I asked, the stain not quite out.

Tension lined his face, but integrity seemed to win out. "Sure. What have you got?"

I plopped into the chair by the door and told him about the interview I had with Griffin Lewis. His protests of the DVA now seemed questionable at best since his son wasn't a witch in the first place. His mother had confirmed his membership with the Greek Orthodox Church, so now because there essentially was no story, I wanted to pitch him another one I thought he'd like.

"I'm listening." He planted his elbows on the desk. I had just begun to launch into the details of the Chinatown Jesus Center when the little bow tie appeared.

"Mind if I interject?" A plastic smile smudged Walter Wood's face as he walked in and sat beside me, coffee mug in hand. I looked at Skip, whose eyes told me to be patient.

"Walter, I think we're okay," Skip said, his grace a contradiction to the thing sitting across from him.

"I've no doubt. But I just wanted to say for the record, Skip, what a fine job I think Joanie's doing for the paper. Let's have more stories like those witches."

Skip saw I was about to venture out of my pacifism when

he intervened. "*Jonna* is one of our best, Walter. That's why she's about to do a profile on the pagan leader who's spearheading this protest against the DVA."

I almost dropped my mug. "But there isn't a story there, Skip. The soldier wasn't a Wiccan, so why profile the grieving father when his son's already buried—as a Greek Orthodox?"

"Because people have never read about a sad witch. Until now." Walter Wood's view of journalism was becoming annoying.

I sat up straight in my chair. The first thing I was going to do when I got back to my desk was order those cigarettes. For now, I pushed around my frizzy hair, reclipped it, and came up with a plan.

"That's a good point, Mr. Wood"—I smiled as plastically as he had—"but I think our readers would be more interested in former gang members in Chinatown who are spending Friday nights in church, not on the streets."

He yawned. Skip asked for a few more details, and I told him about the Chinatown Jesus Center, Danny Bro, and the young Chinese women and men—like Lee, our own mail-room worker—who said they were trading their parents' cultural traditions for a new radical life. Wood shrugged as he listened, as if this were a story he'd heard a thousand times before. Skip tapped his pen on the desk in a low steady rhythm that matched his countenance. Finally, when I tried to explain the vision behind this youth-oriented story, he looked quietly from Wood's face to mine.

"Let's not change game plans just yet, Jonna. Give me something I can use about this Wiccan guy by four o'clock. Go ahead and dig into the Chinatown piece a little more. But no promises. By Wednesday, let's see where we are."

I scratched my head. My dear gentle editor had never denied me a chance to pursue a story with real promise in exchange for one that we both knew was a dud. I was as confounded as I had been at the base of High Anxiety and as chilly as when I'd stood on top of it.

"Good idea, Skip," Wood said. He rose, and though he looked my way, he did not look at me. "Keep up the good work, Joanie."

When he was out of the office, I didn't know whether to punch something or to cry. This was a battle I wasn't familiar with. I gulped what was left in my mug and pulled a chocolate mint from my pocket. I'd come to expect more in how we reported religion news, and Walter Wood's approach did not fit. Skip saw my disappointment.

"Things might be a little, uh, different for a while, Jonna, just until we sort through some budget issues, so be patient, okay?" His voice was kind again, calming and brimming with confidence directed toward me. "You'll have to trust me on this. Now, anything else?"

I took a chance. "When you were at Regal, did you ever hear about the Cherrinard endowment?"

He loosened the cap from his bottle of water. "Doesn't sound familiar."

"What if I told you I thought the university had shifted thousands of dollars designated for one type of religious training and services and used the money for everything but? I believe that's happened with the Cherrinard endowment, Skip, and I'm wondering if you—"

"I'd say don't touch it."

His interruption startled me. "Huh?"

"I said don't touch it. You've got enough on your plate, Jonna. You can't begin to think about a completely new story. Especially something that sounds so, well, hard to believe."

"I thought so too, which is why I have a meeting at Regal today at one about—"

"It just got cancelled. Now, get me that Wiccan story by four and stay on top of them. I think they're about to file a lawsuit with the DVA."

"Did Hartman tell you that, too?"

He tilted his head as if I'd surprised him with my tone. It had taken me aback as well. Yet, with his usual dignity, he rose from his chair and pulled a few of the papers with him. His eyes softened. "By four, okay. Please?"

"But . . ." I mumbled. Skip was out of his office. I followed him down the hall, though he darted into one the VP offices, closing the door behind him. As I watched him disappear, I felt as if I'd just fallen in a pile of snow, like my efforts to traverse across a mountain had failed and I was soaked and tired. I turned back toward my desk. It didn't help that when I glanced out the window, it really was snowing. Hard.

Hannah was buried in her computer, writing her story on Senator Lillian Milton, when I knocked on her cubicle. She did not look up, but she did grunt. Piles of press releases, notebooks, and maps were sprawled across her desk and on the floor. A tiny handheld tape recorder was talking to her from on top of her computer monitor. She switched it off.

"Wood. You were right," I said.

She swiveled around. Her eyes climbed from my boots to my sweater. "Lightfoot, we must go shopping sometime so I can help you look a little more, well, like you're living in the twenty-first century. Anyway, now what's he done?"

I looked down to remember what I'd put on this morning. Boots with gray pants and the old wool sweater I wore last Friday that now had a partial coffee stain in the middle. "I agree. On the shopping point. And Wood seems to think witches—not former gang members turned born-again Christians—will sell papers. So I'm supposed to write a story that isn't a story."

"Tell me about it. He told me to find as much dirt on Senator Milton as I could. The closest I've come is a C-minus in a political science class her first year of college. So what?" Hannah's hands flew into the air with the question, catching the light off her jewelry and tossing it across the ceiling. When she calmed down, she picked up a notebook and flipped through it.

"Come to think of it, her first year was at Regal University. Milton had to transfer to the City University her junior year because she couldn't afford the Ivy League tuition. And guess what her major was?"

"You're kidding."

She flicked the notebook at the spot that apparently revealed the fact. "Wish I were. 'World religions with an emphasis in Christian theology.' She could have qualified for a Cherrinard scholarship—if she'd known about it." She tossed the notebook back on the desk and leaned back. "Early on, the senator had an interest in church history. Even considered seminary after she graduated. Instead, she became an assistant to a district attorney and landed in law school."

"Did you know Skip is a Regal grad?"

Hannah's face contorted in surprise.

"It's true," I went on. "Now Milton. Why does it feel like all roads lead to Regal?"

"You might be right about that, Lightfoot. So he might not have been too happy to hear what you've found out about the endowment."

I shook my head. "Skip said I had too much to do already, especially with the Wiccan profile."

"So what are you going to do?" Hannah asked, picking up another notebook.

"Go to Goldwasser's for a pastrami on rye. Want one?"

"Of course." Hannah handed me a ten-dollar bill, but by the time I'd checked my messages, grabbed my coat, and arrived at the deli, it was 12:31. I wouldn't have time for lunch if I were also going to make the meeting with David at one. Skip had explicitly told me not to go, but he wasn't operating under normal conditions. There were weird vibes in the air, dollar signs floating around the office like evil spirits and affecting the judgment of ordinarily gifted editors. I'd always listened to Skip. But this once, I reasoned, he'd gotten it wrong.

Granted, the principled demands of journalism were not the only reason I scratched Goldwasser's and caught the uptown subway. I was now as curious about David as I was about seeing the documents. Nice had begun to grow on me.

It was snowing big wet flakes when I found the entrance to the campus. I asked the security guard where the offices for the library archivist would be, and he sent me across the commons, where a handful of students were putting the finishing touches on a snowman. Carrot, cap, buttons, and all. I was tempted to join the fun, but it was already 1:05.

I yanked the flaps of my cap down and sloshed through the snow, my stomach a jumble of emotions. Past them, I came to a tall white building with massive columns in the front. I noticed the inscription "In luce Tua videmus lucem" carved over the entrance and remembered David's comments on the college's mission, "In Thy light we see light." I climbed the stairs and entered the library. The clerk pointed in the direction of David's office, but as she did, she seemed puzzled.

"You can try him there, but I haven't seen him come in today."

I found the door that read "Campus Archives" and pushed it open. A red-haired woman in her forties looked up and asked how she could help me.

"I have a one o'clock appointment with David Rockley."

She glanced down a hall and then hurried over to the counter where I was standing.

"You had an appointment?"

I nodded my head. "I'm with the *Clarion* and—"

"David didn't come in to work today. And when we called his apartment, he didn't answer. It's completely out of character for him."

::Chapter Eight

Snow from my boots formed little puddles on the polished library floor. I pretended not to notice by staring instead at the rows of old books that lined the walls, metal ladders leaning delicately against them. The ceiling looked like a spiral castle, and for a second I wondered if I were in a real place or if I'd entered one of those rooms you see when you're sound asleep.

Today was as mixed-up as a dream. The red-haired woman repeated herself—"it's out of character"—but the words still didn't make sense. I'd seen David two days ago and Sarah talked with him on the phone yesterday afternoon. I was sure he'd told her to have me meet him here today. At one o'clock. I shook my head in hopes of figuring it out, and as I did, a chunk of snow dropped from my hair across my cheeks.

"Why not try him again?" My attempt to sound positive wasn't completely convincing, but the woman nodded and picked up the phone. She let it ring and ring, and when it came to his recorded voice in a message, she left another: "David, it's Sharon again. Call us at the library when you can so we know you're all right. Okay? Thanks."

Slowly, she put down the phone and swallowed so that her neck quivered slightly. She was a thin woman with firm high features, who reminded me less of a librarian and more of a dancer on Broadway whose best days had passed. Each gesture she made reflected a grace she seemed accustomed to carrying. Right now, though, it was not enough to calm her nerves. She looked afraid for her colleague.

"He's never done this. In the five years since I've worked here, David's always been the first one in and the last one out." Why wasn't I surprised to hear that? "That's why I'm a little worried. And if you were supposed to have an appointment with him for one o'clock . . ."

She sat down. I tapped my fingers on the desk and pulled out my cell phone.

"Well, I thought I had an appointment. I could have gotten that wrong, you know. I've been meaning to get a calendar. Anyway, hang on." I dialed Sarah and found her at home baking a carrot cake with organic raisins, baby carrots, and cream cheese frosting for a client. My stomach growled. I asked her about her conversation with David yesterday, and she confirmed that he had in fact asked me to meet him at his office today—right now—at one o'clock.

"Why? What's the matter?"

"Well, he's not exactly here." I injected an upbeat note to it. "And his colleague doesn't seem to know why."

"This is weird. I'm sure he said to meet you at one. Let me call Luke to see if he's heard from him, okay, and I'll call you back."

I flipped the phone closed and stood in the majesty of this library. The books, the papers, even the old smells were more inviting than I'd expected. Nothing seemed boring or dull, as I'd always assumed a library's archives would, and there was not a colorless section anywhere in the room. From the mahogany tables and chairs to the bright windows and lines of books, this was a place that seemed as friendly as a park or a coffee shop. Maybe more.

My phone rang. Sarah told me Luke hadn't heard from David either but he would call a few other friends who might have heard something. We agreed to keep each other updated and then hung up.

Sharon was back at her desk, plodding through a stack of boxes with yellowed letters and photographs. She wrote corresponding numbers and titles on various forms and placed them in another box with the letters "RMO—EX" on the side. I remembered David's comment on the records management office "expiring" several old documents after they'd been digitized.

"Looks like you have a little bit of work to do."

"Today I don't mind. It's kept my mind off—"

A door opened at the other end of the office and a round older man stepped out. He wore a three-piece blue suit that didn't quite fit and thick black glasses. He had the type of face that seemed tired all the time, saggy and droopy, as if he rarely emerged from the antiquity around him. He was more of what I'd expected in this place. When he saw me standing at the counter, he glanced across to Sharon.

"Are you being helped, ma'am?" he said, his voice as flat as the sheet of paper in his hand.

"Sure am." I crossed the room and held out my hand. "I'm Jonna Lightfoot MacLaughlin, religion reporter for the *Clarion*. I had an appointment with David Rockley at one o'clock, but I think I must have gotten it wrong since he's—"

"Didn't Sharon tell you?" He shook his head, then adjusted his glasses, and his skin sagged a bit more as he did.

"Ralph, I didn't know what to say about—" Sharon was standing beside her desk.

The lines on his cheeks and jaw moved slightly. "Of course. You might not have known. But today is the first day of David's two-week vacation. I'm afraid—Ms. MacLaughlin, is it?—you'll have to come back . . . later."

Of all the things David had told me Saturday night at the Wet Fish Café, I was sure a two-week vacation had not been anywhere in the conversation. I pulled out my reporter's notepad from my bag and flipped it open, surprised to find the notes I'd written about Emma's encouragement this morning.

This city needs you, Jonna.

"You know what? You're right. I'm way off. We're still in February, aren't we?"

A breathy sound popped out of his mouth, and I thought it might be as close to a laugh as we'd get from this man.

"But since I'm here, mind if I leave him a quick note on his desk? Sort of a reminder that I came by and will try to remember our next meeting? Which way is his office?"

He nodded for Sharon to lead me to David's office, and I followed. She unlocked his door with her master key, and though I still sensed she was worried, she smiled graciously. As she returned to her desk, I turned and walked into the nicest office I'd ever seen. Not nice as in opulent or fancy, but nice as in, well, David.

The walls were pale blue and the ceiling high with rectangular fluorescent lights. On one side of the office, a tall window gazed down on a view of the snowman in the commons. Six or seven plants sat on the ledge. Behind the desk were filing cabinets and bookshelves with reference books twice the size of my *Cromwell's Encyclopedia of World Religions*. Dozens of paperback novels—mysteries, young adult, classics—sat beside the larger books. On the wall across from David's desk hung a large photograph in an old wood frame. Purple and blue flowers in a Colorado mountain meadow filled it, with a snowcapped peak in the background.

Beside Colorado, three small photographs of children's faces hung in a vertical line. The top picture featured a Spanish-looking girl, with bright brown eyes and pigtails; beneath her was a beaming African boy whose expression reminded me of the kind you'd make just before jumping into a cold lake on a hot afternoon. The third was of a shy-looking Asian boy, younger than the others, whose black hair stood straight up in little wisps. The photos did not look like those professional types you can order in catalogs for office supplies; they looked as if David knew these children personally.

They made me curious.

At his desk, folders and papers, academic journals, and opened envelopes created an organized border to a brown vinyl desk pad. I noticed more photos on the desk next to his phone, with David in each: one of a family at a wedding with David standing next to an older man, another of him with a group of friends who looked his age, and another with him and my brother Matt at what I recognized as The Pub of Saint Agnes in Denver, my favorite place there. I picked up the picture and could almost hear my brother's voice saying, "Isn't David a great guy?"

When I set the picture back on the desk, I saw a small pile of newspaper clippings neatly stacked under a shiny glass paperweight. I leaned toward them and noticed that the headline looked familiar. When I looked closer, I saw my byline. I flipped through the pile: Each story in the pile was one I'd written, some even from my days at the *Denver Dispatch*.

I stared at the paperweight for a few seconds, shifting back and forth as if that would help my view. I wasn't sure what to make of the fact that he'd collected so many of my stories. But I had to admit that it felt good to have a fan. I scratched my head and smiled. As I did, I had a sudden craving for sushi at the Wet Fish Café . . . with David.

A German stein filled with pens and pencils sat at the edge of his desk. I pulled out a ballpoint, tore a blank page from my notebook, and scribbled the following note: *"Mon. 2/20/06 Hi David, I came by for our 1:00 appointment. Sorry I missed you. Call soon, Jonna."* I underlined soon and placed the note in the center of his desk pad with the pen over it to keep it from moving. As I did, I noticed he'd scribbled Cherrinard in the top corner of the pad, with two exclamation marks beside it. The second had an upside-down triangle instead of a point, like an arrow facing down. I followed it to a small shoebox on the floor just beneath the desk.

The phone rang. I jumped and knocked my knee against the desk, tipping over the stein so that pens crashed across the floor. I heard Sharon answer it from the other room as I dove to retrieve my mess. And since I happened to be in the area, I lifted open the shoebox lid and discovered . . . brand-new running shoes. I snuck a peek beneath them, but other than a replacement set of laces, I didn't see any secret document or mysterious clue. Just shoes.

With the last pencil back where it belonged, I was careful to put the shoebox lid on as well. That was when I noticed that the filing drawer in the lower-right corner of the desk, above the shoes, was slightly open. I knew I shouldn't, but with Sharon still talking on the phone, I took a chance and pulled it quietly. It was full of files: blue, yellow, green, all of them tabulated, and all of them with the word *Cherrinard* handwritten on the top.

But as I snooped through the first, then the second and third and forth file, I was amazed at what I saw: nothing. No paper, no letter, not even a receipt or sticky note anywhere in the files. Though the entire drawer was full of Cherrinard files, there was not a single shred of paper anywhere among them. They'd been cleaned out.

"Anything else I can help you with?" Sharon was at the door. I shot up and smiled. I'd been so amazed by what I was not seeing that I hadn't heard her hang up the phone. I stepped out from behind the desk and strolled over to the wall.

"Well, as a matter of fact, curiosity has gotten the best of me. Any idea who these children are?" I moved in close and studied each. Sharon slid beside me as if the move helped her relax. The photos pulled her in.

"Absolutely. This is Naomi; she lives in El Salvador. This is Ebenezer, and he lives in Ghana. Don't you love those cheeks?" She shook her head, delighted by each child. "And this is Andre from Indonesia; he's such a cutie-pie."

She admired their faces, and though I agreed with their cutie-pie status, I still didn't know why they were on David's wall.

We walked back into the hall, and she locked his door. "He calls them his children. You know, he sponsors them each month through one of those international compassion groups. Writes them letters, sends them books, and, of course, helps them go to school. Isn't that great?"

"It is great."

"David is such a nice guy, a real class act, you know?"

No surprise there. What was surprising was when Sharon took my elbow and directed me behind a ladder in a back row of books, whispering in what was not a librarian's whisper, but a friend's.

"I think I know why David asked you to come by today, and I think it's a good idea."

Uh-oh. His romantic intentions were about to be sprung. I flicked back my hair, feigning feminine ignorance as best I could.

"Why?" I said wistfully.

She peered around the ladder and back at me. "Because he thinks you can help him. Why else would he set up an appointment with a reporter?"

Why else would he set up an appointment with a reporter?!

The question exploded in my head and down through my heart until it stung all over my skin like a rash. I'd been down this track before when certain Southern bachelors had confused dating with press favors. So this was the reason Mr. Nice brought me bagels? Or introduced me to organic sushi? Or showed me Saint John's? Because he wanted to use my position as a reporter to break the story of some old religious guy who gave money to—

"Ms. MacLaughlin, are you all right? Your face just turned colors. Are you feeling okay?"

I dabbed my forehead with my sleeve and pulled at my hair. "Yes, fine, sure." She put her finger in front of her lips for me to keep my voice down.

I breathed in, then out, as though I'd just run up the stairs, though I hadn't moved an inch. Air felt thin. I inhaled and whispered. "So you have no idea where David would have gone . . . on vacation?"

"None . . . in fact, he usually plans it months in advance. This is so . . . sudden."

"Okay then. Well, I did happen to notice a lot of files and letters around his desk, even new running shoes. Did he always keep his desk like that? Even before vacations?"

"No way. His desk looks like that only when he's near the end of a really big project. Usually it's spotless." Sharon pulled her shoulders back and straightened her neck, a move I imagined she'd learned during her dancing years. "Besides, wouldn't you take new shoes with you on vacation?"

Considering I couldn't remember the last time I'd bought running shoes—or any shoes, for that matter—her question stumped me. It seemed a good point, but I was still trying to step over her comment about why else David would meet with a reporter.

Why else would he want to see . . . me?

I handed Sharon my business card and told her to call me when he came in. Or if she could think of any other particular details about why he might have scheduled our appointment. Or any reason at all why I should bother helping him. Because I did not have time to be running back and forth to this campus for another—

"But . . ." Sharon said.

"Sorry. I have a deadline I need to get to."

I surfaced from behind the ladder, passed her tired-looking Ralph-boss, who was emerging from his office to replace a heavy old book in its slot on a shelf. We exchanged nods and I left. My initial perspective about the archives—that they were dull and unfriendly—had been right after all.

The storm had not let up outside, but I blazed through the commons anyway. I didn't care about putting on my cap or zipping up my parka. I only wanted to get away from the library, away from the ridiculous possibility that I had entertained up until ten minutes ago: that a nice man like David Rockley, whom I hadn't wanted to notice before last week, might have sincerely wanted a date with me. Why else would he have collected my stories, except that he'd know how to use me as a reporter? I should never have listened to my brothers. Any of them. Ever.

I passed the stupid snowman standing in the commons, who by now had been abandoned by the frolicking students who'd created him. Buttons for eyes, rolled up newspapers for arms, and mush for a head—I could relate to him. He stood alone, in the snow, looking idiotic and naïve and vulnerable. I couldn't help myself: I marched over and punched him in the face, knocking his head off and sending carrot and cap scattering.

That helped restore the natural order of things.

Around the corner on the sidewalk, past the security guard in his little box, I found the nearest bodega. Like coffee shops and pizza joints, bodegas—or tiny convenience stores—sprinkled virtually every block in Manhattan. At the counter, I slammed down Hannah's ten-dollar bill and asked for a pack of Marlboros and a ham sandwich.

Tobacco in the winter elements hadn't tasted this good for a while.

Three blocks later, I finished my smoke and half of the sandwich before I hurried down the steps to the subway. Griffin Lewis's non-story suddenly seemed interesting. I began forming the lede paragraph in my head as I waited for the train. The notes from our interview were back at the office, but I had the gist of his story formulated except—

I darted from the subway entrance, up the three blocks, and past the security guard at the corner of the blizzardy campus.

When I stopped for directions again, he pointed to a small gray building on the other corner of the commons, thankfully in the opposite direction of the headless snowman. The nearer I came to the building, though, the more I could make out stone creatures carved above the windows, snow collecting on their tongues and wings: gargoyles.

"It figures."

I stamped the snow from my boots inside the entrance of the old building and followed the sign's directions to the second floor. Several classes were in session, offices were buzzing, and an area with tables and vending machines—which I took note of—was filled with students and staff. Just beyond it, I found the hall I was looking for.

Students in jeans, down vests, and ski hats hurried past me chattering and clowning, which—when I realized where we were—seemed irreverent. The department of world religions covered a catalog of the planet's belief systems: Islamic mysticism, Indo-Tibetan studies, devotional traditions of North India, Jewish Hebrew history, Chinese religion and philosophy, religions of the ancient Mediterranean, early American Protestantism, contemporary social ethics, to name a few. Each specialty was printed beside the doors, along with the professor's nameplate and mini altars of sacred symbols, images of shrines, or spiritual quotations.

Several doors down on the left, I found a square poster taped over the glass, depicting the earth and a silhouette of human figures holding hands around it. They looked like red and yellow flames coming from the center. Stars and moons surrounded the earth-people, and I knew I was at the right place.

I knocked. Professor Evan Hartman peered out from a half-open door.

"Yes?" His bald head was as shiny as his beard was thick, and he wore a black denim shirt with baggy trousers.

I introduced myself, which seemed to annoy him initially, but still he invited me in, pointing to a battered metal chair with a ripped brown seat and closing the door behind me. His office seemed no bigger than a broom closet, and on any other day, that would have amused me. Right now I wasn't in the mood to laugh. I took the seat, in between piles of books, papers, and candles, and waited for the professor to finish typing something on his laptop computer.

It was a messy office, with newspapers and academic journals stacked randomly in between filing cabinets and bookshelves. His desk faced the wall and was cluttered with coffee cups, used sandwich bags, folders, manuscripts, even an empty birdcage. On the shelf above him hung a framed print of a red pentacle on top of what looked like black-and-white pages in a book with the words "Blessed Be" printed above both. In one corner of the desk was a picture frame no bigger than the one I had on mine of my family; this was of the professor with three women under a black-and-gold banner that read, "Pagans for Peace."

He clicked a few more keys on his laptop and looked up.

"So, what brings you here in this weather?" He swiveled his chair toward me and folded his arms across his chest.

I ignored his question and got busy working.

"I hope you don't mind, but I realized you might be able to help me with this follow-up story."

"It's the least I could do. Your coverage of the rally was quite . . . thorough."

Something moved on the corner of his desk opposite the photo, underneath a couple of loose papers. I yanked in my ankles. The professor saw me twitch and reached into the clutter. He grunted and picked out a small tan gerbil with a white belly; he held it in his palm while stroking it with his fingers.

"This is Reginald. He won't hurt you." He looked tenderly at the creature, wooing and calming it the more it tried to wiggle from his grip. "You were saying."

Reginald seemed a fitting name for a member of the rodent family, given my history with one Reginald in particular in New Orleans. I flipped open my notebook and explained to the professor that Skip had assigned me a follow-up story on Griffin Lewis, a profile that might reveal the personal side of pagan life in the city. Though I wasn't sure yet how I would accomplish it, I guessed Skip wanted to show readers that people who believe in Wicca have the same kind of emotions as anyone, that the creepy stereotypes were outdated.

"Well, well, Skip Gravely is finally admitting that careers and money aren't the only religions New Yorkers believe in. Good for him."

"Skip's always known that. Why else would he have hired a religion reporter to cover —?"

"Because he's a savvy businessman, Joan. He always has been." He smirked as if some memory of my editor convinced him he was right and I was clearly not. "But, forgive me, you did not come here to talk about Skip Gravely." And for the next fifteen minutes, Professor Hartman described what he knew about Lewis, his growing involvement as a priest in the pagan movement, and the tragedy of Teddy's life and death. And as if the scholar within couldn't help himself, he also explained more of the customs and rituals of pagan witchcraft, distinguishing again the ancient elements of the religion. He was especially careful to delineate it from Satanism.

"Satan, or any such little demon, you know, is simply a Christian construct, created long after paganism was born, and the opposite of witches. The Devil has only one purpose, doesn't he? Disruption. Witches and pagans, however, are one with all, quite peaceful, really." It sounded like a lecture he'd given a dozen times before that rarely shifted emotions regardless of how the students did or didn't respond. He jumped from that point to the growing population of New York pagans and back to Lewis. Most of what he said confirmed what I already knew, but when I asked the professor about the burial of Lewis's son, a puzzle crossed his face.

"I'm not sure what you mean."

"Teddy's mother told me he was already buried — as a Greek Orthodox because the boy was confirmed in the Greek Orthodox Church."

"Greek Orthodox? Ah, a religion almost as ancient as the pagans'," the professor said.

Reginald squirmed. Hartman cupped his other hand over the pet and placed it in the birdcage, pulling the tiny metal door shut. "Well, Griffin has always felt that witches have been trapped by the stereotypes of the culture."

"Then is he exploiting his son's death for the cause of —?"

"What father doesn't want his own flesh and blood to carry on his ideals? If Teddy wouldn't do that when he was alive, Griffin will make sure he does in his death." Tiny pink blotches appeared suddenly on the professor's skull. He shut his eyes, breathed in deeply, and then opened his eyes a few seconds later, blotch-free.

"This is off the record, Joan, but between you and me, Griffin Lewis needs to believe that what he's doing matters. Wicca has provided him a great amount of comfort and belonging, and as I said before, is the point of all religions now, isn't it?" He picked up one of the mugs, drank some odd-colored drink from it, and set it back among the lot. "For the record, I will say that he cares about the future of his community. He simply wants what all parents, regardless of their religion, want: to be able to bury their children with the sacred respect he believes they deserve. Wouldn't you?"

It was a trick question, I could tell, so I didn't even attempt to answer it, though I did scribble it down. Instead, a question popped out of my mouth, one that had been needling at me since I'd first called the man.

"What do you believe?"

He locked his gaze with mine, and he laughed. It was a rumbling guttural sound, as if I'd just tossed him a dare he could not refuse. "What do I believe? The same as everyone else in this world, including you: I believe whatever I want to believe whenever I choose to believe it."

"No kidding? That seems awfully convenient. To believe anything you want? No God or goddess, Allah or Christ to answer to?"

"Why bother with gods when I am really at the center of what I believe anyway?"

Reginald squeaked. The professor leaned over and pulled the gerbil from the cage, holding it gingerly in his hand. "He's used to having free rein in here. Would you mind?"

I stood to leave as he released the creature to the desk, where it scampered happily beneath a stack of papers. He watched it like a child might a new pet.

"One last question, Professor."

Again, he seemed annoyed that I'd interrupted him, but he

looked up anyway, adjusting his glasses.

"What exactly did it mean when you received the Cherrinard professorship?"

He reached for another mug, but when he saw it was empty, he put it back. "Ah, that. Well, aside from the fact that I don't see how it's relevant to Griffin's story, I will tell you it was . . . a providential moment for my work here. A real godsend."

His eyes became buttons, his nose a carrot, and his skull a cap—but I punched the door instead. "Uh-huh. I'm guessing that was quite the providential chunk of change from the Mr. and Mrs. Frank Cherrinard Endowment for Religious Training. What I don't understand, Professor, is what religious training you might have done with it."

That stubby laugh rumbled again. "I wouldn't expect a young reporter to understand." He rose from his chair, his bald head a good five inches above my frizz. But I noticed the tiniest blotch reappear as he continued to speak: "And because your boss is an old friend of mine, I'm going to pretend I did not hear you imply what I think you implied."

"Ah, that," I mimicked. "I bet he'd be curious to know what you did with it."

Just as the professor was about to blow a fuse, Reginald crawled out from under a paper. Hartman seemed to gather his inner peace again. "Good idea, Joan. I'm always happy to talk with our friends in the media, to help shed light on religious matters. So why don't I come in to the *Clarion*? It's been weeks since I've been down there. The three of us could sit down together and have a nice chat. I could answer any questions then." He picked up a calendar. "When would be convenient for you?"

"I'll call you."

"You do that."

He closed the door gently, and I stared at the earth-people poster for a few seconds before moving down the hall. I stopped at the vending machine for a Hershey's Special Dark chocolate bar, but once the machine ate my coins, nothing dropped into the bin. I kicked it, still nothing. Harder, still empty, until a class of students spilled out into the hallway. With a final fruitless boot, I followed the crowd down the stairs and into the snow. I lit a Marlboro and sloshed through the commons and toward the subway.

This was turning into a very bad week, and it was only Monday.

Hannah wasn't at her desk when I barged by, so I ate the other half of the sandwich I'd bought for her and got to work. I had a little more than an hour until deadline. Even if I felt Griffin Lewis's story had more to do with marketing pagan philosophy in the mainstream news and less to do with his son's noble death, I decided I'd give my boss what he had asked for: something he said he could use.

That was clearly the order of the day anyway, so why fight it? Professor Evan Hartman was using his academic position to do what he wanted, whatever that was; Griffin Lewis was using the *Clarion* so witches could get positive publicity for a change; Walter Wood was using the witches to sell papers; and nice guys were using reporters, rather than dating them.

What difference would it make if I joined the circus too?

::Chapter Nine

f I believed in reincarnation, I would want to come back as a cherry blossom tree in Central Park. I'd never have to move, people would hug me whenever the spirit moved them (which would be every day), and I could count on looking beautiful at least once a year, pink and flowery and stunning. No one would ever take advantage of me because of my position, my roots, or my looks. In fact, they'd admire me only for who I was: a cherry blossom tree. They would even sit in my shade for summer picnics and eat fried chicken and chocolate cupcakes, or build snowmen beside me in the winter.

But I didn't believe in reincarnation. Yes, I had once, when I was twelve or so and my parents encouraged us to believe along with them. But when they learned that their good behavior in this life determined their status in the next, they weren't exactly encouraged by the prospects. After that, we moved on to Judaism or something else, I forget which. And considering my non-pacifist treatment today of innocent snowmen, I understood their reservations. In fact, I was having my doubts about religion entirely, let alone men.

Both seemed too complicated.

It didn't help that it was 4:03 p.m. and I'd just pushed the Send button on my computer. In a few minutes my editor would be reading my 452-word assignment. It was slop; I knew it. He'd know it too as soon as he opened it and saw the lede:

> *Longtime Brooklyn resident and grocer Griffin*
> *Lewis, 46, is like any grieving father who's lost*
> *a child in the war. Except for one thing: He's a*
> *witch, a high priest in one of New York's witch*
> *communities known as the Eastern Order of the*
> *Pagan Sanctuary. Though some might believe he*
> *could cast a spell and bring his son back to life,*
> *they would be mistaken. So the least Lewis can*
> *do is send him off with what he calls "some pagan*
> *dignity" to the Summerland, that eternal resting*
> *place he and other witches call the afterlife. That's*
> *why he's pushing the Department of Veterans*
> *Affairs to allow him to place a pentacle on his son's*
> *grave, even as the young man's physical body returns*
> *to the natural unrestricted process of earth. . . .*

How had it come to this?

Walter Wood, that was how. What had he said? "Nothing is easy in the business world these days. We're all having to make sacrifices, aren't we?"

I simply didn't expect I'd be sacrificing real stories to write slop for Skip Gravely, of all people. In New York City, of all places—the world capital of journalism.

The snow was no longer falling in buckets, though I couldn't stop staring out the window, wishing I were a tree or some such thing. Maybe a polar bear at the zoo, where I could lie in the sun all day long and sleep, take the occasional dip, nap some more, and wake up every few hours when my food was brought to me. I could eat as much as I wanted without having to worry about gaining weight or using a fork or having my entire meal dribble down my chest, because it was supposed to dribble. Polar bears didn't have to be neat and—

The phone rang. I looked at it and debated. After all, it was almost closing time and I'd had my fill of humanity for a Monday. For a month, really. It rang again. I eyed the thing until the better part of valor won. I reached across and picked it up.

An unfamiliar voice identified himself as Daniel Cho, and though it had an undisturbed—even gracious—tone to it, I could not quite place it.

"Yes, Mr. Cho, what can I do for you?" I faked, reaching for my notepad and flipping through the pages. As I did, I came across Emma's words again:

I reckon you and God make a good team. . . . This city needs you, Jonna.

I scribbled a big question mark beside the blurb and tried to listen to the voice on the other end of the phone, who by now was identifying himself as a fan of the *Clarion* and thanking me for joining him and his friends this past Friday night in Chinatown. He was honored that I would have visited their service and wondered if I had any questions about what I'd experienced.

Finally, I saw the tall pastor in my mind, talking calmly behind a podium to hundreds of former gang members and young professionals. It wasn't the sort of phone call I'd been expecting at the end of this day; I'd all but forgotten about the possibility of good news. I floundered and punted.

"Yes, Reverend. I'm wondering—"

"Call me Danny Bro, please, Miss MacLaughlin. I'm not

used to the Reverend thing."

"Okay, then, call me Jonna. Or Lightfoot. I'm not used to the Miss thing; it makes me sound so . . . adult-like." And so single, I thought. He laughed softly. Something lifted from my neck muscles, breaking off a small chunk of the crankiness that had been nestling there for most of the afternoon. I was suddenly curious about how the Chinatown Jesus Center began.

Danny Bro told me first about his youth in Chinatown. His family had immigrated to New York when he was ten years old to run a small business, supplying meats and fish to local restaurants. The long hours often meant Danny was alone in their apartment. Because he never knew how to fit in at school, he eventually joined a gang and soon was a leader of it.

He paused from the emotion that was packed in between the sentences and, from what I could tell, still coming. There was something this man, who spent his Friday nights speaking to the next generation, didn't find easy words for.

He cleared his throat. "My father was killed one night on his way home from the office, a drive-by shooting from one of my own gangbangers going through what's called courtin' in, or initiation." Though the event happened twenty years ago, he spoke as if the memory were fresh. "I'd thought I was a tough kid, but let me tell you, that was hell."

At his father's funeral, a Korean missionary who'd known his family since before they'd moved here talked candidly about the senselessness of the death and the purpose of human life. Danny listened, angry, aching, and completely uncertain of what to do. He'd been guilty by association of his own father's murder, and when that missionary sat down, the young man's heart burst, though of course he didn't dare show it. Not even a crack.

A month later, Danny found the missionary on his own, with questions and regrets tucked behind street talk and cool moves. The man heard the pain in spite of the facade and explained to Danny that his guilt had already been absolved. When Danny asked what he was talking about, the missionary merely handed him a Bible and said, "See for yourself." Then he sent him out the door. Danny spent the next few months away from the streets, consuming the words in the book as though they were food and he'd been starving all his life.

"After that, I went back to school. Seminary next. It was slow and hard but right, you know? And I was as surprised as anyone when the Chinatown Jesus Center was founded." A siren bellowed in the background. "That was ten years ago, and God's been gracious to us ever since."

I jotted down his answers, but the next question came from the pastor.

"Now, Jonna, why all this interest in the Center?"

"Well, I am a religion reporter, you know, and this is a great story for—"

"Oh. I was afraid of that."

I scoured over my notes but didn't see any reason he would be concerned. In fact, if anything, this was the type of story that would encourage readers, the kind I'd always been looking for. It had that spark of inspiration that reminded people of the benefits of religion, not the disasters; it showed how faith could help, not hinder, someone's circumstances. I'd been short on these stories for a long time, especially lately.

"I think your story could be a real service to our readers, if you'd allow me to talk to a few more of your staff members and parishioners."

He was quiet. I heard a ding on my computer and glanced up to see that Skip had sent me an e-mail. I prodded the pastor, but he did not give in.

"I can't tell you what stories to write, Jonna, but please consider that we're young, and attention can be a dangerous thing."

"It can?"

"Absolutely. It can feed an ego, but not a soul. I've seen too many times how distracting publicity can be from our real purpose." Reverend Daniel Cho did offer to help me with any other articles I might work on in the future as they related to new conversions or urban ministries or Christian growth. And he was quick to remind me that I was always welcome to join them for worship services whenever I could.

I leaned back in my chair and considered his words. Here was a spiritual leader who preferred no publicity for the generosity of his work, though it had been profoundly affected by the death of his father. On the other hand, I'd just written what might as well have been a publicity piece for a father who seemed eager for the media to notice his son's death.

It might have been the way the day was going, but both made me uncomfortable. Out of habit, I searched for Daniel Cho's name on the Internet, even the back issues of all New York newspapers; all I could find was his listing in a religious directory for clergy and his seminary graduation announcement. Danny Bro and the Chinatown Jesus Center seemed like a genuine breath of fresh air in the religion world of smoke screens, scandals, and frauds. Even though he'd asked me not to, I couldn't shake the possibility of covering their work.

No wonder Hannah loved to quote Zora Neale Hurston:

"There is no agony like that of an untold story." For now, though, I had to put it on hold and read Skip's e-mail: "See me before you head home for the night. Please."

He was sitting as I'd seen him a hundred other times: reading glasses slipping, green pen in hand, hard copies of daily stories piled neatly in front of him. I tapped on his door. He circled a word and looked up.

"Lightfoot. Have a seat."

I obeyed.

He licked his thumb and flipped through the papers until he found what he was looking for: my story. He held it out to me. "A few changes here and there, but not bad. I have to admit, it didn't feel like you spent as much time on it as usual. Take for instance this graph where . . ."

The day just descended to a new definition of bad. I retraced my steps in my head: the subway, the snowman, the library and David's office, Professor Evan Hartman with his strange little rodent, Reginald, in the world religions department. How could I tell Skip, the man who hired and trained me and believed in me enough to bring me with him to New York City to work for the *Clarion*, that I'd deliberately—?

"Lightfoot, hello? Where'd you just go? You feeling okay?"

My cheeks took flame. It was at least a hundred degrees in this office, yet I was sure I was going to be out in the cold in a matter of seconds.

"I had to do it, Skip. I mean, I know you told me not to, but, well, there's this guy. I mean there was this guy. He's past tense now; in fact, he didn't show up for work today. But I figured you were feeling pressure from Wood and not thinking straight, so I skipped Goldwasser's, but then I found out he was using me anyway, which was when I went and talked to Hartman about—"

"Whoa! Who are you, and what'd you do with my religion reporter?" He laughed at his joke as if it were original. "Now, breathe deeply," he said. "Okay, you want to start over?"

I wiped my forehead and spilled every detail about my afternoon up until deadline: how David had invited me up to his office in the Regal archives but not bothered to show up; how his vacation seemed a surprise to his colleague but not his boss; how his desk had stacks of papers but his files were empty; and how Hartman refused to talk about the endowment when I visited him in his office, though he didn't hesitate to tell me about paganism, witches, and Griffin Lewis.

Skip scratched his chin. He took what seemed an eternal drink from his water bottle and then twisted the cap back in place. "Well, you have been busy, haven't you?"

I fidgeted. I couldn't hold eye contact with my boss. The last thing I wanted to do was disappoint this man. I'd rather ski High Anxiety. Blindfolded. Or be reincarnated as a gerbil.

"First, relax. Fix a couple of things in the story for me, and get this back in the next half hour, okay?"

He held it out to me like a peace offering, though we both knew it was a piece of slop. I took it and wanted to toss it where it belonged.

"We'll talk about these other . . . issues when you've finished, okay?"

I squeaked compliance at the same time I rose from my chair.

"Oh, and Lightfoot, it's going page one."

I was halfway out the door when it registered. "What?"

"Page one. We're following the witch trial."

"What trial?"

"You said they would be filing a lawsuit against the DVA, so . . ."

"No, I said Lewis would fight this thing even if it meant going to court."

"Which it will. No pun intended." He grinned. "Anyway, Wood thinks this will help sell — "

"You're kidding."

"And I happen to agree." He pulled in a heavy breath, then released it. "It's just for a little while, until things get back to . . . normal."

Now it was my editor who broke eye contact first. He turned his wrist and stared at his watch. "See you soon."

I stepped out of his office but stopped frozen at the edge of the newsroom, as if I were seeing it for the first time. I felt like a junior high student on a field trip, watching a room full of living, breathing information; factoids and statistics and quotes fluttered across the room like the birds in Central Park. There was the investigative team in the corner trying to make sense of this morning's shooting at the municipal court building—a former employee versus an unkind colleague; the business reporters across from them profiling another Wall Street CEO who'd fallen from his leadership position because of a lapsed ethical judgment; the sports department with Fred Kordowicz about to announce to New Yorkers that their favorite Yankee was the latest steroid scandal; the arts critics reviewing Hollywood's most recent killing spree on-screen; and the health reporters linking the sad numbers of obesity rates for children in the Bronx. We covered wars and poverty, travel and real estate, food and fashion and families across the city, state, region, and globe, and right now, it was too much.

I didn't know why it struck me at that specific moment, but something in Skip's words tossed a wrench through my entire being. I felt as if my whole body, head, and heart had fused into a single funny bone and I'd just slammed into the sharpest edge in the office.

I turned back to my boss—the one who'd been a steady calm for me in this chaotic profession, who'd invested in me when I didn't know anything but that I wanted to write and I wanted my words to matter. I studied him, still working at his desk, gripping his pen and water. His tie was green and his shirt neatly starched, as always, as orderly as his disposition. And when he sensed my presence in the silence, he looked up from his pile of terrible news and waited.

"What exactly is . . . normal, Skip?"

"Excuse me?"

"You said 'when things get back to . . . normal.' I guess I'm not sure what that is."

I wasn't really expecting an answer, and he didn't offer one. But our eyes locked for a few heavy seconds. He blinked first. I turned toward my cubicle and began to move. An image of my parents dropped into my mind. Normal never described them, either. They'd planted organic turnips, called a casserole we ate for dinner (which was served at 7:30 in the morning) World Peace, and engaged in so many forms of spiritual harmonizing from so many pockets of the planet's faiths that sometimes it felt more like the United Nations, not a family, lived in our house.

Until of course their last dabble. That song stuck for them. But even that one took them away from me and into another world: Costa Rica, where they worked with coffee farmers, poor people whom I hoped I supported with my daily caffeine addiction, though I suspected they were probably getting only the dregs.

I felt guilty about that, too.

No, normal was not anything I knew as a child, though I believed—as most children do—that our family was like everyone else's. The older I got and the more life I saw beyond our organic meadow—and especially in the newspaper business—the less I believed we'd been even remotely close to normal. And now, I was having my doubts about its existence at all. It hadn't mattered before. But looking at this *Clarion* mountain of abnormal in front of me, I felt in my pores this was not how it was supposed to be. Something wasn't right. Something did not click. I checked above me to see if a solitary dark cloud was about to burst, then around me for clues in case some voodoo charm or magic spell had been cast my way.

I pressed my thumbs against the base of my skull and rubbed.

Then again, it could have simply been that time of month. No wonder the snowman lost his head.

"You look like you've seen a ghost." Hannah, who was sitting at my desk like a queen on her throne when I came back, did not help the situation. "You feeling okay?" She stood to give me my chair and I slid into it.

"I don't know. Could just be the joys of womanhood. Or of journalism."

"Ah." She stepped back as if I were contagious. "Okay. Well, besides the fact that I never got my sandwich, I'm expecting to hear something juicy about Regal that made skipping lunch worth it."

Her question sent me back to David's office, to the empty drawers in his desk and the children's faces on his wall. I heard Sharon's librarian-whisper in my ear about how David had thought I could help him, which tossed a grenade back into my stomach again and fire into my neck.

"Why do we do this again, Hannah?"

"Do what?"

"This." I pointed to the madness in the newsroom, the buzz around the desks, the huddles in the corners, the shouts of reporters on their phones, the clacking of fingernails on keyboards. Why did humans care so much about news in the first place? What was the point when nothing ever changed anyway?

"Uh-oh. What happened?" She leaned in. "Tell me you did not get stood up again."

"I got stood up . . . again." I snapped a pencil in two and dumped it in the trash. Hannah pulled a chair beside me and listened as I told her how David's colleague was worried when he hadn't come in, how his boss wanted me to think he was on vacation but how his office seemed filled to overflowing with projects and notes and, well, David. I described the folders of papers on his desk and his empty Cherrinard files in his drawer.

"You looked in his drawer?"

"Well, it was open."

She rose from her chair and leveled her knuckles against her hips. "Guess what, girl? He didn't stand you up." She pulled out a tiny tube of lipstick from her bag and went to work. "And he isn't on vacation."

"I don't care if he's on the moon."

She smacked her lips together, tossing the tube back into her bag and slinging it over her shoulder. "Uh-huh. Think about it. I'd bet good money he was planning on coming in today, but after his apartment got broken into, maybe he thought a day out of the office might be a better—"

"Oh, and he couldn't call to tell me that?"

An eyebrow cocked. "You said yourself his drawer was open. Maybe he left it that way on purpose so that—"

"I also said I don't care." I swiveled toward my computer and clicked on Lewis's story. "Besides, it's the witching hour for me. I have to rewrite this profile for Skip within a half hour."

A slight tsking sound escaped from her mouth. "Okay, Little Miss Attitude, I'm going to dinner . . . with a date, for the record. The first in . . ." Hannah glanced at the ceiling. " . . . five months. Let's hope the stars are aligned on this guy."

"Show-off," I mumbled. "Don't worry about me. I'll just be here, working. But thanks for the sandwich."

"The least I could do, since you're buying tomorrow. At the Russian Tea Room." Hannah snapped her fingers as if it were the perfect idea, because the most expensive five-star restaurant in the city was perfect. She strutted down the hall, her coat draped around her shoulders. There was no denying it: She was an African queen, New York style.

I felt like a court jester, especially when I looked at my story. Skip's edits surprised me. He'd pulled Hartman's quotes up closer to the lede, and he'd filled out more of the pagan rituals than Griffin had discussed, as if he'd heard some of Hartman's office lecture. He also suggested I add a few more details about the man's grief, maybe even include information from Teddy's obit.

The cloud darkened. So I tweaked and rearranged and did what he asked. Sixty-seven additional words and forty-five minutes later, I printed out the profile and rambled back to Skip's office, reading it a final time as I walked. It wasn't terrible, yet I was hardly convinced it was page-one quality, let alone relevant to my ongoing coverage of all things religion in New York. Then again, I supposed if Hartman's perspective of religion was the standard in this city, it qualified.

Skip was not at his desk. His water bottle was open and the stack of papers had grown, but he was nowhere to be found. I glanced into the advertising department, then the VPs' offices, and when I didn't see him in either, I threw the story on his desk, hurried back to mine to send him the electronic version, and grabbed my parka.

The "issues" talk with Skip would have to wait until tomorrow. Maybe *Little Miss Attitude* was getting a break from the cosmic forces in the universe, despite her violent behavior with snowmen and pencils this afternoon.

And though my cell phone was ringing, the cold air outside biting, and the subways standing room only, my mind was mush. In the blur of humanity on public transportation, all I saw were subtitles in a movie, words like *normal* and *believe* and *purpose*. In each eyeball or backpack or shoe, on each advertisement or map or conversation, I saw only questions. Were they normal? Was this right? What did she believe? What was his purpose? Even when I grabbed an electric heating pad and climbed into bed in my apartment, I felt numb. It was only 8:09 p.m., but my body craved sleep. I wanted to be a polar bear. I wanted someone to bring me my food while I napped.

I saw my mom on a beach. She was picking up sand dollars, the white foam of the waves rolling over her toes and back across the sand. Her long chiffon dress swayed in the sea breeze, and her face shot out beams as if she'd swallowed the sun. Giant spectacles of medieval gentlemen surrounded her, walking slowly beside her, wearing coats of armor across their chests. I didn't recognize any of them. One of the giants reached over and handed my mom a sand dollar as big as a grapefruit, though it looked like a pin's head in his hand. She laughed when she saw it and held it gently in her fingers. They kept strolling, barefoot, bright, easy, until my mom waved for me to join her and the giants. But just as she did, an enormous green screen sprang out in front of me, a jittery collage of pigs, straw, icicles, and broccoli—a fog of ugly images that blocked my view. I turned this way and that until finally—

I was in my bed, smelling coffee from the kitchen.

Hannah had already left for work, with a note by the coffee-pot that told me to meet her for lunch at Goldwasser's (the Russian Tea Room would have to wait), or else I'd be in B-I-G trouble. I poured myself a cup and took a long shower, though neither was able to knock out the cobwebs and aches I felt in my muscles. Maybe the winter cold would do the trick, but it had warmed up slightly since yesterday and the fresh air was only a brisk greet-ing. I bought a bagel at the bodega by the subway and looked for Emma at her booth as I descended. Maybe her cheery disposition would get me going.

But she wasn't there. In her place sat a middle-aged man with skinny shoulders. He was bobbing his head to some silent music. Emma must have taken the day off. I slid my MetroCard and made my way through the turnstile. I felt lonely waiting for the train.

I imagined my mom talking with a coffee farmer and strained to hear her voice in my memory until the train drowned it out, screeching into the tunnel. There was an empty space in the subway corner next to a big woman reading the newspaper. I squeezed my way beside her and looked over her shoulder.

"Witches Cry for the Dead."

I rolled my eyes and tapped my toes. The train picked up speed. I was too squished between people to get out my detective novel, so I took to people-watching. A young Asian couple sat across from me reading small leather-bound books that I thought might be Bibles. I remembered Danny Bro standing in front of his congregation, and I made a mental note to call him once I got to work, more for my sake than his. Maybe his story of inspiration could pull me out of these Tuesday-morning blahs. Maybe he'd changed his mind since we talked and he was willing to let me interview some of his congregation.

Maybe I would do it anyway. It was a piece of good news that the *Clarion* could use right now. Or at least I could. I planned how I'd pitch it to Skip, as an exciting story that put the witches to shame. Or something like that.

The big woman turned the page in her newspaper, elbowing me in the process, and I saw Hannah's story on her weekend campaign tour with Senator Milton. It was a long spread with two photos and a pull quote that read, "When the good people of New York work so hard for their communities, it's a day to begin hoping again." My neighbor caught me reading and pulled in the paper. The rumble of the train and the mood of the passengers seemed to match this morning. Even the crowds on the sidewalk outside of Penn Station grumbled. The street noise was loud, but none of it was coherent.

Griffin Lewis and Lady Crystal were waiting in the lobby of the *Clarion* when I arrived. I pulled out a smoke and walked back outside. Too late. They were next to me on the sidewalk in front of the building in a matter of seconds.

"Good morning, Ms. Lightfoot." Lady Crystal's voice was suspiciously charming. "We wanted to personally thank you for this." She held up this morning's paper, and her face almost cracked a smile. Griffin Lewis, who was wearing a black cap over his ears and a black trench coat, nodded.

"Yes, we're so pleased that you're covering this," he said. "It'll make our appeal much easier."

I inhaled so hard the red on the tip of the cigarette looked as if someone flipped on a switch. It went off when I exhaled. "Uh-huh. So I guess you are going to court."

"You bet. Our attorneys are filing the lawsuit today. And we've garnered so much support for our Thursday midnight rally that we're sure even the spirits will be there."

"And the point of that is . . . what again?" I asked, looking at the misty pair. In black from toe to head, they fit in easily to the New York crowd hurrying by us.

"The point? To call for justice, for the gods to listen, for the forces of spiritual energy to meet in the natural convergence we'll bring at midnight." Lady Crystal was clearly rehearsing her lines for the coming performance; I, however, didn't feel any audience appreciation.

"In other words, you're hoping for more press to build your case against the DVA?" The tobacco tasted a little too good this morning.

"Well, since you seem sympathetic to what we're trying to—"

I flicked the cigarette into the street. "Listen, guys, I am not sympathetic to your convergence or your cause any more than I am to the Mormons or the Methodists or the greedy little . . . oh, never mind. In other words, I don't really care if you get a pagan star for your graves or not. Though I am sorry for your loss, Mr. Lewis, you should know I was just doing what my boss told me to."

I stormed back inside and climbed the steps to my office. My phone was blaring when I got there.

"Good morning to you, too, Jonna." Luke was ridiculously happy in the mornings. Why were there so many things wrong with the world?

"I called you last night. How come you didn't answer?"

"I was busy."

"Can you come over tonight? As soon as you get off work?" I could hear tubas in the background.

"Why?"

"Why? Because I talked to every friend I could think of yesterday and this morning, and no one seems to know where David is. I know it's only been a day and this is New York so he could be anywhere, but maybe we should—"

"He's on vacation." I dropped my parka and bag on the floor, looking to see what outfit I'd put on this morning. Green pants with a red sweater. Great. I was a Christmas tree.

"Hello? Did you hear me?" My brother was bringing me out of the holidays.

"What?"

"I said he's not on vacation."

"That's what his boss told me."

"But that's the weird thing, Jon; David didn't have any vacation time left."

::Chapter Ten

I saw giants . . . strolling beside my mother . . . on the beach.

As much as I wanted to tell my brother about my dream, I knew it would sound absurd. Then again, that could be fitting for this morning. I pulled out half of a dark chocolate bar and took a shot.

"Luke, I saw Mom last night."

"What? Are you changing the subject, Jon? Because we need to talk about David, whether you want to or—"

"In a dream, I mean. Maybe you'll know what to make of it, since you've always had a knack for these things. Anyway, I saw her walking on the—"

I didn't have time to finish. As soon as I started describing my dream to my brother, trumpets and drums went wild in the phone, Lady Crystal and Griffin Lewis magically appeared at my desk, still ranting about their Thursday-night convergence, and Hannah tapped me on the shoulder, mumbling something about borrowing a battery for her tape recorder. The sounds morphed into a swift attack on my ears:

"Jonna, I think I need to—"; "Lightfoot, I've been wondering where—"; "Ms. MacLaughlin, why wouldn't you—?"; "What's happening in the—?"

Cymbals crashed, trumpets tooted, and voices rose until

somewhere in the newsroom a reporter sneezed so loudly it stopped all of us in our tracks. Even Luke heard it.

"God bless you," he said into the phone just as a tuba bellowed out a single note from somewhere in his classroom.

"God bless you," I shouted, rising from my desk above my cubicle to see Fred Kordowicz, the sports reporter, bury his nose in a plaid handkerchief. He held up a hand delicately as a thanks, careful not to disrupt the work his other hand was doing. I settled back into my cubicle to see two white witches in black standing beside an African queen—who was wearing a white cashmere sweater—and by now even Skip, in a black jacket and white shirt, had joined the party. Apparently, I—in red and green—didn't get the fashion memo, not that it would have mattered. I pulled the phone to my chin.

"Gotta go, Luke. The gods are calling. See you tonight."

I hung up and waved my hand over the congregation before me like I'd seen preachers do in Pentecostal services.

"Now, who's first?" I said with as much good cheer as I could muster. Which wasn't a lot since all I really wanted was to go back to bed. Or smoke. Instead, I willed myself to be polite. That didn't help much either.

Lady Crystal stepped forward. "Our attorney is filing the lawsuit against the DVA today, so we thought you'd want to be the first to know the details." She pushed back her hair from her face and crossed her arms against her chest in a way that suggested she was doing me a great service. Then she glanced at Skip.

"Jonna will be happy to talk with you, won't you?" He nodded toward me before turning his attention back toward Lady Crystal. "And I'm Skip Gravely, by the way, editor at the *Clarion*. You are . . . ?"

"Lady Crystal Lenowitz, High Priestess of the Eastern Order of the Pagan Sanctuary." She rested her arm around Griffin's shoulder. "And you probably already know Griffin, since he was in your paper this—"

"Front and center," Hannah chimed in, picking up the newspaper. She pointed to Griffin's picture and shook her head slowly. "You know, I have to confess, I didn't think I'd live to see the day when witches went page one in New York. Who'd have thought?" Skip gave Hannah the closest face he had to a glare, but she merely folded the newspaper neatly and put it back on my desk.

"I never expected this day would come either," Griffin said. "It's historic, for pagans and witches everywhere, you know. Finally, we're on the verge of being accepted as a normal religion, and that's very exciting for . . ."

A red flag flapped in my brain and tuned out the man's voice. Though he might have been right about this as a historic moment for pagans, I wasn't so sure about the "normal" thing. Was any religion normal? Or any person, for that matter? I'd yet to experience even a normal day in journalism, especially lately. What did it mean anyway? Conforming to a standard? Forming a pattern or a type? Who set the standards and who formed the patterns? And didn't they shift and change depending on the time period and culture in which a person lived? Or even the part of the world where we were born and raised? Was there anything that stayed the same, any absolute value for—?

"Lightfoot? You there?" Hannah was tapping again.

"What? Oh, sorry, uh, you were—?" I rubbed my eyes to see Hannah turn to the others.

"Jonna hasn't been herself lately. Could be winter flu or some terrible bug going around. I'm not sure she should be here at all, but you know how dedicated reporters can be." Hannah handed me a tissue. I took it, placed it over my mouth, and coughed. Lady Crystal and Griffin stepped back; even Skip stepped slightly toward the hall as Hannah continued: "I'm immune because I happen to live with her. But she might be contagious; I've been wondering for a while why she hasn't gone to a doctor." She shrugged. "So how about if she called you folks on the phone for that interview? Skip?"

"Good idea." Skip led the witches through the newsroom maze as Hannah pulled out the chair for me. My face felt hot. So did my head. Maybe I *was* sick.

"That was a close one." Hannah was sorting her way through my desk drawers in search of the battery she'd mentioned before. Her tape recorder had died after she'd listened to her interviews with the senator for the story that should have been page one.

"Something weird is happening, Hannah. Since when does Skip Gravely bump political scoops for a fluff religion piece?"

"Since Walter Wood began putting pressure on him to increase sales, that's when." She gave up her hunt and leaned against the filing cabinet. "And it could get worse before it gets better. The word on the street about this guy isn't pretty."

"Meaning?"

"Meaning, he's been doing a lot of investments in legitimate media companies and turning them into —"

Skip reappeared at my cubicle, his glasses in one hand and a small white cloth in the other. He breathed on the lens and wiped. Hannah picked a piece of lint from her cashmere. I coughed.

"Sorry to hear you're not quite . . . yourself, Jonna." His voice was soft but not exactly sympathetic.

"Thanks."

Skip pushed his glasses back on and stared at Hannah. He'd hired her a few years before me and liked to boast that she was the best political reporter he'd ever had. He'd also heard her opinions plenty of times on how journalism should never be driven by profits and quarterly earnings — that its first and only loyalty was to the citizens. Skip, of course, would beam as he listened, telling the rest of us that was why she was so good at her job: She never got her priorities mixed up. He'd always been able to count on her to find the right stories for the right reasons.

Lately, though, I hadn't seen much beaming.

"I came by in the first place just to let you both know I got some calls about your stories." He smoothed his hair back before resting his hand at his side. "Good calls, for the record. Keep it up." Skip turned toward his office.

"That's it?" Hannah stood tall.

"That's what?" Skip looked over his shoulder. Hannah locked eyes with him, but said nothing. She waited instead for her editor to offer her more. He raised an eyebrow as if he'd not understood her question, as if he'd expected something else from her. Hannah, though, simply shook her head and told me not to forget I was buying her lunch. For now, she had to find a battery. Skip watched her hurry off before facing me.

"You and I still need to talk about some things, don't we?"

"Don't worry. I'm letting the Regal piece go. You were right: It was too hard to believe."

"So I don't need to schedule a meeting with Professor Hartman?"

My cheeks went flush again and my forehead felt clammy. "You talked with him?"

His eyes softened and the gentleness I'd first admired in my boss returned, his voice sincere. "Look, I've been friends with Evan since we met in an anthropology class twenty-six years ago. I'll admit that he was a little strange then, and he hasn't changed much. But he's a good man and a good scholar who's helped a lot of people in this city. And because you've always shown great respect to your sources, I have to admit I was surprised to get his call."

I thought of the bald professor with the beard, stroking his pet Reginald as they sat in the midst of pagan textbooks and half-empty coffee mugs. Strange was one way of describing him.

"I know. I was out of line. There were just some things that didn't add up." I massaged my neck as I remembered the exchange in Hartman's office. Skip cleared his throat. "But like I said, Skip, I'm over it. I've been down this track with guys who . . . oh, never mind."

"Good. And since you might need to talk with him again regarding this witch lawsuit, I'd appreciate it if you'd treat him as you'd like to be treated. That is the mandate religion reporters swear by, isn't it?" Skip smiled and I relaxed for the first time this morning. "Now, anything else before I go and fend off the vultures?"

"Well, as a matter of fact . . ." I recounted the conversation I'd had with the Reverend Danny Cho, explaining the details of his father's death and his resulting conversion. The last thing the young man from the streets of Chinatown had expected in his life was to be leading a congregation of seven hundred ex-gang members at a church called the Chinatown Jesus Center. It wasn't just a great religion story, I told Skip; it had both inspiration that would hook readers—code for "sell papers"—and good news, which was sorely missing on the pages of our paper lately.

"Reverend Cho is the real deal, so humble, in fact, that he didn't even think I should write about him. Can you imagine? Anyway, I'll talk with a few more folks at the Center and get a broad perspective." He hesitated. I pushed. "I think I need to do this, Skip. I think this one could be it."

It, we both knew, was that elusive story I'd been searching for since he'd offered me the position in Denver as religion reporter—the good news I wanted desperately to find and report.

The side of his mouth curled slightly upward. "Well, dig a little more and we'll see what we can do. But it can't interfere with your coverage of the pagans' lawsuit, okay? This is a story we have to follow, Lightfoot."

If that was the compromise I had to make to pursue the story I wanted to write, I'd do it. I thanked my boss and wandered down the hall. The ladies' room was empty, and when I emerged from the stall, I noticed one of the lights above the sink was flickering on, then off. I stared at it while I ran my hands under the faucet. The warm water felt good on my skin, and though I knew I had plenty of work waiting for me, there was something soothing about standing in the half-lit quiet room. It felt safe. Easy. No one around to bother me.

Until I looked in the mirror. My hair was a mass of tangled frizz, and the shadows beneath my eyes revealed more than I wanted to show about how I'd been feeling lately. My cheeks looked pasty and pale against my red sweater, and if I'd seen the face in the mirror on someone else, I'd have thought the poor girl hadn't slept for days. She also looked as if someone had stolen her comb and a portion of her dignity along with it. There was no denying it: The reflection was a mess.

What was happening?

I turned off the hot-water knob and splashed cold across my cheeks to snap out of it. I smoothed out the wrinkles in my sweater and washed out the tiny coffee stain on my chest. Somehow I even managed to press a brush through the tangles, flattening my hair against my head until it resembled something close to orderly. I could do this. I could be normal.

Back at my desk, I got busy. I waded through last week's press releases and think-tank reports, most of which were more marketing efforts for religious seminars, gospel concerts, or book launches. One was another invitation to a potluck brunch at a storefront church in Queens. I tossed it quickly in the trash; I'd had enough potlucks in my career to last into my next lifetime as a polar bear.

I flipped through the rest of the mail until I came to a letter on the bottom of the pile. It didn't have a return address. It did, however, spell my name correctly in purple ink and clear hand-writing, which, considering my history of annoying anonymous letters, I took as a good sign. I ripped it open at the same time I heard a ding on my e-mail. I set down the envelope and clicked on the computer. The subject line read, "Midnight Gathering Under the Wiccan Star." I rolled my eyes and returned to the letter.

A single sheet of paper fell from the envelope. It was folded neatly in thirds, and as I opened it, I saw there was only one sentence handwritten in purple ink in the middle of the page: "Answer: In Thy light we see light." I turned it over and saw nothing. The other side of the envelope was empty too; only my name, a generic post-age stamp, and a New York City postmark covered it.

I was not in the mood for riddles.

I picked up the phone and called Lady Crystal to follow through on the interview for the story I was now committed to writing. She said that as a result of her mass e-mail and the lawsuit, she expected at least two hundred pagans and witches to gather Thursday night at the steps of the mayor's office. The ceremony would "seek the natural blessing of creative energy over their legal request." They were planning a ritual with specific herbs, songs, and chants to "invoke the favor of Mother Earth" so they could finally send off their loved ones as they were meant to go.

I was still not in the mood for riddles, so I offered a glib thanks to Lady Crystal for her time, scribbled a few more details, and hung up. I downloaded the flyer she'd e-mailed announcing the lawsuit and the gathering and reached for the phone to call their attorney. But as I did, a skinny young man appeared at my cubicle. He wore an oversized brown parka, work pants, and a baseball cap turned backward on his head. He was working his gum like he was in a contest.

"You, uh, Jenna . . . Light . . . foot . . . Mac . . ." He smacked the gum as he stared at a form in his hands, which looked to be about the fourth—and, therefore, faded—copy. "Oh yeah. I mean Jonna Mac . . . Laugh . . . lin?"

"Why?"

"Delivery." He tucked the form in his pocket, still smacking, and reached behind him to grab a vase filled with white roses. "Here you go." Smack. He set them in my hand and turned to go.

"Wait!" I hollered. His face crinkled. "Are you sure? Roses for . . . me?"

"Well"—smack—"you're, uh, Lightfoot Mac . . . Laugh . . . lin, right?"

"Yes, but—" And he was down the hall and out of sight.

I stared and sniffed at the bouquet in my hands, and as I did, both sight and scent loosened some emotion in my soul that felt like it had been lodged there for a while. Tears surprised me. The roses were so bright, the petals just beginning to open. They stood plump and dramatic in a smoky glass vase, even more dramatic when I placed them delicately on my desk, my eyes still wet. I felt as if spring had come inside my cubicle, but its beauty was doing me in. And I wasn't really sure if my tears were hormonal or circumstantial or typical—whatever that meant.

I wasn't sure about much these days.

Attached to a plastic stick in the center of the flowers was a thin white envelope the size of my business card. I pulled it out, and handwritten in purple ink were the words, "Question: In luce Tua videmus lucem."

The connection was obvious, though the message was not. Of course, the Latin phrase was the mission for Regal University, but why the cryptic card with flowers? Or the translation in the letter postmarked three days ago? I reached for a tissue, dried my eyes, and looked toward the window. Two mysterious notes, an archivist's secret discovery, a mass meeting with witches, and now a dozen white roses from an unidentified sender made me feel like I was living in a detective novel.

It was too much. So I did the only reasonable thing I could think of.

Within minutes, Hannah and I were sitting in a window booth at Goldwasser's deli ordering pancakes and scrambled eggs and orange juice. I asked her about her date, and instead of answering, she summoned the waiter back over to our table so she could add an order of two chocolate chip muffins as dessert.

"Does that tell you something?" She sipped her coffee, leaving a bright red lipstick circle on her cup.

"Okeydoke. Let's move on."

"I certainly have. This is New York City, after all. Lots of good single men here, right?" Hannah spent the next ten minutes talking about the date she'd moved on from, the terrible restaurant where they'd met in the financial district and the endless monologue the guy gave about his booming career as a broker on Wall Street. Her descriptions were filled with so many tsk-tsks that I knew the man didn't have a chance.

When our brunch arrived, Hannah shifted gears. Her date wasn't a complete waste, she said. The guy knew Walter Wood—not personally, but well enough to give her an insider's perspective that she said made the evening worth her time. Apparently, Wood had done so well as a stockbroker that he formed his own investment firm called Med-USA. He'd bought a few television stations in the Midwest, some regional magazines, and a syndicated news company that he operated from a high-rise office building on Madison Avenue. He'd also bought a few smaller newspapers along the East Coast and turned their sales around by redirecting the editorial content to include less hard news and more reader-friendly stories. Because the *Clarion* had been struggling financially, losing subscribers to the Internet and television newscasts as well as subsequent advertisers, the family who owned it approached Wood last month to see if Med-USA was interested. He'd been maneuvering the paper ever since.

She poured maple syrup over her pancakes like an artist drizzling paint and kept talking. "I did some fact-checking this morning and sure enough, Med-USA is the rising star of media turnarounds. If he hasn't already, Wood is probably very close to settling a deal as publisher of the *Clarion*." Hannah raised an eyebrow at the idea of the little man becoming her new boss and then dove into her brunch like she did everything else: with a perfect balance of gusto and grace. I marveled at her ability as I wiped grape jam from my sweater.

"It could get ugly, Lightfoot. I mean, the last thing this city needs is another tabloid. I'm not going to take this lying down." She shook her head at the depressing state of the culture, at the general public who was buying into what she called "the mindless infotainment trend." She finished her eggs by lamenting "the decline of the real news that citizens need to govern themselves" and declared it "a sad day for democracy" by emptying her glass of orange juice.

It wasn't exactly the pick-me-up diversion I was looking for, but I supposed it didn't hurt. I broke off a piece of the chocolate chip muffin and decided to tell Hannah about my mysterious letter and delivery. I recited the Latin phrase to her as well as its meaning, told her about its inscription on the library entrance at Regal, and asked her what she thought it all meant.

"You got flowers?"

"Yup. White roses."

She caught the waiter's attention and pointed to her coffee cup. "Lightfoot, there's a reason for everything, you know. I've always wondered why my grandmother insisted on telling me everything she knew about the flowers in her garden since I've killed every plant I've ever owned. Now I know." Hannah explained that white roses were never accidentally chosen. Someone picked them to send a deliberate message because everyone knew white roses symbolized virtue, innocence, and purity. They usually were associated with the start of a friendship, or sometimes even a significant farewell. Whichever the occasion, they clearly did not mean the same as red or pink.

"I think we both know who sent them to you."

"We do?"

She leaned forward.

"And if you ask me, girl, he sent them to you to let you know two things: He trusts you, and he's interested."

"In what?"

"In you."

The waiter set down our check at that moment, and I quickly pulled three ten-dollar bills from my wallet. I pretended to do the math when Hannah tsked me. I looked up.

"Why don't you call him to thank him?"

"Because I'm not interested."

She smiled and looked out the window just as a bicycle messenger rode by. The clouds had formed a grayness over the city that made me wonder if it might rain or snow again.

"Besides, I'm busy, Hannah. Anyway, he's on vacation." I gulped the last of my orange juice. "I think."

"You think you're busy?"

"I think he's on vacation. That's what his boss said, but my brother seems to think otherwise, so I'm not exactly—"

"Your brother?"

"Yeah, he said David didn't have any vacation days left, though I'm not sure how he would know—"

"There's one way to find out."

Hannah rose, threw on her jacket, and waved for me to follow. I left the money under my plate and hurried after my friend, who by now was hailing a cab going uptown on Broadway. He slammed on his brakes when he saw her, and I slid in beside her, thankful for the warmth of the car.

"Where are we going?"

"Where do you think?"

I thought about arguing, but experience told me it wouldn't change Hannah's mind. So I buckled up. I read the cab's license information on the half window between the front and the back-seats and saw that our driver was from India. His hair was white, his skin dark, and he was listening to a talk-radio station. On any other day, I would have asked him about his country or his religion, in case he had some lead to a story I should know about. Today I kept quiet, watching the buildings and crowded side-walks whirl by, listening to the radio as Hannah called someone on her cell phone.

When the local news came over the radio through the speak-ers behind me, I slouched in the seat. The first story was on the mayor's recent shopping spree at a Hasidic-owned electronics store in Brooklyn, followed by the recent controversies at Presbyterian Research Hospital to clone human cells, and another about New York's gay and lesbian organizations petitioning to march in the Saint Patrick's Day parade next month. After that, the stories moved from a Broadway star marrying a local chef to the Yankees lineup for tonight's game and even a television schedule for the evening's prime-time shows. It was a "normal" broadcast, but I found myself wondering again why humans cared at all about news.

Did any of it really matter in how we lived?

Once we were through the traffic, we pulled up to the corner of Regal University, not far from where the pagans had rallied. My stomach dropped, and I pushed an orange acidic taste to the back of my throat. We made our way across the remains of the once-snowy commons—and now-melting snowman's body—to the steps of the library, pausing a moment to take in the Latin inscription about light above us. I pointed Hannah toward the archive library, and she charged ahead. I stayed in the hall by the door to eavesdrop on the conversation.

Sharon, the helpful colleague, greeted Hannah politely, until Hannah asked to speak with David Rockley. The redheaded woman coughed thinly as she asked Hannah a series of questions. Her tone was different from what it had been with me, as if she were more concerned about following protocol than with hearing Hannah's answers: Why did she want to see him? Did she have a scheduled appointment? What was her purpose?

I could relate to that last one.

But the receptionist was no match for my colleague. Hannah said she was interested in researching the religious history of New York's higher education. She was hoping to get a meeting with the archivist since she'd been told he was an expert on such matters generally, and specifically on Regal's documents.

Sharon cleared her throat and asked Hannah to wait a moment. Perhaps she'd like to take a seat at one of the tables. No, Hannah would not. I heard the click-clack of high heels resonate across the room and figured Sharon was heading to her boss's office. I was right.

The click-clack echoed again, and Mr. Ralph began speaking so softly to Hannah that I couldn't make out what he was saying. Hannah compensated, though, and repeated everything she was hearing:

"He's gone for the day? . . . And he won't be back tomorrow? . . . Or for a few weeks, at least? . . . Well, I'm sorry too. This is awfully inconvenient for me. Is there someone else who might be able to answer my questions? Or some files I could look at? . . . Not that you know of? I guess I'll just have to come back later, won't I?"

Hannah stomped out of the library and slammed the door behind her. I joined her as we descended the steps outside and hurried again across the cold gray campus.

"He's not on vacation," she said.

"Why would they say he was if he—?"

"I don't know. But I can't believe an Ivy League school that prides itself on being a world-class institution would have only one employee who would know about its religious history." Then, in the middle of the campus, hundred-year-old buildings all around us, architecturally beautiful structures reflecting an enduring devotion to the academy, Hannah stopped. I circled back beside her and asked what was the matter.

"I wonder what they're so afraid of."

"Maybe they're not afraid," I said, zipping my coat up to my chin. "Maybe it's all just a bunch of hocus-pocus David cooked up to get some attention."

"You said yourself something didn't add up."

"I've been wrong about 99 percent of the time lately, Hannah, so I'm not sure about this or anything else for that matter, or what anyone, let alone a guy like David, would have said to make me believe otherwise, especially since he—"

A gust of snow landed on my face. I shook it off.

"Why'd you do that?" I said.

"Because you're sounding like an idiot."

"Maybe I am an idiot for coming out here and—"

Hannah bent down, threatening to snatch more snow. I shut my mouth. She stood up and pointed at the hurried students and professors on their way to class.

"What one thing do you think could scare the living daylights out of them? These are some of the smartest people in the country, talent dripping out of their ears, who knows how much money and connections and references they have. What could make them afraid?"

I looked from her to them, to the dozens of young women and men with backpacks and earmuffs, some wearing glasses, holding books in their hands or reading notebooks as they walked to class. I saw clusters of older white men in tweed jackets chattering as they walked, gesturing and bobbing their heads—were they on to some breakthrough for curing cancer or space travel? I glanced from their faces to Hannah's. "Is this a trick question?"

She bent down again and I held up my hands in surrender. She laughed. "Think about it, Lightfoot. It's the same thing that scares Wood and Skip. It scares you and sometimes even me."

"Nothing scares you, Hannah X. Hensley."

She plopped her hand on her hip and stared at me. I was shivering from the cold, so I started walking again, looking in the direction of the street, where a dozen yellow taxis were speeding by. She came alongside. "Yes, Lightfoot, one thing scares me."

I held up my hand as a cab pulled to the curb. We climbed in.

"What is it?"

"The truth."

::Chapter Eleven

I t seemed a funny thing for a journalist to say. After all, the whole point of our profession had always been to pursue the truth, to get to the heart of it from as many different angles as we could. A little like choosing an apartment: You never just looked at the outside of a building and said, "I'll take it." Instead, you walked through the whole thing, inspected the bathroom, kitchen, closets, even the neighborhood, to get a sense for the whole. Even then, you looked at other apartments to compare them before signing a lease. A reporter was supposed to run an eyeball across every corner of every room before describing it in print as truth. Readers depended on us for that.

What, then, did Hannah, the most dogged journalist I'd ever met and the most confident woman I'd ever known, mean when she admitted that it scared her?

"First of all, I'll deny it if it ever gets beyond this cab. Understood?"

I crossed myself like I'd seen Catholics do during mass.

"Okay then. Think of the last time you got to the bottom of a story—I mean really understood it. After all the phone calls, interviews, analysis, and fact-checking, what were you left with? Something so ugly and terrible you'd wished you hadn't started in the first place."

I rested my head against the back of the seat and closed my eyes. I knew exactly what she meant. Finding the truth of a story was almost always an encounter with the darkest side of humanity; I learned it first in Denver, then New Orleans. It could be hard and prickly, pressing against every shred of hippie optimism and positive vibes my parents had instilled in me.

"That's why it's scary, right? You know you have to face it, but it's usually never what you want to find. And just as you think you're peeling away the last layer, it gets worse."

A horn honked and a bus roared behind us.

"Then why keep at it?" I whispered without raising an eyelid. "Why bother?"

Hannah smacked my wrist—which caught my attention—and stared at me square in the face, her eyes unflinching. "Because we have to. It's who we are, Lightfoot. It's how we're wired."

Her cell phone rang, and I was relieved when she took the call. I closed my eyes again and imagined beaches. Someplace warm and far away where I didn't have to hear honking horns or blaring radios or hard questions. Where someone else brought me food.

We were climbing the steps at the *Clarion* when Hannah got another idea. She suggested I call Regal's department of human resources to confirm whether David was on vacation. She also said I should call the director of library services to see if anyone else could be considered an expert on the university's religious past and what they might say about David's work or even the Cherrinard archives.

"But I told Skip I'm not working on it," I said as we left the employee lounge armed with coffee refills for the afternoon.

"What does Skip have to do with it? They're just phone calls . . ." We rounded the corner to her desk, where she grabbed her recorder. "Calls . . . about your friend, remember?" She didn't even take off her coat before she turned around again, on her way to attend another press conference with the senator.

"Have fun," I said, waving after her.

"Always do," she hollered over her shoulder. "Just call, okay?"

"If I can fit it in."

I spent the afternoon cleaning my desk around the roses, rearranging piles, and reading an old issue of *ChocoLatte* magazine. I moved my encyclopedia across to the filing cabinet and dumped several files from last year in the trash, eyeing the phone every now and then in case I got an urge to call Regal. No urge came. I did manage to put a few sentences together about the Wiccan lawsuit, though it was hardly prize-winning stuff. And while I was at it, I figured I might as well confirm that the lawsuit had been filed. I picked up the phone.

After spelling out her name slowly and deliberately for me, Bariana Berber, attorney for the group, told me she had in fact filed it this morning in the U.S. District Court of New York and the federal court of appeals. As if she was in cahoots with the witches to take full advantage of the press opportunity, she then offered me a doozy of a quote: "The DVA is clearly dragging its feet regarding Wiccans. By filing litigation today, we're hoping to compel the agency to act and finally honor the pagans' loved ones who lacked the good sense to subscribe to one of the department's officially approved religions." She paused to let me get the whopper down, though I knew she was hardly finished.

I sipped my coffee, swirled it around my mouth for

entertainment, and wondered what kind of weather Denver was getting. Attorney Berber breathed into my ear and asked if I was ready.

"For what?"

"For another comment?"

"Oh, why not."

"Great. Here we go: Why is it that the cemetery administration forbids these devout people from acknowledging their faith the way other veterans' families do? Is that just? Or right? After all, we live in a free society with a Constitution that's meant to protect the religious expressions of all its citizens."

We'd gone into the deep end on this last quote, and I was in no mood to swim around in it. I thanked Attorney Berber for her time. I doodled a picture of a woman with floppy ears and cat-frame glasses and wrote B. B. underneath it. What the Constitution had to do with witches and tombstones was beyond me. But one thing was sure: A quote with hot-button words like "Constitution" and "rights" would definitely beef up the readership. And that would make my boss—or rather his boss, Walter Wood—happy as a hippie at harvest time.

I shaped more of the story, sent it to Skip, and looked for something else to do. I got more coffee. I made another trip to the ladies' room, avoiding the mirror. I called Reverend Cho hoping to set up an interview with him and his staff but left a message on his secretary's voice mail. And I sniffed my white roses every hour or so.

When I hadn't heard back from Skip or Danny Bro or anyone else by 5:06, I pulled on my parka and cap and headed toward the New Jersey PATH. It was another cold February night, but commuters and sidewalk crowds seemed unbothered by the temperatures, moving as they always did—quickly—past the stores and buildings and endless traffic of Manhattan. The street vendors with their hot pretzels and toasted almonds seemed bored on the job, and I felt bad that no one was stopping to support them. So I bought a few bags of almonds I thought would be good treats for my nephews and decided that at least one thing in this world would always be certain: food.

The PATH train was crowded, but I managed to squeeze into a seat between a Latino man in painter's pants and work boots, and a young Indian woman with a bindi on her forehead. Though she wore contemporary black slacks, her jacket and scarf matched the red dot between her eyes and reflected the elegant designs of her Hindu tradition. She read a thick book, the painter napped, and I ate a toasted almond to determine if my nephews would like them, then another in case they did not.

I remembered the excitement I'd felt when I first came to New York and sat beside such diverse faces every time I rode the subway. Tonight I wanted to feel that same enthusiasm again. But it was too hard to ignore the fact that we were riding through the river, too hard to feel anything positive at all. Though this was a city filled with unexpected intersections of cultures and classes, one that had initially captivated me, it had begun to feel as bewildering as, well, a subway in an underwater tunnel.

The train jerked to a sudden stop. The Indian woman bumped into me. I bumped into the painter, and he almost slid off the edge of the seat. All the other passengers also swayed forward and jerked back, clinging to poles or people or seats to keep their balance. Within seconds, everyone settled back into their positions as if nothing had happened, but no one said what I was thinking, what I knew was my impending doom: We were stuck.

One man simply—and loudly—cursed the New Jersey Transportation Planning Authority. A baby began to cry, and two teenage boys in baggy jeans and hooded sweatshirts took advantage of their captive audience and started beat-boxing. The woman beside me apologized quietly for bumping into me and turned the page in her book. Instinctively, I apologized to the painter, who only shrugged before napping again. It was as if being stopped on an underground train in the middle of a river was a normal part of these New Yorkers' day.

I, however, grew desperate for a cigarette. But I'd have settled for a drop of chocolate, caffeine, or any other chemical supplement that would calm me down. My face caught fire. I devoured both bags of toasted almonds, even licking the paper, and wiped my palms frantically across my pants. I started tapping my feet, glancing wildly around the subway car, wondering where the emergency exit was and imagining what would happen if I had to climb out into the tunnel. Or, heaven forbid, into the Hudson River, where who knew how many white sharks or big fish or poisonous snakes were waiting to eat me alive.

My forehead was sweaty. I swallowed, but there was nothing in my mouth to swallow. I tapped more and wondered how the man beside me could sleep and the Hindu woman could keep reading. Maybe they knew survival skills for these urban predicaments that no one had bothered to teach me when I'd first arrived last year. Maybe they had some secret diversion strategy I hadn't yet figured out. Maybe now was the time to learn one. So if I focused on the rhythms of the beat-boxers or the color of my boots or the light in the corner, I'd survive too. Yes, the light in the corner. My head felt dizzy. The white flickering light. I needed air. *In Thy light we see light.*

I sat up straight and knocked my head against the window of the subway. I shut my eyes tight and made a pact with God. I admitted I'd been ignoring him a bit—maybe a lot—lately, but I had good reasons. Not much had been making sense. Work and men and city life were too confusing, and so, yes, I admitted I hadn't been very good at being spiritual or religious or even polite in the midst of any of it. That would change, I promised the Almighty, if he got me out of this alive. I would tithe more. I would exercise. I would—for all eternity—finally quit smoking. If I just made it to my brother's apartment, if God didn't let the sharks or snakes get me, I promised I'd be a better person, a better Christian, patient and kind and all the rest of it.

I heard a voice and my eyes popped open. Apparently, others heard it too. Someone shushed the beat-boxers, and a man's Brooklyn accent announced over the intercom, "Uh, we apologize for the delay. We are temporarily being held until the next train comes out of the station. We should be moving shortly. Thank you for your patience."

I caught my breath. The woman beside me flipped another page, and the painter snored. I stood up and felt the blood rush to my feet. I stamped the right, then left—up, then down. It felt good. The train jerked and the conductor was right: We were moving again. Maybe God had accepted my deal. I hung on to the silver bar above me, still standing, and for the rest of the ride kept my eyes concentrated in one direction: the corner.

February air never felt so good, even if it was only twenty-four degrees. I lapped it up when I emerged from the steps of the PATH station and into the Hoboken neighborhood. I pinched my cheeks, glared at the enemy in front of me—the Hudson River—and almost danced my way up the hill to my brother's apartment building. I was free. Alive. Freezing.

And out of breath by the time I buzzed my brother's apartment. Jesse and Garrett were concentrating on toy dump trucks on the rug in the living room when Sarah let me in the door. She waved me back to the kitchen, where she was chopping carrots and celery for a salad. I kissed my nephews' foreheads, and before loading paper clips and rocks into the back of their trucks, Jesse looked up at me with bright brown eyes: "Did you bring us any surprises, Aunt Jonna?"

"Well, it wouldn't be a surprise if I told you, would it?"

"Ah, you ate it again, huh?"

"You wouldn't have liked it, Jess. Yucky stuff."

He giggled at me and then slammed his truck into Garrett, who was making explosion noises out of the sides of his mouth. I plopped my coat and bag on the kitchen stool, grabbed a tomato and a knife, and began slicing.

Luke had gone around to the corner bodega for milk and cereal, Sarah said, but we'd be eating soon. Whatever meat was in the oven smelled like my day had just moved from bad to better. It helped, too, that while we chopped veggies, Sarah told me that she'd spent her morning "up to her elbows in chocolate frosting and cupcake batter" for a new bakery across from Church Square Park. Each detail made me wonder if I should consider a career change.

I was about to describe my near-death experience under the Hudson when I heard the door open. Two little boys called to us in unison that their dad was home, Luke hollered something about a milk delivery, and soon we were sitting around the table eating baked ham, potatoes, and salad.

It was a happy response from my plea to the Almighty. The

clinking of forks and knives on plates, the boys spitting out silly sounds, the foam of Brooklyn lager in my glass, all made me glad to be joining my family for dinner rather than having become one for some shark in New York's harbor. I was enjoying the simple pleasure, wanting to savor it like a mocha coffee or the cold February air after being stuck underground. But my brother turned serious, then cautious as he looked at his sons sitting across from him.

He turned toward me. "This morning before work, I went to the men's breakfast at the church . . . but I didn't see David there."

I concentrated on the butter melting throughout my mashed potatoes. Luke kept on.

"He's always there. I mean, he is one of the leaders, you know."

"Hmmm." I didn't know David was a leader of their church's men's group, and I wasn't sure I cared. I did care about the carrots and onions I'd moved on to, which I was certain were doing my body instant good, another glad tiding.

"None of the guys knew where he was, which I found a little weird, since at least one of them is usually in touch with him."

He set down his fork and leaned back in his chair as if he needed to think about this last piece of information he'd given us. His jaw was scruffy but his hair shorter than when I saw him last Sunday. Sarah shot him a glance that seemed worried, though I wasn't sure if it was for the boys listening to this adult conversation or for their friend who missed a church meeting. Or both. I took another slice of ham.

Luke watched me. I cut off a piece and popped it into my mouth. Sarah watched too as I kept eating, and by the time I'd made it back to my salad, I felt two more sets of eyes on me. I shoveled in another mouthful of healthy nutrients before slamming my fork on the table.

"What?" I demanded.

Now my brother's eyes were worried too. He pressed his eyebrows, making his forehead wrinkle, and he tightened his lips. Sarah sighed, Jesse froze, and Garrett fidgeted. I gulped my lager so that a foamy mustache remained above my mouth. Garrett tried not to laugh, but a chuckle sneaked out. He stopped altogether, though, when I pulled my napkin to my face.

"Aren't you the least bit curious about where David is?" Luke's tone was gentle but big-brotherly.

"I told you on the phone that his boss said he's on vacation."

"And I told you on the phone that he didn't have any vacation days left."

I picked up my fork, more for defense than anything, and speared a tomato. "Maybe he overslept."

"Not likely, but possible . . . except I called Regal's HR and asked about him so — "

"What's HR, Dad?" Jesse was pulling a string of fat from his ham.

Luke studied his son. "It stands for human resources, Jesse, and it's the office at a school or company that helps people with things like insurance and vacations."

"Is your school's HR going to send us on vacation?"

"Maybe." He pushed around the food on his plate. "Anyway, they told me he'd used up his vacation days for this fiscal year and would have to wait for July before he'd get any more."

"That's private information, so how'd — ?"

"A friend of a friend. The point is, Jonna, he's not on vacation."

I laid my knife across the top of the plate. Apprehension lined my brother's face.

"Is Uncle David in trouble, Dad?" This time it was their youngest son, Garrett, who spoke, his eyes on the verge of a downpour. The sight of tears from a six-year-old boy—who was also related—might as well have been a dagger in my heart.

"We don't know, Son. He's probably fine, but we just don't know." Luke managed another bite of his dinner before laying his utensils across his ham, as if he wanted to eat but was too anxious, which made me realize how serious he was taking this. He was usually eating seconds by now.

Sarah stepped in. "Jonna, were you able to find out anything else about what David told us?" She put her hand on Garrett's shoulder and rubbed it. The rain subsided.

But Sarah's question took me to Regal's archival library yesterday—which by now seemed a week ago—and I thought about Sharon's initial response to me when I first came to her desk: polite, helpful, concerned even. I remembered David's office, his pictures on the wall, the papers on his desk, and felt strangely warmed to it. Until I was transported to the bookshelves where I stood with Sharon. And as if I were hearing it all over again, her question stabbed my fragile and ridiculous dating life:

"Why else would he set up an appointment with a reporter?"

I saw myself swinging again at the snowman, then listening in the hallway of the library this morning as David's colleague deflected Hannah's questions. Each encounter felt like a scene from an independent film—the kind where you're never quite sure what's happening—and it blurred through my mind as if a director had cut back the speed so I'd see each moment in slow motion. None of it made sense.

"Were you, Jon?" Sarah said.

"Was I what?"

"Able to find out anything new? You know, when he asked you to come by the office?"

I narrowed my eyes first at my brother, then his wife, still feeling the sting of Sharon's question as if it had dropped into all of our ears and I'd been exposed.

"No . . . well, yes."

They sat up in their chairs, tension hanging between us.

"I'll tell you what I found out: David Rockley seems to be one of many these days who think the *Clarion* is their personal publicity tool. Maybe he came across some old religious documents. Who cares? He works at one of the best universities in the country with some of the smartest people on the planet, and, I don't know, maybe he feels like he doesn't compare or something. Maybe he thinks he can take advantage of the fact that he knows a reporter who happens to cover religion, and so he could use me to help his reputation. Guess again."

Their faces went blank, except Garrett's, whose eyes grew wide, then full again. But I looked away. I wasn't finished.

"I'm sick of it. He can get his own free press in some other way, as far as I'm concerned. Call some other reporter, for all I care, to get out his stupid story." I dumped my napkin in the middle of my plate. "So much for being such a nice guy."

I shoved my chair back and shot from the table, grabbing my plate in the process as I started toward the kitchen. By the time I'd come back, no one had moved, but my youngest nephew now had watery lines staining his cheeks. His lip quivered. His nose ran.

But he didn't say a word. Neither did his father or mother, both of whom were merely shaking their heads at me as if they'd just watched a monster emerge from the sea—in a really bad television show. Garrett's big brother, though, managed to find language that told me how he felt, language that became a lightning bolt disguised in a nine-year-old voice:

"Uncle David would never do that. He's not like those other guys, Aunt Jonna. He *is* nice." He rose from his chair to face me, his hands balled into fists as he stood tall across from me. His messy brown hair jumped around his head as he spoke: "And if something's wrong with him, you have to help him. You have to . . . doesn't she, Dad?"

Luke's arms swallowed his eldest son, and all my brother could do was nod. Now it was no longer my nephew's eyes that filled, but mine.

I stepped back, knocking over the chair as I did but pulling back the raw feelings at the same time. I stumbled toward my parka and bag and past the dining room table, where my family still sat, stunned or worried, I couldn't tell which.

"Thanks for dinner, Sarah," I mumbled. "I need to get home."

"Come on, Jonna, we can work this out with—"

"Later, okay?" I pulled open the door. "I'll call you later."

When I staggered outside, I scrounged through my bag for a cigarette but couldn't find one. All I came up with was my cap and my wallet. I yanked the flaps over my ears and hurried down the steps. Given the ride over here, there was no way I was taking the PATH back to Manhattan, which left me two options: a cab, which would cost more than I had in my wallet, or the ferry.

Several blocks later, I was at the terminal for the New York waterway, buying a one-way ticket. I couldn't remember the walk through Hoboken, though my face hurt from the sting of tears frozen on skin. My head was an ache of conflicting images, so thick and muddled I thought it might burst. There, in the chaos of my mind, Jesse's innocent face morphed into Walter Wood, who dissolved into Hannah and Griffin Lewis and Skip, even my dad, then my mom, all three brothers, and finally my neglected friends in New Orleans and countless colleagues in Denver, until each flashed all over again like instant replay. Their eyes shot straight through me, making my insides a war zone of feelings and reactions; I was angry and heartbroken, ashamed and defensive, sad and resentful. I'd prayed for a rescue from an irrational underground panic attack but found instead wounds and sores aching within me.

I pulled a tissue from my pocket and took a seat near a window. There weren't nearly as many people on board as the last time I'd taken the ferry, which, of course, had been with David. Somehow, he seemed responsible for this mess.

He'd sat across from me in the cabin, chattering about his dad, happy to remember the trips they'd taken together, hoping for a chance someday to do the same with his own son. The lights of New York's skyline that night—like tonight—had looked like a million stars across a dark canvas. I'd been surprised at both the spread of the view and the reason for the trip: David was also afraid of riding beneath the river. He'd said he'd rather travel over the water than under it. And he'd looked glad that I'd come along.

But that was before I knew what he was really after. My head throbbed as I stared at the buildings across the river, each light challenging the eerie night air, bright and intimidating and expansive. I suddenly wanted to blame not just David but all of New York for this barrage of unwelcome feelings, for the confusion and misunderstandings and distance that had descended on my life like a storm. In Colorado or New Orleans, I'd hardly known such emotions existed, let alone felt them. Now I wanted to blame every part of this city — from the witchcraft of its pagans and the arrogance of its universities to the greed of the media executives and the easiness of its anything-goes religions. All were blending together into a single shred of bad news that was sending my career and my life into a downward spiral. Everything in this city was horrible, hard, at odds with everything I'd learned from my mother and father growing up.

But as I looked overboard at the wake the ferry was leaving in the water, I knew my parents' faith journey was not much good to me right now. Maybe the dreams, the anxiety, the panicked moments were all hints of what I hadn't wanted to admit: that my mom and pop could no longer help me. They were far away, after all, unable to support me or model to me a devotion I'd never be able to match anyway. Even my brothers had their own beliefs, their own lives, which I admired but could hardly compare to. No, I was alone in this moment, aware that the forces in front of me, the bad news of New York City, were the foes I had to fight. And I had to do it on my own.

A religion reporter with a flimsy faith.

The boat rocked for a second, and I slid forward in my seat, jamming my knee into the metal frame in front of me so hard I knew I'd have a bruise tomorrow. A group of teenagers — whom I hadn't noticed before or had subconsciously ignored because of my last ferry ride—swarmed into the seats across from me. They laughed at the waves on the river and competed with one another to see who could be the loudest and most obnoxious. It was the last thing I wanted to endure, another encounter with juvenile delinquents on a night that was already going from bad to worse.

"Can you guys shut up?" I said, my voice firm and the volume slightly louder than civilized.

Four pimply-faced teenaged boys turned toward me and grimaced. One seemed genuinely afraid of the woman who'd just scolded them, but the others merely rolled their eyes and continued their antics, hollering, whining, and mimicking a variety of sounds.

"I said, can you guys . . . shut . . . up?"

One of the boys, who wore a baseball cap with a devil embroidered on it, smirked and raised his arm so that the material in his coat scrunched up as if he were shaping a fake muscle. His friends laughed loudly, nervously. My heart seethed, and my blood boiled.

Just as I was about to blow a fuse from head to toe, the pimply devil-cap turned to me and said quite matter-of-factly, "Did you forget your broomstick tonight, lady?"

My broomstick? Did I forget my . . . what?

It wasn't funny.

Even so, that sent his friends into an all-out laughing spree, where they fell over each other, slapping each other's hands and eventually wobbling toward the back of the ferry, far away from the witch they'd just mocked, tried, and convicted. The boat docked a few minutes later, and I sat dismayed, my body void of energy, strength, or motivation. I hadn't thought it possible that this day could descend to even lower depths, but the boys on the boat had just proved otherwise.

As I watched the other passengers leave the ferry, I wanted to stow away altogether. I wondered if God took pacts seriously. I wondered why every part of me had to feel like I'd just been kicked and jabbed in a boxing match and left only with bruises and broken bones. I wondered why I'd moved here in the first place. I wanted to go home to Colorado.

Slowly, I made my way off the pier and toward the subway. Even at 8:40 p.m., the street was crowded and noisy, the cold air biting. I pulled up the zipper around my collar and walked with my head down. I swiped my MetroCard for the subway turnstile and walked limply toward the platform. As the headlights appeared in the tunnel and the train slowed to a stop, I waited for the doors to slide apart.

And that was when my eyes caught hold of the most terrifying sight of the entire night. More than all the greedy pagans and evil men and stupid teens put together, more than stalled subway trains in the river or teary nephews, there, in the window of a slowing train, I saw the darkest and ugliest sight yet, one I'd tried most of my life to avoid seeing. And when I did, I knew instantly that it—not New York or these other things or even David—was my real enemy. It was the real foe.

It was the curly-haired reflection of a chubby thirty-year-old woman who worked as a religion reporter and stunk as a human being. Her reflection—her hardheaded, faithless, self-centered reflection—was scarier than all the rest.

::Chapter Twelve

Hannah was right: The truth was terrifying.

The devil-capped kid on the ferry was also right: I was a witch. Not the Wiccan kind that I'd been covering for the *Clarion*, but the stereotype of the mean and mad woman more interested in harming others than in helping them. The cackle, the sneer, the self-absorption and self-protection, all of it defined the stereotype. And all of it described Jonna Lightfoot MacLaughlin.

It wasn't that I hadn't known her before. It'd always been easy to see how wretched and flawed and full of shortcomings I was. In fact, my inadequacies had been the clearest part of my personality most of my life. How many times had I quit smoking? Or promised to start exercising? Or fantasized about a long and romantic life with a Catholic hunk or a Southern Baptist or any other gorgeous single man who was not my brothers' friend? And how often had I bartered with God, begging for some miracle or talent or reward that gave me what I wanted when I wanted it?

What was different this time was how completely empty that woman in the reflection looked. It was as if I saw her face, her heart, and her entire being top to bottom, and I knew for the first time that there was not a solitary shred of good anywhere to be found in her. Not one. My family's faith didn't help me, nor did the churches I'd attended or the friends I knew. My job also couldn't do the trick, though I'd secretly assumed covering religion might at least cut me a little slack. Not so. None of it mattered in a department that had long ago been marked "insufficient funds." None could pull me out of this hole where bad didn't just reign consistently; it reigned supremely.

The subway doors took a little longer than usual to open, as if the powers that be wanted to scrub the wound with salt. So there she was, an awful sight to behold: a gloomy, depressing, and completely helpless little waif of a person looking at me. She was the one I'd spent most of my days covering up with secondhand clothes or deflecting altogether with chocolate bars and cigarettes. And if I was seeing her so clearly now, who knew how many other people had encountered her as well?

I thought of the other witches, the Wiccans, who believed in an altogether different approach to life—of Griffin Lewis and Lady Crystal and Professor Hartman, none of whom was the cheery type, but that didn't mean I should have treated them like the enemy. They were still human beings, after all, not stereotypes or foes or even jokes I'd begun to ridicule just because I didn't see what they saw. They were still flesh and blood with families and jobs and heartaches.

And the others whom Lightfoot the Pathetic had scorned? My roommate and my nephews, for starters. No wonder Hannah had called me Little Miss Attitude. No wonder my nephews had cried and confronted me for the way I'd talked about David. They'd seen this terrible mass of frizz masquerading as a person, and they'd responded correctly.

I didn't want to think what my colleagues or my boss had seen: an ego or a freak or a sorry caricature of Lois Lane trying to justify religion to, of all people, journalists. That might have explained why so many kept their distance and why Skip had first given the job to me: Who but someone who was already kind of weird would want such an obsolete or wacky beat? He'd said that as a hippie kid, I'd been preparing all my life for the job. What I now suspected he meant was that I'd grown up around more delusions and hypocrisy than most on his staff and so would spot them easier. I'd disappointed him, too.

Then there was David, the one who seemed to push this snowball down the hill in the first place. I didn't want to think about him, tried not to, even as the train doors finally slid apart and I stumbled into the car. So what that each of my brothers had vouched for his character? That everyone who'd ever met the guy—his colleague, my nephews, my friends in New Orleans—were all drawn to him. I'd ignored all of them, too, and now every time I looked into the subway window or at the shiny steel wall, I couldn't shake the face that stared back at me. She was a bigheaded blob of a wreck getting swept along on a train she couldn't control, watching from the outside as the collision got closer and closer.

We jerked forward, and I shut my eyes tight to block out the hideous mirror. I saw color—red, orange, yellow, green—spilling into patterns that created fingers, then hands, then faces. They were fragile but bright, glass windows with human features. The apostles Paul and John, Shakespeare and Columbus, Florence Nightingale and Abraham Lincoln, martyrs and athletes and disciples, all in a panorama of images spread across massive stone walls that rose into the sky. And there in the middle of them all was one final window—or was it a door?—blue and brown and gray, arms out to his sides, eyes like none of the others. Every other face or hand or figure in the mighty room pointed his direction because he was the center.

I was in the Cathedral of Saint John the Divine on the night David introduced me to its majesty. I heard his question, "What do you see?" I squeezed my eyes tighter as I felt the rumble of the subway beneath me. This dreamy memory was far better than the apparition that greeted me outside. David's voice hummed in my mind: "Common human efforts by great and flawed human beings, all honored in a sacred space like this. And what's at—?"

Someone stepped on my toe. The reverie evaporated when I opened my eyes to see a large elderly woman moving slowly among the passengers. I hadn't noticed that the subway had stopped, and she hadn't noticed my feet as she bumped her way into the train. I yanked them back, smarting from the woman's impact and glaring at her as she squeezed into a corner seat as if nothing had happened. Her hair was a jumble of white curls and her face a droopy pattern of shadows and wrinkles. She plunked her hands on her knees and heaved a great sigh as if this were the first time all day she'd been able to rest.

I didn't want to look away from her, and not just because I was afraid the creature might jump back into my line of vision. As the subway jerked to a start again and the woman gripped my attention, I felt something shift inside me. Not like an earthquake or indigestion, but a shift nonetheless. It was as if a knot that'd been stuck in my shoulders for a long time had been pressed, tugged, and, finally, dislodged.

Maybe it had been the jab from the mirror or the gleam from the stained glass. Or both. I couldn't explain it. I only knew that sitting there on the train, staring at a tired old woman—whose head by now was slightly cocked, her eyes shut and mouth ajar—

I suddenly didn't feel as idiotic as I had on the ferry. Or as angry, though she'd stomped on my toes a few seconds earlier. I still felt blank, numb even, but something else was seeping through me I hadn't felt in a long time: relief. I sighed too.

Fifteen minutes later, I wandered up out of the subway, cold but not frozen, afraid but not haunted. I was exhausted, but I was also amazed that I was still walking. I didn't reach for a cigarette, and I wasn't interested in putting anything in my stomach. I only wanted to turn the key to the door, climb the stairs to my apartment, and crawl into bed.

The next morning, I woke up early. Sunlight streamed into my bedroom, and I lay there watching dust particles from my dresser dance across it. It didn't matter that I hadn't cleaned in days; what did matter was that I could enjoy the sight at all. I popped out of bed to make coffee and took a cup in to Hannah, who grunted something about the time. I ate granola, showered, and was standing on the steps of our apartment building, breathing in the new day, by 7:07 a.m.

The morning air was brisk on my face. I hopped down the steps and rounded the corner to the subway station, passing a small group of schoolchildren waiting for a bus. Their faces were sleepy, but they watched me walk by as if they weren't used to seeing other people out this early. A smile formed on my face, surprising them as well as me. One little girl raised her hand to wave and smiled back at me, reminding me of the sunlight I'd watched in my room. Something odd was happening.

By the time I reached the subway steps, the crowd on the street had filled out, and I strolled through it. Commuters were hurrying to work, clutching coffee cups, newspapers, or briefcases. I reached for my wallet and approached the subway booth to buy a new MetroCard. Emma sat inside.

"Well, look who's here!" She'd been glancing over a book when I came to the window.

"Good morning, Emma. Nice to see you back." I dropped a twenty-dollar bill into the tray, along with the card so she could refill it. But she didn't pick it up. Instead, she peered over her glasses and tilted her head before she spoke.

"Everything okay, Jonna?"

I blinked. "I think so. Why? Did I forget to brush my hair again? I couldn't have lost my driver's—" I scrounged through my bag, but Emma just laughed.

"Baby, you're fine." She took my money, her soft brown eyes never leaving my face. "You look fine. Gorgeous even. It's just, well, I don't think I've seen you this . . . early."

"Oh yeah, that." I picked up my MetroCard from the tray between us and shrugged. "It's funny, Emma, but I just woke up, wide awake, like I couldn't wait to get going."

I scratched my head and watched Emma move in close to the microphone, look around the station as if she had an announcement for the entire world, and say, "See? There *is* a God!"

The minute she said it, I felt as certain as if someone had just handed me a chocolate donut and said, "This tastes good." Of course it does.

We nodded and laughed, and if I hadn't seen it for myself, I'm not sure I would have believed it. But this middle-aged transit worker with bright eyes and kind words jumped off her stool and right there in her toll booth burst into what I would have called an Irish jig, shouting an occasional "Praise be!" and "Glory!" as she danced. She hooted and I hollered and the serious faces of a few commuters looked on and relaxed as they did. My ancestors from the home country would have been proud.

We stopped only as we both acknowledged a train approaching the station. Emma looked and pointed, beat out a final tap, and giggled.

"Now, go find some good news for that newspaper of ours," Emma said.

I shook my head as I turned toward the train. "I'll try, but it's mostly bad, you know."

"Don't worry — the bad news always comes before the good, now, doesn't it?"

I don't know why it hadn't seemed obvious before. Then again, a lot hadn't been exactly clear lately, I realized as I waved to my subway friend. She beamed back at me, her hands swaying above her head, and I heard the doors open behind me. I spun around, stepped on board, and managed to find a place between a Muslim woman wearing a head covering and an older man in a postal uniform. Both looked as tired as I had most other mornings. I could appreciate that.

So I settled in quietly beside them, trying not to disturb them, and chewed on Emma's point. The train pulled to a start, and I considered how her comment worked its way out: vegetables before dessert, exercise before weight loss, winter before spring. Why hadn't I seen it before? Even my career confirmed it. How many bad drafts had I needed to write before I finally produced a good one? And if it were a progression in the natural world, there must be implications for the spiritual world, too. Maybe I'd had to look hard at an ugly old Jonna before I'd see a hint of a new one.

The subway bumped its way through the tunnel, and I jiggled slightly on the seat. A man across from me wore a purple sweatshirt with the Regal University coat of arms on it. The Latin letters embroidered across it were as clear and obvious as the words Emma had said. A lot was becoming clearer this morning.

As we slowed to a stop at Ninety-sixth Street, I noticed an uptown train waiting across the platform. I squeezed my way out from my seat, trying not to elbow any passengers in the process. The doors widened, and I jetted across to the Number 1. Soon we were heading uptown in a near-empty subway filled more with ads and maps above the seats than commuters. I sat under a billboard for a grocery store, startled by a song I couldn't remember the words to but humming its melody nonetheless.

Ten minutes later, we screeched to a stop at 110th Street. The sidewalk outside was busy and cold as I pulled up my collar and dodged in and out of the vendors and neighbors, going this way and that, carried along in the routine of a New York Wednesday as it was waking up. A few blocks later, I found the steps I'd been looking for, quickened my pace, and almost jogged up like an athlete on her morning workout. Almost.

At the top, I pushed the high door and left the February temperatures for a warmth that couldn't be measured in degrees. I strolled slowly into the majestic space, riveted by the colors and wood and candles around me. A few women sat silently in pews; a janitor mopped an area of the floor not far from them. I tiptoed past, all the way to the first row, and sat in the middle, looking ahead to the nave of the great cathedral. I wanted to remember what was in the center of it, what all the people in the stained glass windows pointed to, what I'd brushed off lately as a nice but irrelevant idea some people I loved—my parents, my brothers, my friends—had realized as true.

It was a cross. In the middle of Saint John the Divine, it hung prominently as the worst piece of news the world had ever seen or heard or read about in print. It was horrific. A man executed for claiming to be God because the people who knew him were confused by his miracles and words. Suddenly, that didn't seem so irrelevant.

I gazed at the blue, brown, and gray image of Christ as if it were the most compelling newspaper story I'd laid eyes on, as if I'd never read it before. The facts were all there: the innocent man in the ancient Middle East who didn't fight or defend himself when tried and convicted to death; the details of his claims and deeds that were so shocking they shaped the history of every culture thereafter; the rumors circulated by his critics; and the sacrifices made by his followers long after his death. It didn't seem like just another heroic tale from an ancient religion; it was downright crazy as well.

Or else it *was* true. And that seemed more frightening than anything I recognized last night, especially when I thought of what I saw. I stared a little longer. My eyes stung. As I looked, some of the words to the familiar song came back. I finally remembered it as the hymn we'd sung last week at Second Presbyterian:

Rock of Ages, cleft for me,
Let me hide myself in Thee . . .

I forgot the rest of the words, but I kept humming. Something clicked. And I knew at that moment that no matter how hard I tried or how I was raised, no matter what I'd done or didn't do, I'd never be able to make myself normal—whatever that meant. Now, sitting in the pew, mesmerized by the image in front of me with all its details sparkling off the window, I realized I didn't have to. That felt better than good.

My stomach growled. I nodded forward and wandered quietly past the janitor and the women in the pews, past Florence Nightingale and the apostle Paul, The Poet's Corner and the information table. I picked up a calendar of listings for free concerts and Bible studies, tucked it in my bag, and left.

The sun was still bright outside as I found a corner bodega. I bought a small coffee in a blue cup. The clock behind the clerk said 9:03. I glanced across the headlines of today's many newspapers—nothing like what I'd just read—and hurried back toward the subway. I caught a downtown train, got off at Ninety-sixth Street, headed out to the street, and waited for the crosstown bus that would take me through Central Park, past the cherry blossom trees covered in snow, to the Upper East Side—to a campus I'd visited more in the last week than in the entire year I'd lived in New York.

When I found her at her desk in Regal's archives, Sharon was wearing a forest green sweater that made her hair seem redder than usual. She was concentrating on an open file, unaware that anyone had walked in. I bumped into a chair to make a little noise so as not to startle her too much. She looked up, her eyes pools of tension.

"Oh. Hello."

It seemed as though I were the first visitor in the library this morning, and her voice echoed off the bookshelves. She tapped her pencil against the documents.

"Good morning. I'm wondering if I could see David."

"Did he call you?" Shades of pink filtered into her otherwise pale face.

"Did he call *you*?" I repeated, picking up a paper clip from her desk and bending it backward.

"Uh, well, as a matter of fact, no, he didn't." She stood behind her desk, the pinks still moving across her skin. "But why would he? He's on vacation, remember?"

"See, I'm thinking that's not exactly the case."

She tugged some of the green sweater down her thin frame and ran her hand across her skirt as though she were getting out the wrinkles. "That's what I've been told, Ms. Lightfoot. There's nothing more I can—"

Her boss, Ralph, opened the door and entered the library. He was coming into work, his cheeks frosty from the cold, his overcoat buttoned fully to his neck. He glanced from me to Sharon and back to me again. I smiled.

"Yes?"

"Morning," I said. "Whew, it's cold out there, isn't it?" I set my bag on the floor, took off my parka, and hung it on the back of a chair at one of the study tables in case I needed to stay awhile—or at least look like I might. Mr. Ralph-boss watched me, not exactly perky as he began to unbutton his coat.

"I'm wondering if you know when David Rockley might be back because—"

"I told you the other day he's on vacation for a few weeks." His coat was off now and his shirt beneath was crumpled. His tie was too, though he didn't seem to notice. He adjusted his glasses, which were as round as his head. "I'm not sure how else I can help you."

"How about telling me the truth?"

Not a muscle on his face flinched. He simply brushed his hand against his hair and glared at me.

"I beg your pardon?"

"Here's where it gets a little confusing for me. HR said that David had used up all of his vacation days, and his friends don't seem to think he would have taken one anyway since—"

"I can't help you." He draped his coat over his forearm and started toward his office.

"No? What can you tell me then about the Cherrinard endowment? Wasn't that what David was working on?"

Mr. Ralph stopped and turned so suddenly I thought he might strain something. Sharon gasped. "That's private and classified information," he said, a hint of weariness blended into his reaction.

I pushed around my hair to rearrange it and pulled out a chair in case the man had hurt himself. "That's too bad. I was hoping to get to the bottom of some sort of crazy claims David told me about last week. See, he seems to think folks here, you know, at this world-class Ivy League university, have been helping themselves to the money from the endowment. Can you imagine?" He walked to the chair and gripped the top of it, but he did not sit down; Sharon did. I returned to fiddling with the paper clip. "I know it sounds nuts, which is why I thought maybe you could show me some of the files he's been working on. Or I guess I could wait until he gets back from the vacation he's not on. At any rate, I'd rather not write something for the *Clarion* without a little more confirmation than what he's already given me."

The two exchanged glances. Sharon returned to the file she'd been engrossed with when I first walked in. Her boss collected himself.

"I can assure you that is not the case."

"No? But David said he'd been digitizing all sorts of old files for a while now and he came across these documents that suggested the Cherrinards wanted their money used for one specific purpose. According to David, the university hasn't bothered. Could be just another conspiracy theory in the world of religion, but, hey, I've got to do my homework, so—"

"It's true we've been transferring several of the university's archives for the past eleven months or so as part of President Coen's restructuring plan. But most of David's work has merely involved, forgive me for saying it this way, rather trivial files and records from the registrar and departments that no longer exist."

"Hmmm. If they're so trivial, why are they, let's see, what did you call them? Classified?"

"Again, standard protocol dictated by our general counsel. The records are confidential, or only available by special request. In our case, I'm afraid once we scanned these documents, we shredded the surplus or sent them to a warehouse in White Plains. So we couldn't help you even if we wanted to."

I looked around the library and saw a dozen or so computers on desks. "Sure you could. How about letting me take a peek at those trivial digital files David scanned, to see what comes up from the Cherrinard endowment? Then I wouldn't have to go all the way up to White Plains. I have to confess, the subways alone can be so confusing for me. Forget about Metro-North and Amtrak and all the other—"

He squeezed the back of the chair. "I'm sorry. No."

"No?"

"No."

"Rats. Well, how about an official comment at least as to why they're unavailable to a curious reporter?" I flipped open my notebook and clicked my pen. "You know, for the record?"

He swallowed. "You mean besides it's standard procedure?"

"Yup. Besides that."

"No comment."

"Maybe the computer crashed? That happens to me all the time, so I'd completely understand—"

"No comment." He picked up the chair and tucked it closely—and loudly—beneath the table.

"But you are confirming that David's been digitizing a bunch of old stuff; you just can't tell me which files? So that means he could have come across these Cherrinard documents?"

"I must ask that you direct any inquiries from here on to the president's office of communication . . . or the general counsel." The elder librarian turned around and walked quickly into his office behind the bookshelves. I twisted my paper clip back into form and returned it to Sharon's desk.

"That went well, don't you think?" I said, shrugging. She didn't look up but busied herself with papers, forms, and receipts on the desk. I waited and watched, but she stayed as pink and tight-lipped as when I'd first walked in. Hannah's question surfaced in my mind, and I wondered which part of the truth Sharon might be afraid of. It certainly seemed to be in the air.

I slid my business card near her phone. "If there's anything I can do, please—"

"You left your card with me last time."

"I did? Wow, I'm better than I thought. . . . Well, not really. In fact, I'm a mess of a religion reporter because—ah, never mind. Anyway, when you do hear from him or you think of anything else I might be interested in knowing"—I pointed to my business card—"now you'll have backup. I'm forever losing things, so I guess it never hurts to have two, right?"

She nodded as she picked up my card, filed it in her drawer, and smiled politely before burying her nose back in her papers. I grabbed my parka and strolled past a row of yearbooks. Bright purple letters covered the spines of the books, spelling out *The Torch* on each with the year marked beside it. They went back as far as 1910. Some were thinner than others or slightly more weathered, but each was purple and gold. Instead of seeming frail or as if they might dissolve if I touched them, the yearbooks appeared surprisingly sturdy, considering their age.

I pulled 1921 carefully from the shelf. The cover of *The Torch* included the type of lamp held by Lady Liberty in New York Harbor, and beneath the emblem were the words, "Sending the light into all the world." In the corner was Regal's coat of arms with its Latin inscription, "In luce Tua videmus lucem." I pushed 1921 back into its spot and pulled out 1934; beside the same emblem was the same mission and coat of arms. Each yearbook cover, all the way up to last year, printed the same phrase, torch, and symbol across it.

I turned back to Sharon. "Excuse me, Sharon." She glanced up from her desk. "Why do you think Regal's yearbook has this phrase, 'Sending the light into all the world'?"

The pink now was gone from her face and there was no mistaking the strain in her eyes. "What do you mean?"

"I could be biased as a religion reporter, but isn't that kind of a term you'd read in the Bible?" I pointed to the symbol. "And the Latin phrase here, doesn't it translate, 'In Thy light we see light'?" She shrugged. "Any clues? Whose light? God's?"

"Yes."

"Yes?"

"I think you already know that the university was founded as an Episcopalian institution." She glanced toward Ralph's door, then at me. "Some traditions—like *The Torch*—don't change, even if their meaning does. I suppose now the light refers to the enlightened mind that's shaped here in the classroom."

I flipped through the 1999 edition of the yearbook and saw photographs of clubs that had more to do with confirming Sharon's perspective than they did the Episcopalian roots of the school. I turned over the firm book, ready to return it to its spot on the nineties shelf, when I noticed one more image that had been sketched in the middle of the back cover—one that made me gasp when I saw it.

White roses.

I stared at it. Then I put back 1999 and pulled out 1921 again. There on the back was the same sketch of the same white roses. Each of the books I'd looked at had a sketch of roses imprinted on the back. My mouth dropped. I ran my finger atop the last roses, tracing the image.

Sharon was staring at me when I looked up. "I was hoping you'd catch that," she said, her voice barely above a whisper.

"White roses?"

She nodded, reaching for a tissue. "They symbolize friendship because a lot of students leave here with some of the best friends they'll ever have." She dabbed her nose gently, but her eyes gripped mine. "David's always been a friend to me, too, Ms. Lightfoot. He's talked about you since he met you in Denver, so I feel like I can trust you. I'm worried about what's going to—"

Ralph's door squeaked open. She dove back into her desk, picking up her pencil and erasing something with manic deliberation. Her boss looked dryly at me.

"I told her I was leaving. She didn't have to get nasty about it," I said. A smirk formed on his face, and I brushed past the yearbooks toward the door.

Outside, the air was fresh, and I walked slowly down the library steps, looking across the expanse of the campus. I wondered what the place would have been like a hundred years ago, or even when it had first been established two hundred some years ago. I tried to imagine young seminarians and theology students hurrying to class, inspired by the verses and mission everywhere they looked. From the Latin inscriptions above the library to the Bible verses and roses still carved on the sides and entrances of the buildings, it wouldn't have been hard to remember why they were here. And I couldn't help but wonder what New York City would have been like if the services and programs Frank Cherrinard wanted for the poor had been carried out.

But times had obviously changed. No one seemed to pay attention to much of the religious heritage that marked such a majestic campus. No one looked like a tourist, gawking or pointing at the symbols or verses as they passed. And no one that I'd noticed or talked to seemed interested in anything more than the academic disciplines and rewards that came from attending a prestigious university like Regal. Yes, it was a lively atmosphere I watched as I walked — students and professors in animated discussions, ideas perused like books in the library — but how would this place have looked if it had retained its founding mission? Or if the Cherrinard endowment had been . . .

David had talked about me since he'd met me in Denver?

I wandered over to the security guard, who pointed me to a building that looked like a small castle amid the stately academic halls. A few minutes later, I found the door to the president's office and walked in. Leather furniture and mahogany desks sat elegantly throughout the room, with several ornate doors facing opposite portraits of past presidents mounted on the walls. The administrative assistant—a perky young woman with neat black hair and perfect makeup—laughed when I asked to see the president. She stopped laughing when I told her what it was about.

Instead, she ordered me to follow her through one of the doors and down another fancy hallway to an office marked "General Counsel" on the outside. She pointed to a chair for me, disappeared for a few minutes, then reappeared with a tall older man in a three-piece suit. A bright yellow handkerchief, matching his tie, peeked out of his coat pocket. He carried a manila folder in one hand and a ballpoint pen in the other. The assistant introduced him only as the senior assistant to the general counsel and left us alone.

"You're inquiring about the Mr. and Mrs. Frank Cherrinard Endowment for Religious Training?" His voice was low and bored.

"Quick question. Is it true that the Cherrinard's gift was . . . a whopper?"

He smirked. "It was generous for the time."

"Probably gained a lot of interest by now, yes?" Another smirk, so I kept going. "But didn't it have some sort of condition tied to it? Something about using the money only for the study and integration of Christian doctrine for all sorts of programs on campus and in the city?" The man shifted slightly but showed little notice. "Anyway, that's what a library employee named David Rockley told me. He seems to think that the Cherrinard endowment hasn't been used as it was intended, and when Mr. Rockley raised it with his superiors and trustees, no one seemed too interested."

He shrugged.

"Here's the funny part: He claims he sent a four-page letter to President Coen but got only a tiny little one-sentence response from your office here, the general counsel. That can't be right, can it?"

"We deal with many issues each day."

"I'll bet. But did you really say it'd be too difficult to produce the information about the fund?" My reporter's notebook rested in my palm, a pen in my hand. This suddenly felt more important than any story I'd worked on.

"No. I believe the letter to Mr. Rockley actually said, 'It would be extremely burdensome for the university to produce any detailed information.' I should know; I wrote it myself."

I scribbled his comment and went for broke. "Yeah? Then why do you suppose Mr. Rockley would tell me he found evidence that confirms the university has misused those funds, even illegally?" He sighed as if I were clearly a bother in his day. I pressed him.

"Like property acquisition, stock options, you know, things like that. He even thinks the president and some of the other administrators dipped into the fund to redecorate their offices, maybe even apartments. Can you imagine?"

"No."

Judging from the looks of this office, I wondered if he'd heard me correctly. "No? But Mr. Rockley used terms like *embezzlement* and *fraud* as if they might apply to—"

"I am aware of the legal terms, none of which can be applied in any way to the integrity of Regal University."

"What if Mr. Rockley's documentation confirms the misuse of such an endowment?"

He held up a hand. "You must understand that occasionally

we have a fanatic who comes along and, for some reason, isn't happy with the University. He moves on." The man yanked the sleeves of his suit and stepped away from me.

"He moves on?"

"Actually, this one in particular . . . resigned. Little wonder, since, you have to admit, he made some ludicrous claims."

I stepped toward him. "David Rockley resigned?"

"According to the memo."

"But his boss said he's on vaca—"

The hand went up again. "These types can be unpredictable." He thumbed through his folder and pulled out a letter. "Yes, it seems Mr. Rockley submitted his resignation this morning." He held it out for me to see David's signature at the bottom before sliding it back in its place. "I can appreciate your concern, but I'm sure the *Clarion* has more relevant matters to pursue." An eyebrow peaked. "Good-bye."

I watched the nameless senior assistant to the general counsel pass the leather chairs and paintings, but only one thought occurred to me as I did: David Rockley was no fanatic.

::Chapter Thirteen

'd known fanatics. A few had wandered in and out of our home growing up, hair disheveled, baggy wrinkled clothes, militant glares in their eyes that sometimes mystified my brothers and me. They'd rarely talked about subjects we were used to hearing from Mom and Pop's other friends, things like where they'd grown up or how many lovefests or protests they'd attended with our parents in the old days. These were peaceful enough hippie-fanatics, but they seemed hypnotized by another world, one marked only by extremes. Eventually, they'd find the MacLaughlin household not quite radical enough and wander off to the next commune.

Since I'd been on the religion beat, I'd seen a different side of fanatics. Some screamed condemnations at Wiccan rallies. Others abused immigrants in the name of religion. Or evicted old people to develop the property where they lived and called it God's will . . . or progress as if they were the same thing. The fanatics of my youth had been harmless, though admittedly a little weird. Whatever the form, one thing was clear this morning: David was not one of them.

I left the lawyer's leather office. The temperature outside had dropped, turning the February sky a pale gray that looked like it might unload at any moment. But I didn't feel cold. If someone had asked me, I wasn't sure how I would have described what had happened in my soul. I did know I was more relaxed and more focused than I had been in a long time: strangely warmed, but with a taste ten times better than hot mocha.

I walked beneath the gargoyles and rounded the corner into the Hallway of World Religions, each professor's office advertising its creeds like mini-billboards. My eyes scanned the mottos, icons, and symbols of the department's spiritual flavors: Indo-Tibetan Studies, Jewish history, the ancient Mediterranean, even modern Western sects such as Latter-Day Saints and Jehovah's Witnesses, which I hadn't noticed the last time I was here.

I wondered what subjects the hall might have housed when Regal was first formed, and I imagined those early Protestants scratching their heads at today's religious offerings if they were walking with me now. Other questions jumped out at me as well—When did this shift begin? What else was happening at the time?—stirring in me so much curiosity that I hardly noticed the vending machines when I walked by. I bobbed in and out of a group of students, came to the office door with the earth-people poster, and tapped.

Evan Hartman's eyes widened when he opened it, as if mine wasn't the face he'd been expecting to see. Over the next few seconds, his expression fluctuated between apparent irritation and surprise before finally landing on politeness.

"Miss Lightfoot. How nice to see you this—"

"I'm sorry to barge in like this, Professor, but could I get your expert opinion on something?"

He grinned. The bald-headed man returned to his desk and pointed to a brown metal chair for me. His office was messier than the last time I'd visited, only this morning there were also several recent copies of the *Clarion* atop two piles of papers and folders in the corner. I noticed my Wiccan articles.

"You did a good job with those," he said, his voice nasal as if he'd been fighting a cold. "Griffin and the others were thrilled. I think we'll see some movement at the station, so to speak, as a result." He reached for one of his mugs and slurped. Reginald, his pet gerbil, was rolled up in a brown little fur ball, asleep in its cage.

"Ah, I don't know what to say," I said as I pulled out my notebook. "But I am wondering if you could help me with something else. I'm trying to understand a little about the religious heritage of the university."

"I'm a professor in ancient religions, so I'm not sure how I can —"

"Just need a little perspective. Regal got its start as a Protestant college, didn't it?"

He nodded and stroked his shaggy beard.

"Which denomination was it again?"

He fiddled with his cup. "I believe it was Anglican, or what we would know today as Episcopalian."

"That's it. And do you think the university founders were pretty serious about their Christian mission?"

"Most men in New York were at that time."

I lodged my elbows on my knees, resting my chin on my knuckles. "So what do you think happened, Professor? Why the shift?"

Professor Hartman set his cup gently on his desk and folded his fingers together across his lap. He looked as if he'd been asked a question that was either so big he'd never have enough time to explain the answer, or one that was so small he'd been insulted. I couldn't tell which. He coughed.

"Honestly? I think things got too easy."

I squinted. I wasn't sure what I'd been expecting to hear, but I knew that wasn't it. "Excuse me?"

"Let's re-create the scenario, shall we? You've left your country, where you were persecuted for believing that the Bible said something altogether different from what the government of the time legally allowed you to believe. In this case, the Church of England had gotten a little, oh you know, power hungry. So you conquer an unforgiving ocean, arrive in a hostile territory, and then turn around a few years later to have to fight the very people you'd just fled. You with me?"

I nodded.

"But you win the battle. Barely. And so you set up things the way you want them because, doggone it, you've earned it. You start your own school in your own way. You enjoy the freedoms of this new and young country and decide you're going to shape it how you think is best. The problem is, everyone else in New York is thinking the same thing—merchants, bankers, capitalists of all kinds—and the snowball gains momentum."

This was sounding familiar.

He glanced at Reginald, who was still sleeping, then back to me. "You asked what I think happened? A new religion was formed, that's what, and they later called it the Industrial Revolution. Progress moved so fast it made people's heads spin. Factories produced machines that made life more convenient, more comfortable than ever. Some of the University's own professors were responsible for such advances and inventions. Soon people began to question those early beliefs. After all, why would you need God anymore when you could create your own life and it's better than it had been?" He ran his hand over his shiny skull, then down his beard, as a slight shadow of mischief formed in his eyes. "To keep up with the progress, I suppose Regal simply adjusted its beliefs and its mission. Does that answer your question?"

"Sort of. I mean, I guess you're saying it's hard to serve two masters, aren't you?"

"Exactly." Reginald's head rose, but Hartman continued. "And certainly no one would dispute the fact that such advances have made our lives better. Today, as then, Regal is at the center of it all."

I leaned back in my chair and looked at his chaotic office. "So if our lives are so much better, why do you suppose people still believe in such old religions?" I pointed to the picture on his desk of the professor with two women. "People like your friends there or Griffin Lewis and Lady Crystal. Even you and me. Why do we still need to believe in God—whatever our version of him is—if everything's so good outside?"

I glanced at the books stacked on his shelves, with titles ranging from *Pagan Idols for Today* and *Ancient Paths for Contentment* to *Spiritual Transcendence for the Twenty-First Century*. He cleared his throat and looked toward the window as if there were an answer out there somewhere he would find if he looked long enough.

"Humans are complex beings, Joan, forgive me, Jonna. I don't need to tell you that." He angled his head back my direction, and I had the impression he was actually taking my question seriously. "Besides, religion has always provided a moral compass for people, tools for knowing right from wrong. The problem is we haven't always followed them very well."

"That's for sure. I don't know about you, Professor, but I stink at following rules or doing what I should do." I smiled, and to my surprise, he did too. "I need help. Every day. Living, breathing help that doesn't change with the times, you know?"

Reginald awoke and started running circles in his cage. Hartman looked admiringly at his pet before turning over his wrist to check the time: 10:50 a.m. His face grew serious again. He collected some files and a notebook.

"Could I ask you just one more question?" I dropped my pen and notebook into my bag and stood to leave. "Do you think Frank Cherrinard was a traditional Protestant?"

"Actually, I believe his diaries confirm that he called himself a devoted follower of Jesus Christ."

"You've read them?"

"A fascinating case study." He rose from his chair and fingered the texts on his shelf until he found what he was looking for: a small frail book hidden behind the others. He pulled it down and opened the cover to show me the title page: *The Diaries of a Protestant Businessman in The Year 1833 of Our Lord and Savior Jesus Christ*, by Frank Cherrinard, Regal College, Class of 1820.

"It's a reprint of the original, after he'd established his endowment. Friends and partners of his business apparently kept it in print." He held the book as though it were an unusual artifact or fossil and he was thrilled and humbled to hold it. "I came across two copies at the rare-book store around the corner, shortly after I'd received the Cherrinard grant. Of course, I gave one to the archives and kept this one for my own collection. It's a gem, don't you think?"

I took a breath. "I think it's amazing. Is it true, then, Cherrinard worried that all those advances might steer Regal's mission off track?"

He shrugged, returned the diary to its spot, and rested his hands across his chest. "He was a man of his times, so naturally his Christian faith guided his decisions."

"But how do you think he'd have felt if he knew the money he gave was being used to study witches and pagan religions?"

Professor Hartman opened the door. "God only knows." He picked up his files and his jacket. "I've got a class now, but I'll look forward to your next story on the Wiccan movement."

He locked his door and wobbled down the Corridor of Beliefs until he rounded the corner. The thought struck me that Hartman seemed to study religions like a doctor might diseases, hoping someday to find a cure while yielding to the fact that some people would never be able to shake it. I'd been surprised at our interaction this morning, partly because he seemed to view me now as an advocate for the Wiccans. But as I walked slowly past the offices of his colleagues, I found another surprise stirring inside me: I felt sorry for the man. Not pity or disdain, but genuine sorrow — the kind you feel when someone's just received a diagnosis at the hospital and you know there's nothing you can do.

Then I saw the vending machine. I studied my options, dropped in some quarters, and punched the button. I waited. Nothing. I punched it again. Still nothing. I pressed the money-return lever and heard the clink of coins at the same time I saw the package of plain M&M's drop into the bin. I chuckled. Free chocolate might not have qualified as a bona fide miracle on any other day. On this particular morning, however, in this place, I recognized it as a reminder that most of life was filled with gifts we didn't earn or create on our own. I popped a handful of the candies into my mouth and left the quarters. Maybe Professor Hartman would find them.

Across campus, the sidewalks were busy with students and

teachers scattered in a dozen directions. The hallowed markers and buildings behind them now seemed a lonely backdrop to their modern-day interests. Though Hartman had read Cherrinard's diary, I doubted many others had. I didn't remember David saying anything about the book, but he had said he'd found enough other evidence to confirm what Hartman had said about Cherrinard. Both he and David had identified young Frank as a devoted follower of Jesus Christ who wanted future students and academics—like those I was now walking beside—to consider the author of his faith as more than another man in history. He seemed to want them to know that learning was based on more than distant philosophies or ancient traditions; it was the life of Jesus that inspired not only the founding of this university but also the talents and contributions of people across the ages. Even modern believers who'd once relied on their parents' faith but now owned it for themselves—like me.

I waved to the security guards, caught the crosstown bus back through Central Park, and skipped down the steps to the subway on the Upper West Side. The midmorning train had filtered out most of the rush-hour congestion, so I easily found a seat. Diagonal from me, a young couple rested on each other's shoulders and clutched each other's hands. They were quiet and sleepy, but both wore tiny grins across their faces as if there were no happier place they could be. Even after they yawned, the grin didn't go away.

I yawned too and closed my eyes. Though M&Ms melted inside my cheeks, I felt a sting in my soul for the ways I'd dismissed David in the past. I thought of when I'd first met him at The Pub of Saint Agnes in Denver, then of his visit to New Orleans, and even last weekend with bagels and sushi and an introduction to the cathedral. Each memory hurt in the grip of hindsight; I had been so busy with my own ridiculous fantasies about romance that I'd been blind to David's kindness and character. I knew that now. But that didn't make him magically reappear.

The train jerked, pulling the couple across from me closer together as I shot to my feet. The doors slid apart and I all but sprinted through the tunnel and out onto the street at the corner of Seventy-second Street and Broadway. I got my bearings and pulled out my phone. My sister-in-law answered.

"Sarah? It's me Jonna." I stepped back from the crowd and into the doorway of a store that was under construction. Yellow tape reached across the entrance. I leaned against the wall.

"Hey, you okay?"

"I owe you—and Luke and especially the boys—an apology. I got a little—no, a lot—off track. Sorry." My throat clogged thinking of my nephews.

"But are you okay?"

"I . . . think so."

She paused. I stared at the sidewalk, my eyes misty, as I listened then to the softness in my ear: "Good. You know what? Last night during bedtime prayers, Luke and I sat on the edge of the boys' beds. We started reading to them, but they insisted we stop and pray . . . for Aunt Jonna. Garrett was so worried he asked Jesus to save your hair!" A small burst of laughter came through the phone. "He looked up at us, dead serious, and said, 'I got the words mixed up, but God knew what I meant, right?'"

We snorted over the need for my frizzy salvation as I stepped aside for a guy in a hard hat. He hollered something to some other workers. Sarah asked me where I was.

"Actually, I've just come from Regal. David's boss claims

he's on vacation, but the general counsel said he resigned . . . this morning." I scooted closer to the building wall, away from the passing construction team. "I don't know how legitimate it was, but he showed me the letter he said was from David. Have you heard from him?"

"Not yet. His dad doesn't seem to know where he is either."

"You called his dad?"

"Luke did. Nice man, but he didn't know much more than the rest of us. Just that his son probably had some perfectly good reason for missing work."

That was a relief. I exhaled and felt the support of the wall. "Sarah, when David called you on Sunday from the police station, he didn't happen to say which precinct, did he?"

"Only that he was in his own neighborhood. Hang on a minute." I heard the phone smack against something hard and the sound of footsteps on hardwood floors. A door creaked and then there was the fuzz of the extension being picked up, all while horns honked and crews hammered by me. "I found it. His would be Precinct 20, I think, and it would be around Eightieth or close by. Why?"

"I thought I'd stop by, see if I can learn anything."

"Good idea. Luke and I will keep checking around. Let's talk later."

I dropped my phone into my pocket and spun around to head back uptown. I passed the Manhattan Movie Complex, then an independent mystery-book store called The Poisoned Pen and made a mental note to come back when I had some time off, especially when I saw Best Bagels beside it. A few blocks up, past a dozen shoe stores, bodegas, and cafés of the entire world's cuisines, I began to formulate a pitch to Skip about his alma mater. This was a story I now had enough details to report, even without David to confirm things. Of course, talking with him would help provide clearer direction, leading me to specific verification of the issues in this story. I picked up the pace and rounded the corner on Eightieth. No precinct. I walked another to Eighty-first — still no precinct — and up another to Eighty-second, where finally I saw the gray brick building with still grayer block letters on the side: NYPD Precinct 20.

It was a noisy office — conversations flying, phones ringing, doors slamming. I approached a chubby older man in a police uniform who was filling out a form behind the counter. I showed him my press pass, but he didn't seem impressed. I told him I was inquiring about a burglary that occurred Saturday night on Ninety-fifth Street, between Amsterdam and Broadway, and needed to confirm what the resident of the apartment had reported. He sighed and told me to wait. He walked across the room to a desk and dug through a drawer, shaking his head and mumbling as he did. He wandered back empty-handed, except for a stick of gum he was shoving into his mouth.

"No break-ins and no burglaries on Saturday night." He began flipping through the form he'd been looking at when I'd first interrupted him. I blinked.

"What?"

"No burglaries. Zip. It was a good night for the Upper West Side."

"But a source of mine said he'd come here on Sunday, said someone had broken into his apartment on Saturday night." I gripped the edge of the counter. The officer sighed again.

"Where'd your source live again?" He cracked the gum as he said it.

"Ninety-fifth Street. So this would be the right precinct to—"

"Yup"—crack—"but I'm tellin' ya, nobody reported nothin' about a burglary in an apartment on Saturday night. Or Sunday."

"Are you sure?"

"What, I don't look sure enough for ya?" Crack. He pummeled his gaze at me, but somehow it bounced off like it had hit a shield.

"You look more than sure, Officer, um, let's see, H-a-r-v-e-y-P-a-l-l-o-w-s-k-i, right?" I studied his name tag as I jotted down each letter in my notebook. The cracking stopped. "It's just I'm positive there was a burglary on Saturday night and that the tenant—a Mr. David Rockley—reported it here Sunday morning. So maybe the report was, uh, misplaced? Those things happen all the time in my office, so I'm wondering if—"

The chubby man turned around and walked to an office. An older female officer emerged from it and blasted toward me.

"You the one inquiring about the break-in on Saturday?"

"Right. My source says he reported the burglary on Sunday, and I just wanted to confirm for the *Clarion* that—"

"We have no such report." She stood expressionless across from me. The gum-cracking officer returned to his file, and the woman planted her fist on her hip. "Now, anything else?"

"Yes. I think I might need to report a missing person."

She looked bored. "How long?"

"Since Monday—make that Sunday afternoon. That seems to be the last time anyone talked with him. But none of his friends know where he is, and his boss says he's on vacation, except, well, someone else says he resigned so—"

"Can't help you. If an employer has confirmed his vacation, you'll need to come back at the end of that period—if he's still missing."

"But what if—"

She picked up a pen, pulled a piece of paper from the recycle bin, and scribbled.

"Here's the city's phone number for the Missing Persons Squad. That'd be a good place to start. They'll take it from there. Now, are we finished?"

"Nope. One more thing: Would your precinct happen to patrol Regal University?"

"Only when we have to." With that, she thumped back to her office, shaking her head as if there were a fly nearby. I heard the gum-cracking officer grunt as she bristled by. Then he shuffled his forms together on the counter. He stopped moving altogether, though, when I pushed my business card into his hand.

"So in case anyone remembers where that report is, please give me a call, okay, Officer Pallowski?" I tapped the counter to punctuate my request, smiled as politely as I could, and found the door. It was almost noon, and because I hadn't yet made it into the newsroom this morning and didn't particularly feel like walking back to the subway, I opted for a cab. I stepped off the curb and put up my hand. Four yellow taxis with passengers passed before a vacant one stopped in front of me.

I buckled up and watched the city swirl by as we drove slowly in the traffic down Broadway, toward the theatres of Times Square and, beyond that, the garment district. At each stoplight along the way, I'd see a brown-haired man about David's age and height and feel a jab of worry. I'd stare closely, in case it was David, and scour the next set of faces when I realized it wasn't. I pulled out my cell phone and called directory assistance for David's number. No answer. Why hadn't he checked in with his friends? Would he really have resigned? And why didn't the police have his report? Was he safe?

"Lord, have mercy," I said aloud, whispering the words but letting them go freely—rather, sincerely—for the first time in months. "Yes, God, please help David." I spoke so loudly I noticed the cabdriver's eyes in the rearview mirror. I meant it. I prayed with all my MacLaughlin bones—and some of my newly garnered independent faith—that David would have some perfectly good reason for missing work, as his father said. I wanted him to be right. And as the taxi pulled to the entrance of the *Clarion*, I knew I couldn't stop hoping.

Hannah was at a press conference when I checked her desk. I left a message on her phone updating her on the events of the morning and telling her to see me ASAP when she returned. Once I arrived at my desk, I pushed the mail to the side and realized I didn't have any tangible evidence about Regal's schemes. Though I knew it existed, having held it in my hands over sushi and even this morning in Hartman's office, I'd need to find it somewhere else to verify the story.

I clicked to the *Clarion*'s morgue on my computer, but the back issues dated only as far back as 1877, when New York's third daily paper began. Though the *Clarion* had mostly been in circulation since 1877, give or take a few tough years, the current technology staff had managed to scan most of those old issues from the actual morgue into an electronic version, with easy access for all employees. I wasn't sure it helped me today, though, since it had been almost fifty years since Cherrinard had graduated.

Still, I figured I had nothing to lose, so once I was into the e-morgue, I typed "Frank Cherrinard" and clicked "search." Nothing. I typed only his last name with the word "endowment" and got a short list from about 1950 through 1993 associated with religious conferences, charities, and events throughout the city. That gave me another idea. Maybe it would help to know what the world of religion might have looked like even fifty years after Cherrinard established his endowment. I didn't have to scroll far to find out. Hartman was right: Cherrinard might have been a man of his times, but he also would have fit in well beyond his years. Even up until the early-nineteenth century, Christianity had been the public language and apparent value system of the times. There were stories on church services and prayer rallies calling citizens to ask "the Lord's blessings on the harvest." The more articles I read, the more the *Clarion* itself seemed like a Christian publication.

But by the early 1910s and into the 1920s, stories began to appear that had a lot more to do with factories and inventions than with congregations and prayers. There was a noticeable shift in headlines alone, but it still didn't give me the evidence I needed. I typed "Regal University" in the search engine and began to see that Regal's own change of focus began to turn around during the 1920s. The headlines began to report the university's sudden acquisition of property, the expansion of the campus, the creation of new departments, and even the increase in salaries for administrators. By 1941, one article reported the development of a "new, broader world religions program" to replace the "outdated Christian history and theology department." I printed out a few of the stories and began to piece together a loose timeline of Regal's changes—recorded directly in my own newspaper's morgue.

Journalism was the first draft of history. In this case, I was piecing together the second. I got out my yellow highlighter and began to underline specific markers on the timeline. This was at least a starting point to show Skip.

Hannah tapped me on the shoulder. I'd been so absorbed in the city's history that I hadn't noticed five hours had gone by. And though lunchtime was over long ago, I wasn't hungry. Hannah pulled up a chair beside me as I showed her the articles. She tsked and nodded as I explained each, jetting her jaw back and forth as though she were chewing on the information. When she laid the last article on my desk, she tapped my shoulder again and sighed.

"Don't forget I've got the notes from your sushi night," Hannah said quietly. "You can use them as backup to outline the story, because face it, Lightfoot, you're going to need it. And you better hope your man reappears with a wad of paper to prove all this." She rose from her chair.

"What do you mean?"

"Are you kidding? Regal is New York. Coen and his board practically run the city. They're buddies with the mayor, the police chief, and who knows who else. I wouldn't be surprised if Walter Wood knew—" Hannah stopped herself. "I'll check it out." With that, she was out of my cubicle and gone, leaving only a slight scent of perfume behind as evidence of her presence.

I shuffled through the copies of articles on my desk and glanced at the vase filled with white roses. I had to keep going. I knew it was risky, pitching a story to Skip at the end of the day when he was putting finishing touches on other pieces and fighting for space with the advertisers and copy editors. But this was too important not to.

He sat as he always did at his desk, calm and focused with a stack of papers in front of him. Wearing a pale blue shirt under a tweed jacket with elbow patches, Skip looked less like a New York editor and more like a professor this afternoon. Even his red pen matched the image. I knocked anyway and he waved me in.

He propped his hands behind his head and looked quizzically at me. I gulped and sank in the chair.

"Lightfoot, you okay?"

I felt warm. "Sure. Why?"

"Can't put my finger on it, but you look . . . different." He leaned back slightly, his hands still hidden behind his neck. I scrunched my hair and shrugged off his observation. "Anyway, what's up?"

I stared at the clippings on my lap. "It's kind of hard to believe."

"It always is, right?"

If it hadn't been my gentle, supportive editor sitting before me, whom I'd always known as fair and respectful of all things newsworthy, I might have thought it was another man who'd made the remark. The Skip I knew was careful with his words, so his comment surprised me. It also firmed my resolve.

"What if I told you I had proof that a local institution has been taking money from two of its constituents for years, money the pair intended for one specific mission, but the leaders of that institution had ignored them?"

"I'd say it sounds familiar. Sounds like the story you broke in Denver with that creepy guy who called himself a minister and all but enslaved immigrants. Remember?"

I hadn't thought of it that way, but Skip was right. The similarities were obvious.

"Except this is sort of the opposite." I picked up my pencil and scratched behind my ear. "This involves a genuine minister and a whole group of folks who never wanted to listen to him."

He pulled his arms back in and placed them across his chest, signaling that he was ready for more. So I went for it. I told him the story of this faithful Christian man who'd done so well in the city that he and his wife set up an endowment at a local institution they'd come to love, but the man had placed very specific conditions behind the administering of it. I told him that this prominent organization had willingly taken the gift, but ignored those conditions, though was now claiming it had properly disseminated the funds "in the name of progress." That, however, was stealing.

"It's fraud. Embezzlement." I took a breath. "I know, it's more bad news for religion, Skip, but maybe the bad has to happen before the good stories can come." I held my eyes on my editor's and waited.

"Okay. So which church is it this time? Or is it a synagogue?"

I shook my head.

"Don't tell me it's an entire diocese? Because that would be depressing if—"

"It's Regal, Skip."

He adjusted his glasses and ran his hand across his beard. "Regal? As in the university?" It wasn't really a question as much as a way of processing information. "I thought I told you to let that go."

"You did."

"Uh-huh. So now you seem to think there is a story here, a religion story about a reputable university?" He picked up his red pen and tapped it against the papers on his desk.

"It sounds crazy, I know. But even Professor Hartman

confirmed for me that—"

"You talked with Hartman about this?"

"About the history of Regal first, you know, its religious heritage, and then about Cherrinard. He's actually read the guy's diaries."

"He's a scholar. He does things like that. So what?"

"So he had no problem calling Frank Cherrinard a devoted follower of Jesus Christ, which I thought was a big deal for a pagan scholar. He even said that Regal had digressed from its original mission, and now I think—"

"So what?" His voice was so loud and firm I recoiled in my chair.

"What do you mean, so what?"

"So who cares? So a university redirected some donor's money? Did anyone die in the process?"

"Well, no, but—"

"Anyone physically harmed?"

"No."

"Then why will anyone care that some well-meaning Christian from a hundred and fifty years ago gave some money to the university and they put it, I don't know, in sidewalks or new offices?"

"Why? Because they didn't do what they were supposed to."

Skip shrugged. "Who ever does what they're supposed to do, Jonna? Come on."

He looked the same as my editor. His voice was identical, but the words—the words were not . . . his. The other Skip had always been adamant about upholding the truth, about pursuing it and then reporting it—no matter what. For his sake—and for

David's—I pushed forward.

"There are a few people left in this world, Skip, whose faith still matters to them. And who still insist that it helps them do the right thing."

"Ah." He rubbed his beard as if he'd been charmed by the idea. "Okay, then. Where's the proof of this . . . corporate stealing?"

"Proof? There's plenty. Documents, letters, forms, you name it. Even articles from the *Clarion* morgue confirm it."

Skip stood up. He walked to the door and gently closed it before returning to his seat. He took a sip of water from a plastic bottle and scratched his head. Then he folded his hands together.

"Lightfoot, you know where I stand as a journalist. I'd be the first to print a story with facts and proof that exposes the clowns who think they can get away with playing God, but I'm afraid this doesn't qualify. See, it wouldn't matter how many letters, copies, or actual pieces of documentation you find about Regal."

"But that's how we can prove—"

"I can't print it, Jonna."

"Why?"

"Maybe a better way to say it is, I *won't* print it."

::Chapter Fourteen

I felt like a snowman whose head had just been knocked off. Even when I stood to leave Skip's office, the room was still spinning. I walked backward toward the door, still centering on my editor as if that would help my balance. He always had before.

"It's Walter Wood, isn't it, Skip? He's putting pressure on you to—"

"No, Jonna. I mean, well, yes, things are a little . . . uncertain. But that's not why I won't print this." He rose from behind his desk, gripping his bottle of water as he came toward me.

I pulled open the door. "Then why?"

Skip stopped at the doorway, cleared his throat, and adjusted his glasses. He looked at the ceiling, then out the window as though he were forming a sentence in his head. I waited, feeling the awkward tension that hung between us, the first I could remember with my boss. Even my palms grew sweaty. Finally, his eyes landed on mine: "Why?" he asked, gentle as always. "Because there are some stories the public doesn't care about knowing. This is one of them."

I stepped back. "What? Did you just say—?"

"Yes. There are some stories the public doesn't need to read."

"Since when?"

"Since . . . today, at least."

Now it was Skip who'd lost his head. The champion of the people's right to know was suddenly discriminating? The man who'd taught me to get to the bottom of every story so readers could decide for themselves was now denying them that option?

I stood frozen in front of him. "But what about the people who—?"

He held up his hand like the general-counsel man had and grinned. "Trust me on this one, Lightfoot. I said I won't print it and I won't. Understood? Besides, there are plenty of legitimate stories out there waiting for you to . . ."

I knew he was still speaking because I saw his lips moving, but no words connected to my ears. The language had stopped making sense when I'd heard him say, "I won't print it." Even after he hurried into another office and out of sight, Skip's presence lingered like a ghost. I stood dazed for a few long minutes, and I didn't know what to make of the editor who'd always guided my reporting, who'd supported every story I'd written and taught me most of what I'd learned about the noble profession of journalism. I staggered down the empty hallway, still stunned by the realization that this same man had just killed the one story I knew was as important than any I'd reported so far. Maybe more so.

It seemed I wasn't the only person who was changing these days.

My eyes were stinging when I finally made it back to my desk. The newsroom looked fuzzy, and now it also seemed as if someone had turned up the volume during the short amount of time I'd been in Skip's office. The sounds of the end of a typical day, those I usually welcomed as the energy of getting out the news—editors hollering, phones ringing, and reporters frantically typing—had turned into a grating noise that hurt my ears. Today it was too loud to mean anything exciting.

I put on my cap and parka and was a few steps outside my cubicle when my desk phone rang. I deliberated. I wanted to get out of here, as far from Skip and shattered images as I could, to stay as focused and warm as I had been at Saint John's. Even so, it was that same memory that moved me back to my cubicle so that by the fourth ring, I was on the phone.

Sharon's voice was breathy. She was crying. When I asked her what was wrong, she collected herself and whispered as if she were in a part of the library where you weren't supposed to be talking, let alone on the phone.

"David's been fired, Jonna."

She sighed into the phone. "I just talked to a friend in HR. He's not on vacation."

"The general counsel told me he resigned."

"It was either resign or be terminated . . . for insubordination. Can you believe it?" She sniffed. "The nicest employee they've ever had, and look what's happened."

I sank into my chair as Sharon explained how President Coen and the trustees pressured her boss either to let David go or risk losing his job as well. When they'd received David's letter about his research and about how the Cherrinards had not just requested but insisted that their money be used exclusively for theological education and ministries for the city's poor, things turned ugly.

"They brought in general counsel to get rid of the problem. It took them a few months, a lot of meetings and discussions, pressuring David to resign, but he refused," she whispered. "Until finally, when they threatened to fire all of us, he turned in his letter . . . sometime yesterday. But I shouldn't be telling you. I can't afford to lose my . . ."

"You did the right thing, Sharon." The word reverberated in my head, and I was instantly conscious that there actually was a right and a wrong way to approach this. I knew why: The truth had long ago been established and set such conflict in motion. I pulled out a pen and wrote down the details Sharon had just revealed.

She sighed but seemed to find some resolve. "I wanted to get you copies of his research, but the files in his desk are empty." Though Sharon had seen some of the letters and forms David had found, she said they were no longer around the library office. And there were only a few selected documents stored in the electronic files under the Cherrinard endowment. It was as if the others no longer existed.

"Did you see David?" I thought of his face, his glasses and goatee.

"Just for a second. They're packing up his office now."

"Holy cow, they don't waste any time, do they?" The photo of my brothers beside my computer caught my eye. "Was he okay?"

"As usual, he was more concerned with how I was feeling than what was happening to him." She coughed a dainty little cough and whispered so I barely heard her: "I told him you came by . . . Oh, sorry, Jonna, I've got to go." The line went dead.

I hung up and scribbled a few words across the top of my notebook: truth, insisted, electronic. I thought about calling Luke and Sarah but decided to wait until I got home. I wanted to get out of the office, so I pulled my folder of old *Clarion* clips and tucked them into my bag along with my notebook. When I turned around to leave, I almost ran straight into the one person I did not want to see: Skip. He was standing beside my cubicle.

"So we're clear?" he said. "You know what you need to do, right?"

I pulled back my shoulders and gripped my bag. "More than ever, Skip." I hurried around him, waved above my head, and pushed the door to the stairs. I reached for my cell phone and left Sarah a message about David.

By the time I'd made it outside, I'd found my pack of cigarettes in the bottom of my bag. The winter air was cold and rugged, a perfect temperature for a smoke. I put one to my lips and rummaged for a match, but as I did, the flavor shocked me—like it had the very first time I smoked—and I coughed and choked and snatched the thing from my mouth. It looked like any other cigarette, but something about this one made me cringe. Shivers shot up my spine and into my neck. I zipped up my parka and found the nearest public garbage bin on the sidewalk in front of the *Clarion* building. I smashed the cigarettes in my fist and dropped them into the trash.

Lee Cheung was coming out of the office as I turned toward the sidewalk crowd. He waved for me to catch up with him and we blended in with the commuters rushing toward the subway.

"Hey, Jonna, whoa. It's funny to see you, cuz, like, just as I was, you know, lockin' up in the mail room and I saw a package for you." He flipped his baseball cap around so that the bill was covering his neck. "I'll bring it by first thing in the morning, cool?"

"Cool," I repeated as we turned the corner. Up ahead, I spied a hot-dog vendor—a tall African man who reminded me of Big Wendall the beignet maker in New Orleans—and remembered how hungry I was. I asked Lee about lunch.

"What? But, it's dinnertime, yeah?"

"Oh yeah. Well, how about if you let me buy you a hot dog?"

He bobbed his cap forward, then back. "Cool."

We stood on the corner of Seventh and Thirty-sixth, squirting mustard across two German franks and smearing pickle relish on the bread. Lee talked about his week and how he was on his way to a night class at the Jesus Center that was "cooler than dope." I laughed, not really sure what he was talking about, and bit at the same time a straight line of yellow descended onto my red parka. He laughed too but grabbed a napkin for me from the vendor, who by this time was also laughing. We could all see our breaths in the frigid air, but it didn't really matter. Something about laughing and eating German hot dogs, sold by an African vendor, with a Chinese street kid on a corner in the fashion district of New York City was a curious reprieve from the stinging encounter I'd just left. None of it was normal, and that felt good on its own.

Nicotine didn't compare. I was even thinking about buying another frank and would have if Lee hadn't been eager to get to the Chinatown Jesus Center.

When we arrived at the steps to the subway, Lee started toward the downtown trains while I stepped toward the uptown. But first I reached for his hand.

"Could you do me a favor when you see Danny Bro?"

"Totally."

"Could you let him know I won't be able to write his story after all? There's just too much going on right now and—"

"He'll be down with that. See ya."

Lee was through the turnstile in no time, and I was heading

home to Harlem, my mind a mix of images and thoughts. I waited on a semi-crowded platform for the uptown train, watching mothers push their children in strollers and listening to two young men beating bongos as I wondered where in the city David might be. I tried his cell phone, but no answer. Again. A prayer formed on my lips. Though the cadence of the drummers echoed around me, drowning out even the tiniest of sounds, it didn't matter. I knew my plea was heard above the city's rhythms.

A few beats later, as headlights approached the tunnel and the train stopped, I thought of my editor standing by his office door. His response still stunned me in a way I'd never expected. The subway doors spread apart, and I wobbled toward a seat beside a student who was devouring a textbook with a yellow highlighter. She took me back to my first meeting with Skip Gravely in Denver: I was as eager as this young student, he as kind a mentor as I could have hoped for. Now on this New York City uptown subway, I saw how much we'd both changed since then.

I closed my eyes and felt in my body the bruises and throbs of the last few weeks. There had been so much to think about, to confront and admit and consider. It had worn me out. Every ounce of me suddenly ached for sleep. My shoulders jiggled with the movement of the train, and a half hour later I peeled myself from the seat and climbed out of the subway.

My phone rang. I bumbled through my bag for it and turned the corner to my apartment as I answered. Luke's voice was tired too.

"Hey, Little Sister. You okay?"

"Just getting home." I pulled my keys from my pocket. "Luke, I'm sorry I've been so awful lately."

"Someone wants to say something to you . . ."

I heard my brother cough, move the phone, and whisper something at the same time I was unlocking the front door.

"Hi, Aunt Jonna. You know what I did at school today? Our teacher showed us a frog and I got to touch him. It was slimy and . . ." I imagined Jesse's eyes bouncing with the excitement of his day as I listened and made my way to my room. Though I was more tired than I could remember, my nephew reminded me that some things covered a multitude of shortcomings. And by the time he'd finished his story, I was under the covers. He passed the phone back to his dad, and Luke turned serious. He told me that one of the guys had finally tracked down David, but David hadn't had time to explain what had happened. He was hoping to call soon. I closed my eyes.

"You were right," I said. "He didn't have vacation time left."

"What do you mean?"

I explained the details of Sharon's call, how she confirmed that he'd been fired for what he'd discovered and how everyone but David seemed determined to cover this up.

"We have to keep going, Luke," I said. "It's only right."

"That's my sister." We agreed to talk later the next day, and within a few minutes of hanging up I'd fallen asleep.

At least, that's what I think happened, since I was still holding the phone in my hand when the light drifted through the window the next morning. My parka was still wrapped around my shoulders and my boots still covered my feet. I heard Hannah in the kitchen and staggered out.

"What happened to you?" Her eyes rolled over my bed-head hair on down to my feet.

"I like to be prepared—in case there's an emergency."

"Since when?"

"Since I came home last night."

She poured me some coffee and smirked. "Well, guess what I found out?"

"What?" I stirred sugar in my coffee and sat down.

"Nothing. Absolutely nothing." Hannah, who was already dressed for work in a red sweater and black slacks, said that from what she could tell, there were no connections between Walter Wood and Regal trustees. There were no records that showed he'd ever done business with any of them, and they'd never invested in the media industry at all, let alone his company Med-USA. "But that's the good news," she said.

"It is?" I rubbed the sleep from my eyes.

"Sure. It means the *Clarion* can do an investigative piece on Regal without risking the loss of all those juicy advertising dollars in the education section from Regal." Hannah picked up her spoon and dropped it in her mug.

"No, it doesn't."

"Yes, it does," she said, raising her eyebrow.

"I mean, the *Clarion* can't do an investigative piece on Regal . . . ever."

"What are you talking about?"

"Skip." I gulped my coffee. "Skip said he'd never print it. Period." It was a hard exchange to recount, and I still felt a little queasy as I told my roommate about Skip's decision to kill the story. It wasn't the kind of news that the *Clarion* was interested in printing, he'd said, and so it seemed to me this was the one—and only—time his standards for serving the public good had fudged.

"He can't do that," she said, standing by the kitchen sink

and rinsing her cereal bowl.

"He already did. It's as good as dead."

Hannah whipped around to face me, planting both fists on her hips and glaring at me like a woman on a mission. "And you're going to let him?"

Groggy was no longer an option this morning. I leaned back in my chair and found some confidence. "I don't want to, Hannah. But it's not like I have hard evidence. I only have your notes, a few clips from the morgue, and some conversations."

She shrugged. "It's a start."

"It would be for any other story, that's for sure. But for some reason, Skip won't go there."

Hannah went into the living room to grab her briefcase and coat before returning to the kitchen. "Meet me at the office in an hour. Let's see if we can't change his mind."

Before I could answer, Hannah was out the door, leaving her usual perfume scent trailing behind her. No matter how many changes I'd go through, I was sure I'd never catch up with Hannah X. Hensley's ability to look good, smell good, and do good all at the same time. But this morning, I had to admit it was the first time in a long time I didn't mind.

Emma was at her subway booth when I scrambled down the steps a half hour later. Her head was bent over a book as I tapped on her window. She looked up with a grin and pulled the microphone to her mouth.

"Good morning, Jonna! And it is a good one, isn't it?"

"So far!" A train was screeching into the station, so I waved to my friend, hoped her pronouncement on the day was right, and hopped on board. It was standing room only, so I grabbed a railing and hung on. I managed to pull Gideon, my tiny pocket

New Testament, from my bag without jabbing the woman beside me and opened to a passage I hadn't read in a while. I had all but ignored Gideon lately, but this morning I was ready for his encouragement.

I was surprised when I heard the conductor say that the next stop would be Thirty-fourth Street/Penn Station. I'd been completely absorbed by Gideon's words this morning, tuning out the usual subway commotion and all but forgetting about disappointing editors and missing friends. Until the doors pulled apart, that is, when I found myself asking for mercy, hurrying off the subway, up the stairs, and onto the street. I stopped at Goldwasser's only long enough for an orange juice and bagel before diving into what I supposed would be a whirlwind of a Thursday, in spite of Emma's optimism.

Hannah wasn't at her desk when I arrived at the *Clarion*. The newsroom was alive with discussions, but I couldn't find her anywhere. When I dumped my bag and parka at my cubicle, I saw her note: "We're in the conference room." I grabbed Gideon, my folder, and my notebook and hurried down the hall.

Through the conference room window, I could see Skip sitting next to Walter Wood, whose green plaid bow tie made him look Scottish. It seemed a funny contrast to Skip's plain dark necktie and jacket. As if the two men were sizing up their competition, they'd spread out a pile of other New York newspapers in front of them. Hannah sat across the mahogany table, her hands punctuating points in the air. An unopened folder sat in front of her on the table. I knocked on the door and Skip waved me in.

"Joan, so nice to see you this morning." Walter's words were as counterfeit as his tie.

"It's Jonna, Walter," I said, "not Joan, with all due respect."

I pulled a chair out beside Hannah and smiled politely at the man. He blinked but did not respond. "Good morning," I said as I nodded toward Skip, who gave me the tiniest edge of his attention.

"We were just discussing Hannah's recent political coverage."

"You were?"

"Do you know she's scooped every other newspaper in town?" Wood straightened his bow tie as if he had something to do with it. "That's why we were talking about her work and how—"

"Only until you got here," Hannah said firmly as she turned to me. "Now, go ahead."

I glanced from her to our bosses and back again, wondering what words would drop from my mouth. I swallowed and scrolled through my mind for the events of the past few weeks, not sure where to begin, especially since Skip had killed what I'd wanted to present. I studied my notes. The others looked at the clock.

"Is it about the street gang in Chinatown?" Walter asked. "Because I've been reconsidering that and think that might help us with some advertisers we haven't been able to reach, so—"

"No, sir. I think you were right to begin with. There's not a story there . . . yet."

"Is it the witches? They're boosting sales," Walter said.

"No, it's not that, either," I said. His shoulders sagged.

"But you're still covering them, right? Isn't there—?"

"Yes, a rally tonight at city hall. I'll be there." I tucked my hair behind my ear, struggling to remember if I'd brushed it this morning. It didn't matter. "I think Hannah was referring to another story, one that could expose a major New York institution for—"

"Oh, this sounds good. Scandals always sell papers," Walter said, his thin lips turning upward.

Hannah nodded. "We knew you'd think so."

Skip didn't move. And he didn't look up from the newspapers in front of him as I presented the story of Frank Cherrinard and his endowment. I detailed what I suspected as the use of the funds—according to past clips of the *Clarion*—as well as the accounts from David, Sharon, and Professor Hartman about the university's heritage. And to top it off, I suggested that Regal's leadership had intentionally terminated the archivist who'd discovered the abuse in order to cover up what had been happening.

"They fired him?" Wood asked, sitting forward with his hands resting on the table.

"Actually, one source said they gave him an ultimatum: either he resigned or they'd fire the entire department. So he resigned."

Hannah's eyes widened at the new information, and a slight grin formed as if that confirmed what she'd believed about David Rockley all along. Wood tapped the table and kept going.

"So this fellow was sacked because of some old endowment?"

"Because he confronted administrators with evidence of the institution's wrongdoing about the endowment, and they didn't like it," I answered. I glanced at Skip, who by now had formed an expression on his face that suggested he wasn't sure which was the bigger disappointment: his alma mater or his religion reporter.

Wood raised his shoulders. "I'm still not sure what the big deal is. A religious quack from a hundred years ago gives a bunch of money to his university, and a librarian loses his job over it?" He held up his palms. "I thought you said there was a scandal here that would sell papers."

"But it's wrong." I felt my cheeks grow hot. "They

shouldn't have misused these funds, and they shouldn't have fired . . . David."

Walter Wood fiddled with his tie again and referred to my editor with a nod. Skip cleared his throat and moved his glasses onto his nose. He looked only at the man beside him.

"I've already told Jonna, Walter, that we can't rely on the word of one disgruntled employee to challenge the reputation of an academic institution like Regal just because he doesn't like what they believe."

"It's more than that, Skip," I said.

"Then what evidence do you have?" His tone was more disturbing than his question.

I looked at my notes. "Conversations, clips from the *Clarion* . . ."

"Any hard proof?"

"Not yet. They've cleaned out most of those files, even the electronic—"

"So you have nothing?"

Hannah chimed in. "She has enough to go on, and you know it, Skip."

He shook his head. "Not this time. No way." He rose from the table. "Meeting adjourned."

Skip left the conference room with Walter close behind. Hannah and I sat quietly at the table, the buzz of the heating system a gentle backdrop to our disappointment. She clasped her hands together on the table as if she were resting. Finally, she shook her head and stood up.

"Well, girl, it might be over."

The words stung. I'd never known Hannah to quit . . . anything. I sat glued to my chair.

"So we let them get away with it?"

She shrugged. "Well, Wood had a point. It's not a very sexy story, is it? It won't sell many papers."

"Not you, too, Hannah."

"I didn't say it *was* over, only that it might be." She turned toward the hallway. "But we'll have to regroup in a—" Hannah was interrupted by a knock on the door. Lee Cheung stood holding a package.

"Yo. There you are. I've been looking everywhere, you know. This looked important." He bobbed as he said it. "Like, I had to get it to you, see? Cool." He dropped the package into my hands and nodded. I ripped off the tab. And as I thumbed through it quickly, I knew that this story was not over. It had just begun.

I was in Skip's office in seconds. This time Hannah had to struggle to keep up with me down the hall. And when Walter saw us in his office, he charged in behind us as well. Like a gust of winter cold, the three of us hovered around Skip's desk.

"Yes, Skip, I do have proof. Here's a copy of Cherrinard's original letter, a few follow-up letters from his lawyers challenging the administration about the endowment, and even a letter from Regal's own general counsel to a certain David Rockley suggesting that it was too burdensome to provide him with the materials that are all—how about that?—right here." I placed them in front of Skip and glanced through the rest of the package. "It looks like there are even a dozen other letters, documents, and contracts here that will confirm Regal's abuse and misappropriation."

The lights in his office flickered above us. I'd never noticed them before. Hannah and I stared at the letters on Skip's desk, waiting for him to move or fidget or say something. History's first draft was sitting in front of us, and it felt both daunting and exhilarating.

And then Hannah started clapping. Walter scratched his head. But Skip merely picked up one of the letters, glanced over it, and calmly returned it.

"It doesn't mean anything," Skip said. Hannah's clapping stopped.

"Of course it does," I answered. "It means embezzlement, fraud, to name a few—"

"Let me rephrase that, Jonna. It doesn't mean I'm changing my mind," he said quietly. "I won't run this story."

Hannah dropped her head forward as if she hadn't quite heard right. But she didn't ask him to repeat himself. Instead, she swayed into the desk, looked hard at Skip, and said, "If you don't, I'll resign."

She paused to make sure the words settled in and then continued. "I won't work for a newspaper that confuses the public's right to know with some political or financial agenda. It's that simple." She locked eyes with Skip, whose expression hadn't changed. Hers hadn't either. Neither moved. The lights hummed.

Walter looked at the two, then at me, as an awkward grin spread across his face. "Now, now, let's everyone calm down. After all, this is still just about a librarian and some old minister, nothing a little ingenuity can't solve if we—"

"I won't print it."

"I'll resign."

I swallowed.

Walter sighed, walked over to the door, and closed it. "Well, then, that would be disappointing, Miss Hensley, since your work has certainly helped the *Clarion*. But I have to support my editors. You understand," he said smugly. "So unless you want to reconsider . . ."

Hannah crossed her arms against her chest and held her head firm.

"Okay," Wood said. "Then I'll accept your letter of resignation by the day's end. We will, of course, pay you through the month . . . as a gesture of good faith." I wanted to laugh at his choice of words, but I was too shocked by what I'd just heard. Then he grinned again. Skip stood up, his jacket hanging lightly across his shoulders.

"I'm sorry it came to this, Hannah," he said.

"I think it was time anyway, don't you?" She never missed a beat. "In fact, I don't know how you can live with yourself, Skip Gravely."

Hannah X. Hensley stood taller than anyone in the entire building at that moment, though in truth she was only five foot four. And when she walked out of Skip's office, she left a beautiful but noble aroma that descended on all of us. I watched her stroll into the hall like the African queen she was, but a mix of feelings collided against my insides. Had Hannah just quit her job because of—?

Skip prodded me before pointing me toward the door. "So, Lightfoot, I'll expect your story on the Wiccan's rally first thing in the morning." I stood dazed. Walter Wood nodded to me and reached for my elbow.

"That was unfortunate," he said. "These things happen. You, though . . . I'm sure you'll keep up the good work, Joan." I pulled my elbow from his grip and collected the papers from Skip's desk, avoiding my editor's eyes as I did. The interaction that had just played out in front of me was the last thing I'd expected. Ever. I walked quickly to my cubicle, dodging the emotions that confronted me with each step.

Hannah was gone. Her cubicle looked the same, but her coat and bag weren't there. I called her cell phone, but she didn't answer, so I left a voice mail. I sprinted down to Goldwasser's but I didn't see her there either. I called Sarah to tell her what had happened but only got their answering machine. Now, with Skip's betrayal, I was on my own in figuring out what to do next.

Except I wasn't alone. I picked up Gideon. I could keep going.

I called Hannah about a dozen more times by lunchtime, and considered going to the apartment in case she was there, but I didn't want to miss her if she came back to the office. So I alternated between calling and stalling. When I still hadn't heard back from her or Sarah or Luke or anyone else besides clerics and religion scholars, I opted for pizza. Mushrooms and tomatoes. But that didn't help either. I tried David again, but no answer still. So I moped around the afternoon avoiding my editor, cleaning out the piles of old press releases, scouring each detail in the package delivered, and feeling miserable, confused, and generally lonely. But I didn't feel alone.

By 4:38 p.m. I left the office with the Regal package, caught the uptown subway, and hurried toward our apartment, hoping to find Hannah. I barged into each room, but there was no sign she'd come home yet today. No one answered my calls. So I cleaned the bathroom, organized my closet, anything to get through the longest afternoon and evening I'd ever had.

I decided to give myself a little extra time to get to city hall, just in case I got lost—or the Wiccans wanted to call it an early night. A little before ten, I grabbed my parka and cap and left Hannah a note to "Call me immediately!"

By 11:03, I was rounding the corner to the steps of the government building in lower Manhattan. The night temperatures hadn't dropped as low as they had the last couple of days, and I took that as a sign of grace, especially because I wasn't exactly excited about being out on a February night with some of New York's stranger citizens. Or maybe I was in that category. Or maybe we all were.

Lady Crystal was putting candles on top of boxes and helping a crew of men dressed in black trench coats and jeans set up a microphone and sound system. She greeted me politely when she saw me, thanking me for coming to cover what she was sure would be the first of many more public events helping "usher in a new age for pagans." I jotted her comment down and chatted with the *Clarion* photographer that Skip had sent, waiting for a crowd to come.

Griffin Lewis stepped to the microphone just before midnight, inviting the "spirits of the ages to invoke a celestial power across the authorities in helping change their status." I stood freezing, watching a dozen or so older women straggle into the group beside some police officers, who represented standard procedure for gatherings at city hall. Griffin encouraged the hundred or so men and women who'd come to light candles and chant. He joined hands with Lady Crystal, creating a chain reaction around the steps, swaying back and forth in the moonlight.

I yawned and listened and wrote, watching a group of people who looked no different from my own family acting and talking like any other group of people, just wanting to belong, just hoping their presence together would send a clear message to those in power to do the right thing for them. For everyone.

As I leaned against a street sign, I was surprised by the sympathy I felt toward the Wiccans' journey. For the first time since I began covering their story, I realized they were seeking what I had been taught to pursue all my life: peace and truth and justice. I might not agree with their spirituality or theology, but I now knew I could understand and respect their desires to get there. We'd all been wired the same way, even if we—all of us—sometimes lost our way.

Witches weren't so scary after all.

A half hour later, a chill in my bones from the winter air, I decided I had gathered enough details to report the story and headed toward the subway. I was tired, my heart and my head weary. I adjusted the earflaps of my cap down as far as they would go and picked up my pace, seeing my breath in the cold with each step. I wanted to get home.

But a block away from the government building, someone took my arm, whispered my name, and pulled me gently behind a parked car on the street. There in the shadow of a Manhattan streetlight on a February night, with a group of lonely pagans behind me chanting for world peace, David Rockley never looked so . . . nice.

:: Chapter Fifteen

The hotel ballroom was busy with chatter. I tugged on David's arm as we found seats a few rows from the stage. He and Luke and Sarah followed me by way of the coffee table to the chairs not far from the podium. Photographers sat in the front row, and reporters from weekly magazines, daily newspapers, and even major television stations were stretched across the aisles. For a Friday morning before most of the city's workers had even made it into their offices, this was a crowd that matched the everyday energy of the city: alive, engaged, excited.

A knock on a microphone up front brought silence over the room. I looked up and felt Luke's hand on my shoulder, pointing to the celebrity behind the podium. I couldn't help grinning at the presence who had taken center stage.

Hannah was greeting the crowd as though she'd done this a thousand times. Cameras flashed and people whispered at the woman who was opening this meeting. It was clear she was not the same representative they were used to seeing. Or hearing. But when she finished a few comments, no one questioned why she was there:

"Please welcome this morning, the Honorable Senator Lillian G. Milton."

Applause circulated around the room as a woman twice

Hannah's age strolled across the stage, reflecting a nobility both stern and gracious. She greeted Hannah with a handshake and a smile, then placed a folder on the podium and reading glasses on her nose. She shuffled a few pages and looked at us.

"Thank you all for coming to this morning's important press conference. What I have to tell you will be both shocking and sad, yet it is exactly because of our ongoing commitment to justice and integrity that we are here in the first place." She paused for a moment. Reporters shifted. Cameras rolled as Senator Milton then outlined in detail the story Skip Gravely had refused to print.

"Today it is my duty to tell you that one of New York's finer institutions has forever damaged not only its Ivy League reputation but also our city's very well-being. By wandering far from its founding mission — 'In Thy light we see light' — its administrators callously misappropriated the hard-earned donations of one of its own graduates, funds intended exclusively for religious training and social service programs to the city but that were used for personal greed and academic hubris."

She stopped reading, shook her head, and looked up. "As if matters of faith are no longer relevant in the academy."

A few people whispered. A cell phone rang and was quickly shut off as the senator continued. "Along with the office of the New York State Attorney General, we are launching a full investigation into Regal University's offices of corporate accounting, internal development, and general counsel. Together we will pursue the truth behind the dissemination of the Frank Cherrinard endowment, not just for the sake of its legal consequences but because, well, it's simply the right thing to do."

Senator Milton paused, and her gaze moved slowly across

each of the faces in front of her. Her presence was so penetrating it wasn't difficult to see why she'd been elected to public office. I sat forward in my chair and listened as if it were news I was hearing for the first time, which in some ways it was. She told us they'd be doing all they could to ensure that Regal's future administrators would no longer turn their backs on any ethnic or religious minority for the sake of financial gain. Then she leaned close to the microphone and took off her glasses.

"Now, this might surprise some of you, but I was once a student at Regal. I'd grown up in the Bronx and, you know, I'd always loved the Christian church. So when I attended Regal, I wanted to study church history in their religion department. But you know what? This poor girl from the Bronx couldn't afford to stay. I had to transfer to another university—and look what happened to me!" She held out her hands to her sides and laughed. The audience clapped. A photographer moved in close to catch her picture while she moved back to the microphone. She gripped the sides of the podium.

"So my vow this morning is that Protestant and Catholic faiths would always be affirmed in our great city's institutions. They must not be disparaged anywhere, especially in the halls of academia, because the heritage and contributions of those with Christian beliefs in this city has been monumental, as important as anyone's in this room—that is, if anyone in here has any faith." She laughed again, teasing the journalists and photographers as though they were old friends. They laughed too.

But when reporters around me began bombarding the senator with questions, I tuned out. My attention landed instead on a sparkling chandelier above the stage, and I was lost in a collage of thoughts, conversations, and events from the last few weeks.

I remembered Hannah leaning on our editor's desk and resigning from the *Clarion*. Though she never once mentioned it to me before this morning, the senator had been trying to recruit her for months to join her press staff. Hannah saw the Regal scandal as a perfect opportunity to "jump ship," as she put it. She'd said if the *Clarion* was no longer going to be "a voice for the voiceless," she'd go to work for someone who would. And she'd do it in her usual way, with style and professionalism—and breaking news at her first press conference.

I remembered David last night on the subway. How surprised I'd been to see him on the street and equally surprised when he sat across from me on the subway, looking calm and relaxed and nice—as if nothing spectacular had just happened.

Though we both knew it had. He'd looked deep into the web of Regal's darkest corners, its tentacles reaching coldly throughout the city—including the police precinct in his own neighborhood—yet he'd managed to challenge them all. He'd believed there was no other choice, even after someone had broken into his apartment looking for evidence of his work. Even after he'd lost his job. None of it could change his mind. So he sent copies of the Cherrinard files to the only person he said he could trust with them: the religion reporter he'd met a few years before in Denver, whose work he'd followed through New Orleans and into the city he loved, hoping his friendship with her would grow in the process.

We'd been quiet at first on the subway, as if it were a miracle to be there together at all—humbling, strange, but somehow right. I'd been the one to break the spell.

"Why didn't you call anyone about where you—?"

"I meant to, Jonna. But it was a whirlwind, so much was

coming and going and well, do you know what I did?"

"That's the million-dollar question."

He'd smiled. "It is?" David had lifted his Yankees cap as if he'd not considered this response, rubbed his head, and put the cap back in place. Then he lifted his shoulders slightly and looked at me so intently I wondered if there were any other humans in all of New York City. "Ah, it doesn't matter," he whispered, his eyes still sure and riveted. "Nothing as exciting as seeing you right now."

The subway had hit a bump and shook us around the seat. But I didn't mind.

"How'd you know where I was tonight?"

"I read your story, of course, about the Wiccans' rally. I figured you'd be covering it and would need an escort home." He'd shrugged. "Here I am."

I was sure that David kept talking all the way to Harlem, but this morning I only remembered that his jaw looked smooth and firm, his eyes soft and—

"That's going to have to do for now, folks." Senator Milton's words slapped me out of my reverie and back into the ballroom, which was abuzz again with noisy crews trying to get the story on the midday television news. In the process, it scooped the *Clarion*. But no matter: Walter Wood ran the other news of the day. A front-page spread of Lady Crystal and Griffin Lewis at city hall and the headline "Pagans Cast Spell for Victory." The Department of Veterans Affairs had agreed to a settlement out of court. They would be adding the Wiccans to their official list of approved religions along with almost forty others recognized by the government. It was all the incentive Wood needed to move his newspaper into the entertainment tabloid he'd wanted it to become from the second he offered to buy it.

Hannah learned from old sources that Skip had been offered a job back in Denver teaching journalism at a state college. He'd held out, apparently hoping to join his old pal Hartman as a professor at Regal, but the senator's announcement didn't exactly bode well for anyone at the university. Of course, no one expected Senator Milton's investigation would turn anything around in higher education. But at least it meant that a voice once heard in the city and in the halls of academia might begin to resound again.

Me? I decided to join the thousands of other New York writers by trying my hand at freelancing. An editor from a national newswire had been nagging me to cover a few religion stories, and I told her I'd give it a try—after I returned from a long overdue trip to visit my parents in Costa Rica.

But of all the decisions I'd made in my life, one of the best came that morning during Senator's Milton's press conference when Luke and Sarah and Hannah stood talking near the stage in the hotel ballroom. I knew I had nothing to lose. I turned to David. But before I could say what I wanted to say to him, he asked if I would join him for dinner that night.

"We don't have to call it a date, Jonna. I mean, it's only—"

"No, David, I think I'd rather we . . . did . . ." And instead of my cheeks catching fire, they actually relaxed. "What the heck? Let's call it dating. Okay?"

He grabbed my hand and we joined my brother, my sister-in-law, and Senator Milton's new press secretary for another cup of coffee and a chocolate chip muffin.

And when I finally got a chance to listen to the messages on my cell phone, I heard an unfamiliar but wispy voice identifying himself as God. I sighed. If I were a true seeker of religion, he mumbled so that I could hardly understand him, I'd come to worship him in Central Park Sunday morning for a "celestial symposium of spiritual harmony and mass love." And then, of course, I'd tell the whole world about him by writing a story.

Instead, I dumped my phone into my bag and got ready for sushi. Because if I'd learned anything by now, I knew God did not mumble.

bonus content includes:

::Reader's Guide

1. Jonna Lightfoot MacLaughlin has come a long way from home. She grew up in Colorado's ski country, but her career took her first to Denver, then New Orleans, and now New York City. How do you think these places shaped her? Can you identify with her moving from city to city, and if so, how did the transience affect you?

2. No matter how hard she tries to shake it, Jonna still has a "thing" for coffee and chocolate, now supplemented also by bagels and hot dogs. What do you think these culinary devotions say about her? (Take a minute to indulge in a cup of coffee or a piece of chocolate to better appreciate her situation.)

3. What roles have Lightfoot's brothers, colleagues, and friends played in her life? Of the many characters in her New York life—Skip Gravely, David Rockley, Emma, Luke and Sarah and their boys, Hannah X. Hensley, Griffin Lewis, Professor Hartman, Walter Wood, or Lee Cheung—which most stood out to you in this story and why? What qualities of friendship or professionalism does Hannah X. Hensley exhibit? What attributes do the others display that you find either admirable or unattractive and why?

4. As Lightfoot covers the Wiccan rally and subsequent
    story with Griffin Lewis, she's also forced to confront
    the stereotypes that come along with certain religions.
    What religious stereotypes does she have to work
    through? What religious stereotypes do you think still
    exist in our contemporary culture and why? How can
    they best be challenged?

5. How does Jonna perceive her singleness and
    dating relationships with men? Why does she seem
    ambivalent toward David Rockley, and what changes?
    What advice would you give her?

6. What does David Rockley discover about Regal
    University, and do you think such an accusation could
    actually have happened at an Ivy League university?
    Why do you think David is so driven about the
    corruption he's uncovered? Have you ever faced a
    similar situation? What did you do?

7. Though many might not think Jonna is a terrible
    person or has committed any grave sin, something
    happens that forces her, for the first time, to see
    herself as she really is. What do you think it is? Who
    is *that* Jonna Lightfoot MacLaughlin? What specific
    "demons" does Jonna have to confront? Have you ever
    felt that way? And what hope is there for individuals
    who come face-to-face with who they really are?

8. Throughout Lightfoot's career as a religion reporter,
    she's always wanted to find good news. Why do you

think she's looked so hard for good news? And what does she realize about it on her journey through New York City?

9. When David Rockley goes missing for a few days, where in all of New York City do you imagine he would—or could—go? Where would you like to go in New York City? Which, if any, part of city life in *A Minute Before Friday* surprised you? What do you think cities can teach us about: religion, culture, God, character, compassion, service, and/or diversity?

10. What themes have surfaced throughout *A Minute Before Friday* specifically and THE LIGHTFOOT TRILOGY generally? How have Jonna's personal quirks and qualities, passions and perspectives, stories and insights most affected you?

::Sacred Sites to Visit in New York City

(in no particular order)

There are hundreds of churches, synagogues, cathedrals, and temples in Manhattan and the surrounding boroughs that make up this world capital. The following are only a few "must see" spiritual sites. (For more specific information, any local or online bookstore offers a variety of real-life references on sacred spaces and religious sites to visit in the Big Apple. Or you might want to create your own list once you've explored the city on your own!)

• The Cathedral Church of Saint John the Divine (1047 Amsterdam Avenue on the Upper West Side) is every bit as beautiful in real life as it is when Jonna experiences it in these pages. Its history, location, and community make this Episcopalian cathedral well worth the visit. www.stjohndivine.org

• The New York Society for Ethical Culture, a humanist religion community (2 West Sixty-fourth Street at Central Park West) has an intimate eight-hundred-seat auditorium that's a favorite to many New Yorkers for lectures and concerts. Its history and architecture are admirable, and its building literally sits across the street from Central Park. www.nysec.org

• Saint Patrick's Cathedral (460 Madison Avenue in Midtown) is the largest decorated Gothic-style Catholic cathedral in the United States. Its doors opened in 1879, and the community remains active to this day. From its steps, you'll also have a grand view of Fifth Avenue and the Rockefeller Center. www.saintpatrickscathedral.org

• The Masjid Malcolm Shabazz Mosque (102 West 116th Street at Lenox Avenue) is the mosque in Harlem where Malcolm X preached. It's walking distance from Central Park and numerous African-American Protestant churches as well as great southern neighborhood cafés.

• Union Theological Seminary (3041 Broadway at 121st Street) is New York's oldest independent seminary, founded in 1836. Some of its famous faculty and students include Dietrich Bonhoeffer, Reinhold Niebuhr, and Paul Tillich. Its gardens, library, and campus are inspiring in beauty and history. www.utsnyc.edu

• Mahayana Buddhist Temple (133 Canal Street in Chinatown) is both colorful and massive. Seated at the foot of the Manhattan Bridge, it is the largest Buddhist temple in New York City. The temple contains a sixteen-foot golden statue of the Buddha sitting on a lotus, with a blue neon halo glowing behind him, and is one of the largest statues of Buddha in the city. Around the hall are numerous depictions of events in Buddha's life. Mahayana is one of the two primary sects of Buddhism, which place more emphasis on the teachings of Buddha.

etc.

• Eldridge Street Synagogue (12 Eldridge Street, between
Canal and Division streets in Lower Manhattan) was New
York's first congregation built by Eastern European Jews. The
building is currently undergoing a restoration project that
includes a museum and educational programs that celebrate
more than a century of Jewish life in America. www.eldridg-
estreet.org

• Abyssinian Baptist Church (132 Odell Clark Place,
formerly 138th Street, between Adam Clayton Powell, Jr.,
and Malcolm X Boulevards, also known as Seventh and
Lenox Avenues in Harlem) has served the African-American
community there for almost two centuries. Its outreach
ministry, worship services, and community-development
programs along with its history have made Abyssinian a local
and cultural leader. www.abyssinian.org

• Trinity Church of Wall Street (74 Trinity Place at Wall
Street and Broadway, just blocks from where the World Trade
Center once stood) is the oldest Anglican parish on the island
of Manhattan. The Gothic cathedral offers a unique contrast
to the bustle of Wall Street and links its history to 1697, when
it received its charter and land grant from King William III of
England. The city's first ministry to African-Americans, both
enslaved and free, began at Trinity in 1705. Its cathedral,
churchyards, museum, exhibits, programs, and modern active
congregation mark its importance on any tour of New York.
www.trinitywallstreet.org

• The Cloisters Museum (in Fort Tryon Park in Washington Heights) is a branch of The Metropolitan Museum of Art devoted to the art and architecture of medieval Europe. The Cloisters Museum was assembled from architectural elements, both domestic and religious, that date from the twelfth through the fifteenth century. www.metmuseum.org/cloisters

• Redeemer Presbyterian Church is a contemporary evangelical congregation that "seeks to renew the city socially, spiritually, and culturally." Though its offices are located at 1359 Broadway Fourth Floor in Midtown (near Penn Station), it holds five services each Sunday at various locations around Central Park and attracts many New Yorkers from a variety of professional industries and communities. www.redeemer.com

• The Jewish Museum (1109 Fifth Avenue at Ninety-second Street) is the preeminent museum in this country devoted exclusively to the scope and diversity of four thousand years of art and Jewish culture. Its many exhibits, collections, and special events make the museum an important and memorable stop. www.jewishmuseum.org

::Lightfoot's Instruction Kit: Top Ten Things Every Reporter *Still* Needs

By Jonna Lightfoot MacLaughlin

As I've learned since I started in this job, religion stories are all around us. On every street corner of every city, through every route of every public transportation system, there's a story just waiting for a reporter to discover it. I know. I'm always looking myself.

So even after I moved from the Big Easy to the Big Apple, I'm convinced you'll still need the following ten things if you want to be the best reporter you can be:

10. A pen that works and paper that's easy to keep with you at all times. I like to have a notebook the size of a candy bar with me every time I step out the door. No scraps of paper—they're too easy to lose. For writing utensils, I favor those fancy mechanical pencils or pens so I can erase if I have to.

9. A clear mind and a rested, semi-fit body. These usually go together, so get a good night's sleep after some semblance of exercise, *before* you go out looking for a story the next morning. Keep your mind fresh and open by reading everything you can and by talking with lots of people.

8. Chocolate and coffee. They speak for themselves as a constant source of inspiration and tend to help if #9 has been overlooked.

7. A healthy and engaging curiosity. As you pay attention to the people and places around you, you'll begin to notice things you hadn't before: the church that's got a new sign out in front, the men and women gathering at the entrance of the mosque, the construction crew outside the old cathedral, even the person sitting next to you on the subway. You get the idea. Keep your eyes and ears open. Each could lead to a story.

6. Good questions. Every reporter needs to answer the "who, what, why, where, when, and how" of a story. These not only guide your interviews, they shape your writing.

5. A telephone. You don't have to have a cell phone with you at all times but just access to the ingenious contraption Mr. Bell gave us. This way, you can call before you go for an interview, call your editor if you oversleep, call the Chinese delivery guy if you're starving, or call the people in your story to double-check—and triple-check—your facts.

4. Organization. It helps to figure out your own system of organization—where you file your notes, how you find research to fill out and confirm your stories, where you left your pencil and notebook—so that you're not wasting time looking when the deadline is looming. Just as good organization helps the reporter get the story, it also helps write a story your reader can follow.

3. Good sources. Current magazines, experts at local colleges, spiritual leaders in the community, and sacred books like the Bible all can be excellent sources for helping you understand the many belief systems that exist within our pluralistic

culture. So can credible websites on the Internet, commentaries, and reference books. Remember, everyone believes something. A good religion reporter knows this and knows where to look if she doesn't understand some of those basics of a person's faith.

2. Good manners. The most professional journalist will be polite but firm with her sources, respectful of the people whose stories she's telling, and nonjudgmental in her coverage of both. Religion is deeply personal and absolutely essential to many people; the good religion reporter understands and appreciates this by being as nice as she can be. Or as nice as David Rockley. Either one. Period.

1. An audience. Obviously, the number one thing a religion reporter needs is someone to read her story. Lots of eyeballs are always best. Once you've written your first draft, ask someone to take a look before you submit your story to your editor. (He'll like you for it, believe me.) Then once your story is published, pick up extra copies of the paper and clip out your story. Send it to your grandma, your neighbors, and especially your high school English teacher. Even the folks who are mentioned in the story. And don't forget to keep a copy for yourself as a way of remembering how important religion reporting is in serving a community.

Write on!

Acknowledgments

A trilogy can be as much of a journey for a writer as it is the reader, maybe more so. It can be grueling and exciting, terrible and exhilarating, putting characters on paper, watching them grow into plots and eventually become stories that we hope challenge and change us for the better because that's what stories are supposed to do. But make no mistake: Writers are often a wimpy mess when they start the trek, but step-by-step their muscles fill out and they end the climb stronger than they started, hoping someday for another go of it.

Along the way of building THE LIGHTFOOT TRILOGY, I would have been a complete weakling, lost in the woods and starving for creative sustenance, had it not been for the help, support, and encouragement of many, many people. I list some of them in the following: The kind folks at NavPress Publishing (Kris Wallen, Darla Hightower, and the rest of their capable team of pros); Lee Hough, my agent and friend at Alive Communications, who continues to extend grace and wisdom when I'm pretty sure I don't deserve either; Kelly Monroe Kullberg of the Veritas Forum, whose friendship and experiences in higher education have always inspired me; the students in my fiction writing class (spring 2007) at Gordon College, who allowed me to move with them through this wacky process and who offered ears and ideas for Lightfoot's journey; Shirley Hoogstra, Andrea Mungo, Mary Burke, Sue Semrau, Katherine Leary, Elisabeth Coen, Eileen Sommi, Sally Lloyd Jones, and the Atomic Engineers of New Jersey, all of whom have offered me friendship, concern, and gentle prods to have fun and keep going; Vinita Hampton Wright, whose ongoing professionalism in the realm of creative storytelling astounds me; Jack Kadlecek, my dad and number one marketing executive, who has encouraged me with each book and each step; and my patient and gifted husband, Chris Gilbert, who had to live with me while I lived in each of these stories and who never once said no when I asked him to "listen to Lightfoot."

Thanks mostly to you, my reading friend, who has stayed with me throughout Lightfoot's romps and rolled through three cities, countless broken hearts, a lot of religion stories gone bad, and finally the good news of truth and grace.

To each of you, and to those friends, colleagues, and reviewers who have kindly introduced Lightfoot to other readers, I'll always be grateful.

Please keep in touch and visit me at www.lamppostmedia .net.

About the Author

J o Kadlecek has worked as a full-time writer, reporter, retreat teacher, and adjunct writing instructor. She is a member of the faculty at Gordon College in Massachusetts as assistant professor of creative writing. *A Minute Before Friday* is the third novel in the Lightfoot series.

CHECK OUT THESE OTHER GREAT TITLES FROM THE NAVPRESS FICTION LINE!

Bottom Line

Kimberly Stuart ISBN-13: 978-1-60006-077-9
ISBN-10: 1-60006-077-3

Heidi Elliott has joined the elite ranks of stay-at-home moms, a world of cartoons, toys, and lactation. When her husband's business experiences financial problems, Heidi decides to take a part-time job at a pyramid scheme dressed up in women's clothing: "Christian" lingerie by Solomon's Closet, a company created by her new friends Kylie and Russ Zimmerman.

The Restorer

Sharon Hinck ISBN-13: 978-1-60006-131-8
ISBN-10: 1-60006-131-1

Meet Susan, a housewife and soccer mom whose dreams stretch far beyond her ordinary world. While studying the book of Judges, Susan longs to be a modern-day Deborah, a prophet and leader who God used to deliver the ancient nation of Israel from destruction. Susan gets her wish for adventure when she stumbles through a portal into an alternate universe and encounters a nation locked in a fierce struggle for its survival.

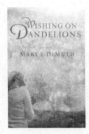

Wishing on Dandelions

Mary DeMuth ISBN-13: 978-1-57683-953-9
ISBN-10: 1-57683-953-2

Like every teenager, Natha tries to sort out the confusing layers of love—of friends, of family, of suitors, and, desperately, of God. Natha struggles to find herself before she gives in to the scared shadow of a girl.

To order copies, visit your local Christian bookstore, call NavPress at 1-800-366-7788, or log on to www.navpress.com.
To locate a Christian bookstore near you, call 1-800-991-7747.